PROLOGUE

The dust of the cotton mill clung to the insides of Katie Turner's airways even though it had been half an hour since she'd left the squat, smoke-belching building on Mule Street. It stung and tickled, making it feel as though a cough hovered permanently at the back of her throat.

She tried clearing it, which only made her sneeze miserably, and swung her arms in a bid to keep warm. The sky was a hateful, leaden grey, and despite the staid buildings that loomed around her with their windows boarded up or as narrow as angry eyes, a breeze still somehow found her as she stood on the corner nearest the marketplace. It threatened to slice through to her marrow. It certainly had no difficulty piercing her threadbare coat, which clung around her shoulders, an inch too short on her arms. The gap between her sleeves and her holey mittens stung with cold.

Katie stepped from foot to foot and coughed. She thought that perhaps it was silly to be standing here on this corner instead of going home to the cozy tenement with her big sister, Molly, but hunger had overruled her cold when they'd split up the chores. Molly and Henry would be starting the fire in the tenement and tending to their ever-ailing mother. Tessie Bailey and her parents, Joan and Peter, were stopping by the coalmonger's for fuel for tomorrow's fire.

Michael Bailey had been given the task of going to the marketplace to get fish for supper. Katie hadn't thought twice about going with him.

A milling crowd of factory workers like them moved through the marketplace, peering into cauldrons of questionable soup or buying loaves of stale bread from an old man with a cart on the corner. They all looked like Katie and her family did: their clothes tattered, their shoes held together with loops of string, their hats crumpling on their heads as though the task of protecting each lice-ridden crown was itself too monumental to face.

Michael emerged from the crowd like something out of a storybook. Not just for the fine halo of fair hair that caught the light, but for the way her heart eased when she saw him. He was kind, and strong, and safe—everything a seven-year-old needed in a world full of fear.

"Sorry for the wait, Katie. There was an awful line at the fishmonger's."

"It smells so good," said Katie.

He handed her one of the parcels, freeing up his left hand, which he wrapped securely around hers. Michael was a whole eleven years old; to seven-year-old Katie, he seemed like a pillar of strength, his big hand wrapping so thoroughly around her little fingers.

"Come along," he said. "Let's go home—but first, I've got a little something for you."

"You do?" said Katie.

THE FORGOTTEN DAUGHTER OF LONDON

TURNER FAMILY SAGA BOOK 3

IRIS COLE

Michael chuckled. "Let's get away from the crowd and I'll show you."

The merry excitement in his eyes turned into a spark of anticipation in her chest. It gave her a fresh surge of energy despite the nagging exhaustion in her legs from twelve long hours in the cotton mill, and somehow she was almost skipping beside him, cradling the precious fish under one arm, her hand secure in Michael's.

The crowd was thick. Men and women pushed past them, all smelling like soot, dust, and the uneasy aroma of many days' sweat. Yellowed eyes flashed in grimy faces, many dipping to Katie as they did so, dwelling on her golden locks and bright eyes. But even the frightening old tramp huddled in an alley, who reached out toward Katie with a yellow claw, didn't frighten her. Michael tugged her away before the old tramp could come anywhere near her. She was safe because she was with him.

He led her back toward the tenement, but not by their usual road. Instead, he chose a little side street that wandered aimlessly toward the inn, crossing a humpbacked bridge over a Thames tributary.

"There we are!" he said. "A nice spot to stop for a second."

"What do you have for me?" Katie giggled.

"Sit down and I'll show you." Michael perched on the bridge's edge, dangling his feet over the water.

The current dragged sluggishly by beneath them, stirring up murky eddies that seemed black and brown in the faint light of the streetlamps. Katie carefully hugged the fish to her chest as Michael reached into the pocket of his near-transparent coat and drew out something that smelled gloriously of butter and sugar. Katie's mouth immediately began to water.

"Is—is that a sticky bun?" she gasped.

"It's just for you," said Michael.

She eagerly wrapped her fingers around it and held it up to the light to admire the glazed golden-brown surface. It was still warm from the oven, and the thought of that sugar made her tremble with joy.

"I love it," she whispered. "Is there one for everybody?"

Michael shook his head. "I found a penny farthing in the gutter by the cotton mill this morning, and I knew just what to do with it. It's all yours, Katie."

Katie brought the bun close to her mouth and inhaled its glorious scent. She sank her teeth into it, and the warm, doughy texture made her sigh with pleasure even before the buttery sweetness filled her mouth. She would gladly have wolfed down the whole thing then and there, but she ate slowly, savouring every piece until half the bun was left.

"This is yours," she said, holding it out.

Michael shook his head. "No, no, Katie-pie. It's for you."

"But you can have some, too."

"It's much more fun to see you enjoying it than to enjoy it myself," said Michael, and judging by the warmth in his eyes, he meant it.

Katie finished the bun and sucked every last drop of sweetness from her fingers. "Thank you."

"You're so welcome." Michael smiled.

Katie leaned her head against the stone railing of the bridge and gazed down at the murky water beneath. "Mama's sick, isn't she?"

Michael said nothing.

Katie sighed. "Mama's been sick a long, long time. I don't think she'll ever get any better."

"Oh, Katie." Michael laid a hand on her shoulder.

"I think she's getting sicker. Maybe she'll even die, and

then what will we do? Molly always says we'll go home to Papa when he gets the farm back, but I don't even remember Papa. I don't even remember the farm."

"It'll be all right," said Michael.

Katie looked up at him, trying to fight the tears that stung her eyes. "Will it?"

Michael studied her. The light from behind made his fair hair look angelic again.

"Yes, it will," he said. "I'll tell you why. No matter what in the world happens to us, we'll always find a way to be together."

A weight lifted from Katie's little chest. She sat straighter. "We will?"

"There might be times when we have to be apart for a little while," said Michael, "like when I'm in the weaving room and you're in the spinning room at the mill. But eventually, we'll always find one another, Katie, and we'll be together in the end. Always."

"I think so, too," said Katie. "We'll always be together."

"I don't just think so," said Michael. He squeezed her shoulder. "I promise so."

Katie leaned her head on Michael's warm hand, her belly full of sticky bun, her heart suddenly full of the same warm, satisfied feeling.

"I promise so, too," she whispered.

PART I

CHAPTER 1

CHAPTER ONE

Five Years Later

The mud was so cold.

It closed around Katie's feet, engulfing her legs up to the knee. She could feel it grinding in her holey socks as she dragged one foot forward through the grey-green slop. She'd learned, in the months she'd spent mudlarking, that lifting her foot above the muck only made the cold bite worse and wore her out faster.

Best to shuffle through it slow and steady. Sometimes her shin would knock against something buried. Could be bone, could be glass. Could be worse. So she kept her arms down in the muck to the elbow, dragging her fingers through the filth in short, careful strokes, searching for anything that might fetch a coin.

Her back and shoulders ached. Long hours had passed like this today, and many more would come before the tide rolled in and forced them up the bank. She tried to keep her mind blank, focused only on the feel of mud and the faint hope of finding something good.

But sometimes, when the ache set in too deep and her stomach gnawed too loud, her thoughts strayed—back to easier times.

She remembered sitting on the humpbacked bridge with Michael, a sticky bun warm in her lap, the air smelling of river and sugar.

"We'll be together in the end. Always."

She huffed out a small laugh. He'd been eleven. She was seven. They'd made that vow while she still had jam on her fingers and crumbs on her chin. It had sounded grand then. Like a promise carved in stone. But they were children, and the world had other plans.

Another memory pushed its way through before she could stop it.

They'd spent the morning in the park, and she'd kept pestering him, asking why he looked like he might cry. He didn't answer, not really. She thought maybe it was about his sister. Even though Tessie had been gone for years, Katie still cried for her sometimes, too. The tenement felt hollow without her.

She'd held Michael's hand on the walk home, thinking it might make him feel better somehow. But when they reached the building and saw the cart—Peter and Joan standing beside it, not with their usual fruit and vegetables but with bundles of clothes and bedding—her stomach dropped.

"Where are we going, Michael?" she'd asked.

His throat moved like he was swallowing rocks. "You... you're not going anywhere, Katie."

She frowned. "Are your mama and papa going to sell

things somewhere else?" That didn't make sense. They sold cabbages, not blankets.

"Katie..." His voice cracked. "I'm going with them."

She couldn't get the words out. "What do you mean?"

"We're leaving."

She didn't know what it meant yet, but something inside her went terribly still.

"Mama and Papa and me are going to live somewhere else," he said, "but you and your mama and siblings are staying here."

She gave her head a sharp shake, trying to drive the memory off. It was done. Michael was gone, and he hadn't come back. That part of her life had been packed up and wheeled off in a cart.

A small, hard shape bumped her fingers. She froze, then closed her hand around it, careful not to slice her palm.

She drew it up through the muck and held it to the light, bracing herself for something foul. But it was a glass bottle. Whole, with only a small chip near the mouth.

Her breath hitched. She wiped it clean with shaking fingers. It might be worth a tuppence. Maybe enough for a whole loaf of bread—soft and fresh, still warm if they were lucky.

She scrambled to her feet, heart thudding. She had to find Molly. But she'd lifted the bottle too high, too long.

"Oi! You!" someone shouted.

Katie flinched. A boy slogged toward her through the mud, face pinched and hungry, his yellow teeth bared.

"Give me that!" he snapped.

Katie screamed and lurched back, but the muck held her fast. He swiped at her with a twisted hand, and she toppled backwards into the cold, sucking mud.

He lunged—and then a clump of slime struck him square in the forehead.

He shrieked and staggered.

"Leave her alone!" James Harrison's voice rang out like thunder. He waded through the muck toward her, legs long and sure despite the sludge. His clothes were as filthy as anyone's, but something in him glowed bright and fierce.

The boy turned and fled.

Then Molly was there, warm hands pulling Katie upright.

"Katie, you poor thing!" she said. "Are you hurt?" Her voice was soft, eyes worried. She was only seventeen, but Katie felt safer beside her than she ever had next to their late mother.

"Look what I found, Mol." Katie held up the bottle, still shaking.

"Oh, my! Well done." Molly beamed. "Have a look at this, James!"

James reached them and took Molly's hand in his own, fingers fitting together like they belonged. "Well done, Katie. You sure you're all right?"

"I'm all right," she said, brushing at the muck on her sleeves. "Maybe we'll find another. Only... only could you stay a little closer, this time?"

Molly gave her arm a squeeze. "Of course we will."

They went back to work, James to her left, Molly to her right. The fear hadn't left her entirely, but something steadier moved in to take its place.

With James and Molly at her side, nothing could touch her.

THE BOTTLE FETCHED a whole tuppence *and* a penny farthing. Along with the few nails and bits of pottery they'd dug up from the mud the day before, the rag-and-bone man who bought their things had given Katie four pennies, which was more than they often found.

She kept a hand curled around the coins in her apron pocket as she hurried down the street, keeping her head low to avoid the glances from passersby. None of them were good. There were men who leered and made Katie's toes curls; and then there were the better-dressed women who looked on her with disgust or, worse, pity.

The smell of the docks was thick in her nostrils—somewhere, there was a salty undertone of the sea, but mostly Katie smelled raw sewage, rotten fish, and tar. It was far less of a stench than she was used to; there was nothing worse than the piercing reek of the sour mud each time she drew her hand from the filth and exposed more of the pungent gases. In comparison, this was fresh air, and Katie drank it in.

Ragged stalls lined the docks here, selling everything from sticks of firewood to pretty trinkets for wealthy folk returning from their travels. Katie threaded through the strangely mixed crowd, dodging petticoated ladies who turned up their pert noses at her passage, and made for the stall hidden away in a corner where one could buy hard, coarse rye bread—only a day old, and hardly at all mouldy —for a penny a loaf, or a farthing perhaps, if the loaf was small and old Mr. Quibble was in a good mood.

She joined the line of miserable paupers awaiting the damp loaves that came wrapped in bits of old newspaper and kept her head on a swivel, her hand clenched tightly around the coins. Trouble was everywhere, she'd learned, and it wasn't often that she walked to the rag-and-bone man's stand without Molly and James. They had sent her away while they mudlarked; they said it was because the rag-and-bone man was more generous with his few pennies later in the day, but Katie knew it had something to do with the ever-growing stench rising from the Thames.

Molly tried not to tell her too much, but everyone said Mama had gotten cholera from the bad air. Katie wondered what one could catch from air so bad it was almost too disgusting to breathe.

She spotted it swiftly: a flash of trouble. The furtive form of a boy, a few years older than her, darting through the crowd. She turned quickly, keeping her money safely in her hand, and watched as the boy snatched a pocketwatch from an unsuspecting gentleman so quickly and deftly that the man didn't notice.

No one would take her coins. Katie clung to them.

The boy scampered off to rejoin a group huddled behind one of the stalls. He showed them a flash of the copper watch and the other thieves pounded him on the back in congratulation. Katie wondered what they would get for that pocketwatch. She supposed it was much more than tuppence, and it made her prize of yesterday's glass bottle seem measly.

Then, it happened. The boy glanced around, and her gaze caught on his face; rakish, freckled, a spray of hair over his forehead.

It was her brother.

"Henry!" Katie cried, stepping out of the line.

But if he heard her, he didn't show it. He simply turned and vanished into the nearest alley with the other children, leaving Katie staring after him, aghast.

Molly was right. Henry *had* spent the past four years as a common thief.

She hadn't wanted to believe it, but now she had no choice.

Katie was trembling, and not because of the damp fog that swirled between the giant ships looming beside the docks. It was cold in her shoes, which never quite managed to try, and her holey shawl could do little for the bone-deep chill rising inexorably from the ground. Nor did the sight of a snoring, drunken sailor sprawled over some broken boxes nearby concern her that much. She could tell her was far too inebriated to pursue her if she ran away.

It was the thought of Molly that left her shaking in her boots.

If Molly knew she was out here all by herself, her big sister would wring her neck, Katie was sure of it. But there was no talking to Molly about Henry. The gentleness instantly left Molly's eyes at the mention of their brother's name, turning to a pain-soaked fury instead. Katie couldn't possibly tell her that she'd seen Henry at this very marketplace.

So she waited, blowing on her frigid fingers, as the morning crowd flowed between the stalls. Mr. Quibble was already there with a shipment of bread collected from the local bakeries. It wasn't quite fresh enough to smell good, but Katie's mouth watered anyway.

The church bell somewhere tolled eight. They had mudlarked until midnight, and only gotten to sleep at two in the morning; the tides were tyrannical masters that cared little for a good night's sleep. Katie knew she had to be back at the shack where they lived before nine.

Impatience made her dance in place. *Where are you?*

Finally, she spotted them: a furtive gang of children slinking through the crowd like a pack of hungry street dogs, largely unnoticed, their shrewd eyes scanning for their next target. Henry was among them. Though his coat was much-mended, Katie realized that he looked very different from the emaciated Molly and James. There was a roundness in his cheeks she hadn't seen there before.

She knew better than to cry his name. Instead, she followed the thieves, clumsily shoving her way through the crowd. More than one curious hand reached out as if to grasp her, but she dodged around them and finally reached a nearby alley just as Henry darted down it.

This time, he couldn't escape her.

She scurried into the alley. "Henry!"

He spun around. None of the other thieves were in sight, and his eyes widened at the sight of her.

"Katie-pie!" he cried. "What are you doing here all alone?" He hurried to her, and he smelled like woodsmoke as he flung his arms around her. "Where's Mol?"

"She's at our house." Katie leaned into his embrace. "I had to come and find you, Henry, I just had to."

He crushed her against his chest for a glorious few moments. Henry's embrace felt like home, even after nearly four years apart.

"Did something happen?" he asked.

His hands fell to his sides, and Katie stepped back to stare up at him. "Well... no," she said. "I just wanted to see you, Henry." The words came out in a whisper. "I miss you."

His gaze darted sideways as if searching for an escape. Katie seized his lapel and clung to it despairingly.

"Come back," she begged. "Why won't you come back to us? We have a little house of our own now."

"It's a shack, Katie," said Henry softly.

"But it's mostly dry, and some nights it's quite warm, and we eat almost every day!" Katie pleaded.

Henry shook his head. "I... I can't."

"But why not?"

"It doesn't matter, Katie. I just can't." Henry shook her off.

A tiny sob escaped her. "Henry, please..."

"You need to stay with Molly and James. They're good people. You'll be safe with them," Henry rasped.

"So will you!"

"Molly doesn't want me." Henry backed away.

"She didn't mean that. Of course she wants you. She misses you."

"Do you believe that?" Henry's eyes darkened. "Do you truly? If you do, then why didn't you bring her with you?"

Katie had nothing to say to that; no words would come past the sudden lump that lodged so firmly in her throat.

"I didn't think so," said Henry.

"Henry, please... Please. Don't you love us anymore?"

He stopped in his tracks, staring at her. "Of course I love you, Katie. I always will."

She tried to swallow the sob, but it choked her a little. "Then stay. Please. Don't go."

Henry's lips hardened into a firm line. "I'm sorry. This is how it has to be. I can't change it, and neither can you."

"Henry!" Katie cried.

But it was too late. He had already whirled around and disappeared down the shadowy alley, into a dark world where Katie couldn't follow.

CHAPTER 2

The river's stench had only worsened.

It clung to Katie as she dragged herself, foot by aching foot, up the slippery, muddy riverbank toward the little shack. The smell hung over the river, so palpable that Katie could almost see it. She imagined it as a green mist that rose from the noxious waters—if they could be called that. The Thames was like a steady current of sludge, with every manner of flotsam drifting in the slow stream: swirling bits of excrement, the damp, hairy forms of dead rats, and a bloated white thing that Katie did not look at too closely. She had already seen more than her fair share of bodies in that river.

She kept her eyes on the shack instead. It wasn't much —a ramshackle little dwelling made of bits of rotting driftwood—but it was warm and dry inside, and the choking smoke from the fire would soon drown out at least some of the smell.

"Has it ever been this bad?" she whispered to Molly.

"What?" Molly asked, slithering along beside her as they climbed toward the shack.

"The smell."

A glint of fear flashed in Molly's eyes. "Well... no. Never."

They squeezed through the old piece of sail that formed the shack door. The interior had a mouldy whiff to it, but at least the sail kept a little of the smell out. The ramshackle wooden walls protected them from the worst of the wind, and Katie went at once to her sleep pallet, where she folded up like a wind-up toy whose clockwork had whirred to a halt.

"Come on, Katie," said Molly. "We need to cook supper with these nice turnips and carrots. Soup will be nice."

"Give me a minute," Katie whispered.

"But aren't you starving?" Molly asked.

Katie closed her eyes. "I'm so tired," she whispered. "Every bit of me hurts."

Molly crouched beside her and touched her forehead.

"Am I sick?" Katie asked.

"No," said Molly firmly. "Not at all. You're fine." She stood up, a jerky movement. "You're tired, that's all. I'll make the soup—you can have a little nap."

Katie closed her eyes. Sleep came easily. Molly woke her to eat the hot, vegetable-laden soup a little while later, but Katie barely stayed awake long enough to clean the bowl. She stirred only slightly when Molly came to bed, wrapped her arms around Katie, and pulled their threadbare blanket close over her shoulders.

The stinging in her throat woke Katie sharply. Her eyes snapped open as she felt her stomach contract and the contents rise queasily in her chest. She took a deep breath, trying to hold back the nausea, but the stench of rotting flesh rolled through her lungs and made it worse.

"Go to sleep, Katie," Molly mumbled, her arms tightening around her. "It's early."

The nausea surged. Katie threw the blankets back and rolled away from Molly, her eyes burning as the acidic bile filled her throat.

"Katie?" Molly gasped.

Katie stumbled to the waste bucket in the corner. She barely made it onto her hands and knees before she was sick.

Soft, cool hands swiped her filthy hair away from her face. Every part of Katie's body ached and trembled with the violent effort of expelling last night's soup. The rolling nausea didn't ease when it was over; she retched, her stomach empty, and came up only with more belly pain.

"Katie, what on Earth is the matter?" Molly's hands shook on her hair.

"What's going on?" James' voice was still thick with sleep.

Katie dragged a hand over her mouth. The horrific smell of the Thames only worsened with every breath she took; it felt as though the filth had penetrated her, sinking into every cell in her body. "I don't feel well."

Molly's hand was ice cold against her forehead. Katie could tell that she was trying to be brave, but her voice quaked so that she could barely squeeze out the words. "James, go for the doctor. I think— I think—"

Katie's heart lurched. She thought of the dozens of funerals they'd attended back in their old neighbourhood until it seemed everyone they knew wore the black of mourning. Fresh graves cluttered the cemetery beside the old church; their gravedigger had had to make room in the corners around the back for small children and babies, since he could fit their coffins there. She remembered the terror in Joan and Peter's eyes, the tremor in Henry's voice when he told her later that they didn't think it was safe to stay, not with that monster stalking the streets and claiming their children. They had taken Michael away because he was their only child left—and they couldn't bear to lose him too.

Then she remembered the way her mother smelled in her last few days on Earth. The way her skin wrapped around the bones of her shoulders and face like it had suddenly grown too small for her. The despair in her eyes; the horrible, weeping sores on her chapped lips from the constant, endless vomiting.

It had all happened because of a monster whose name she was almost afraid to speak, but she squeezed the words out anyway. "Do you think it's cholera?"

Molly's voice grew firm and certain as she gently guided Katie back to bed. "No. I'll fetch you a little water. Don't worry at all. The doctor will be here soon." The words came out stiff and cold.

Katie wasn't so sure she believed Molly—or that Molly believed herself. She lay back on the pallet, her heart pounding, and stared pleadingly at James.

"I'll be back in a jiff, Katie," he said, putting on his coat and grasping the tin that contained their life savings. "Don't you worry. He'll take care of you."

Katie watched him go, her heart thudding in her throat. Hope seemed a stupid thing in this reeking place.

Dr. Connors was a quiet, gentle man, but the sight of him terrified Katie. No, not the sight of him—the *smell* of him. He smelled like soap, but also like death somehow as he leaned over Katie, poking and prodding her painful body.

She lay back on the pallet and hung onto Molly's hand for dear life. The nausea washed over her in sickly waves, making it difficult to focus on anything except holding it in. She draped her arm over her forehead and concentrated on its weight against her skin, on anything except the clawing feeling in her stomach.

Dr. Connors was saying something to Molly. Katie wasn't concentrating on the words, but between waves of sickness, she caught the end of a sentence: "... has killed hundreds by now."

Katie's eyes snapped open. "K-killed?"

Molly gripped her hand more tightly.

Dr. Connors' eyes were soft as he crouched beside Katie, ignoring the filth of their surroundings, and lightly touched her arm. "You may well yet live, my dear." He gave Molly a bottle of medicine. "Here—take a few drops of this tincture morning and night. And for Heaven's sake, move away from this river."

He paused at the shack's doorway and ran a pitying eye over the three of them as they stared after him mutely. "Godspeed to you all."

Then the doctor was gone, and Molly and James were staring mutely at each other over Katie's head.

Katie's body retched, but there was nothing left to bring up, so she curled into a miserable and shuddering heap.

"Why... why did he say we have to get away from the river?" she whispered.

Molly stroked her hair. "Because of the smell, my love. It's not only a smell. It's bad air—miasma—and that's what's been making you so ill."

Katie closed her eyes.

"I'm sorry, Katie," Molly whispered. "I should have moved us away from the river as soon as it started to smell like this."

"But where will we go?" Katie moaned. "What will we do if we can't mudlark? There aren't any jobs. We tried to get them after the cotton mill burned down. There just aren't any!"

"Hush, Katie-pie," said James, touching her shoulder. "We'll work it out. Don't you worry."

"It'll all be all right, Katie," said Molly, her voice now much stronger.

Katie closed her eyes. With their soft, gentle voices resounding above her, it was so easy to drift away into a sweet, peaceful sleep.

"Lavender blue, diddle-diddle, lavender green,

"when I am king, diddle-diddle, you shall be queen."

Papa's hand was big and rough, but the fingertips traced over Katie's cheek with incredible gentleness. They were warm and comforting as his deep voice filled her world while she rocked back and forth in her cradle.

"Call up your men, diddle-diddle, set them to work.

"One to the plough, diddle-diddle, one to the fork."

Katie opened her eyes and gazed up at her father. His face was a vague haze in her memories, but she'd never forget his smile, with the dimple so deep on the left cheek and so little on the right.

"Katie, my sweet, diddle-diddle, why won't you sleep?" he sang.

Katie giggled.

"No giggling." His big hand tickled her neck. "None of that. It's sleepy time for you, my little Katie-pie."

"Sing again," Katie cried.

"Oh, one more time, then. But after that, you must sleep," Papa teased.

His smile shone into her world like the sun.

"Lavender blue, diddle-diddle, lavender green..."

Papa's voice faded into the patter of rain on canvas. Katie woke slowly, and only halfway. Weakness clung to her like wet cloth, blurring the world.

The canvas roof leaked. Water dripped steadily onto the ground beside her.

She nestled her cheek deeper into Molly's warm lap. Her whole body throbbed—dull, hollow pulses from the hunger and the sickness that hadn't quite won. The bread they'd eaten earlier seemed like something from another life.

She wanted the dream back. That voice, that warmth. It was the only memory she had of her father, John, left behind in Yorkshire when the drought stole the farm and scattered their family.

She didn't know if he lived anymore. Didn't know if he'd want to.

Maybe, when she had more strength, she'd ask Molly to write to him. Or, she might've once asked Michael.

Her breath caught.

Michael would've known what to say. He always had. Back then, anyway. Before he vanished from her world like everyone else.

Papa's voice faded away into the patter of rain on the canvas. Katie woke slowly and only halfway, weakness still clinging to her, making the world into a strange and blurry swirl. The canvas roof was leaking, she vaguely realized. Droplets of water pat-pattered on the ground by her face.

She nestled her head into Molly's warm lap. Exhaustion throbbed in her, accompanying the aching starvation in her belly. The river's miasma had not been able to kill her, yet this hunger felt as though it might. The stale bread they'd eaten earlier seemed a long way away.

Katie longed for the dream to return. It was the only memory she had of her father, John, whom they'd left behind in Yorkshire when the drought robbed him of the family farm. But that was a long time ago. Now she didn't know if John lived or died anymore. What would he think of them living in the shack.

No, not the shack. Katie blinked, staring at the little river of rainwater trickling past her face. They weren't in the shack anymore; they'd had to get away from the river. They had made a quiet alley their home now, with the canvas stretched between the two buildings that flanked them, and the wind sliced through this place and chilled Katie's damp clothes.

She closed her eyes, and Molly's gently hand brushed her hair back from her face. Sleep wrapped its arms around her, yet her stinging hunger made it so difficult to fall asleep.

As if from a long way off, she heard James and Molly talking in quiet whispers.

"Don't say it," Molly was saying, her body trembling. "Please don't."

James' voice was quiet, but held firmness and strange courage. "My precious Molly, I know you don't want to hear it, and you have every reason not to. I don't want to think it, either. But you and I both know the only choice we have left is the workhouse."

Katie clenched her eyes tightly shut and pulled her blankets over her ears, focusing on the pattering rain instead of their voices. She didn't want to hear the word *workhouse* again—a word that her mother used to spit like something dirty.

No... no... She was so tired. She must have heard wrong. Maybe her hunger was making her see and hear things that weren't there.

Sleep came like a mercy.

MOLLY SHOOK her awake early the next morning. Waking up was piercingly cruel. As soon as Katie's eyes opened, she knew discomfort, hunger, cold, and the throbbing pain that ruled in her limbs after yesterday's long stint from one factory to the next, seeking work.

She moaned.

"I know, Katie, I know," said Molly softly, "but it's time to get up. Maybe we'll still be in time for breakfast."

Katie raised her head from the pallet that left painful kinks in her neck and hips. "B-breakfast? We haven't had breakfast since we left off mudlarking. Where will we find breakfast?" Her pain and hunger spilled into irritation. "Leave me alone, Mol. Let me sleep."

Molly tugged her blanket away from her. "We have to go, Katie-pie. Come along, now. Get up."

Katie forced herself to her feet and stared blearily around at the alley. A clutter of rubbish lay in a mound along one side, which they had used as a windbreak. The threadbare canvas dripped water onto the muddy floor. Their few things lay among them; a pile of newspapers for James to sleep on, the rotting wooden pallet for the girls, and a few sticks of firewood burning out slowly in the middle. All their other things—their cups and pots and spoons—had long since been sold for food.

Food. Katie swayed where she stood, longing for it. "Did you mean it, Mol? Where will we find breakfast?"

Molly took her hand like she was a little child. "I did. Come along. You'll soon see."

Katie clung to her hand, asking no questions, as they walked away from the alley. James was waiting at the alley mouth. His eyes darted to Molly's, then dipped away. Usually, he gazed at her the way Katie eyed the sticky buns in the bakery windows when they scavenged through the rubbish heap nearby for scraps, but now it was as though he couldn't look at her.

"What's wrong, James?" Katie asked.

"Nothing, Katie-pie." James managed a smile. "Nothing at all."

Katie wanted to ask why they weren't rolling up and hiding their blankets to keep them from being stolen, but it took so much out of her to speak. Instead, she held Molly's hand and followed behind her in obedient, exhausted silence as they left the alley behind and wandered through the streets.

Neither Molly nor James said a single thing. It was as though a curtain of ice hung between them, the way there used to be silence between Molly and Henry sometimes, too.

It had been so long since Katie last saw Henry. She missed him with an unexpected pang of agony that made her gasp and touch her chest.

"It'll be all right, Katie," said Molly softly. "Don't worry. We'll have enough to eat very soon."

Katie wondered if Molly was telling her lies to make

her feel better. She had long since stopped feeling hungry; even the painful hunger pangs had ceased their pointless assault on her empty stomach. She felt nothing but weak now. Her feet dragged across the rough cobbles as they left the slums behind and wandered along a broader street, stopping now and then as hansom-cabs drove by much too quickly in a flurry of whirring wheels and sweaty horses.

Molly's hand trembled on Katie's at first, but it magically steadied after a few blocks when they turned down an even larger street and passed a church and a row of little shops. Katie barely looked at them. She kept her eyes on her feet, willing them to keep moving, one after the other, to keep carrying her forward despite the exhaustion that sucked them down.

Finally, Molly stopped. Katie leaned against her, hoping they didn't have to keep moving.

"I'm tired, Mol," she whispered.

Molly's voice trembled a little. "Do you feel ill?"

"I'm just so, so tired." Katie scraped the words out with the last of her strength.

Molly's hand gripped hers more tightly. "We're nearly there."

They stood a few moments longer, long enough for Katie to find the energy to raise her head. Great walls towered before her on either side of an iron gate. A little guardhouse leaned against the wall by the gate, and iron spikes lined the top, looking dull and dangerous in the sun.

Katie had no idea what this place might be, but she felt too tired to wonder as Molly led her across the street to the guardhouse.

The man inside the guardhouse smoked a reeking pipe and looked at them with less interest than Katie once regarded faeces-encrusted nails she found in the Thames. Katie hated that look. She stared at the floor to avoid it.

"What's all this, then? I suppose you're intakes, are you?"

Intakes? Katie lifted her head. Where were they being taken into?

"Yes, sir," said James. "Three new intakes, please."

Katie gasped. "Intakes? Where are we?"

Molly's warm arm surrounded her shoulders. "It's all right, Katie. It's going to be all right."

Her voice sounded so strange; steady, yet flat and lifeless. Katie looked up at her and saw the same dull blankness in her eyes.

Her stomach churned. If it had contained anything, she might have vomited.

The man opened the gate. "Go on, then. First door on your left—that's the intake office." He made a disgusted sound through his nose. "Rather you than me."

James moved forward, but Katie couldn't get her feet to stir. "Molly, where are we?"

"It'll be all right, Katie," Molly repeated. "Trust me. Please. You have to trust me."

Her voice cracked a little on that last word, and Katie stared up at her big sister, terror thudding through her body. Molly's voice was still steady, but tears now shimmered in her eyes.

It couldn't be, Katie thought. "It could not—must not—be true, that Molly had brought her here. She had dreamed her and James talking about it last night, hadn't she? It couldn't be true.

Trust me. The same plea echoed in Molly's eyes, and Katie knew that she did. She trusted Molly with everything she was. No one else in the world had ever been so devoted to caring for Katie and protecting her; it would be pointless *not* to trust Molly.

She gripped her sister's hand more tightly and nodded, and Molly led them forward.

The gate shut behind them with a terrific crash that made Katie jump, but Molly's arm around her shoulders stopped her from looking back. Her mouth felt dry as they walked into a gigantic, cold building with tiny windows. It smelled musty inside, and when the door thudded shut behind them, it seemed very dark.

The bare room contained nothing but a desk. The walls and floor were all of grey stone, cold and heartless, easy to scrub.

The woman behind the desk looked as though she'd been sucking limes. She held up a pen like a weapon and fixed them with a cold glare. "Come on, then. I haven't got all day. Name."

James approached the desk, his limbs moving twitchily, like those of a puppet.

Katie could barely squeeze the word out through the terror strangling her chest. "Molly…"

"Hush, hush." Molly rubbed her arm. "It's all right. You're all right."

James gave his name and birthday, and the woman scribbled it, then gestured at a door off to their left. James turned and walked up to it. He paused to look back at Molly for a long moment, and Molly made a small, strangled noise in her chest before James disappeared through the door.

The sound Molly made chilled Katie to the bone. She had never heard her big sister emit a sound of grief or dismay before, despite all the hard things Molly had gone through.

"Mol, where's he going?" Katie whimpered.

"Names!" the impatient woman at the desk barked.

The sound made Katie jump. She tugged herself away from her sister and backed toward the door. "Molly, tell me what's happening!"

Molly turned to her. Tears danced in her eyes again, and she gently reached for Katie's arms, but Katie moved back despite the trapping pressure of the door behind her. "We're in the workhouse. Aren't we?"

Molly's face crumpled. "I'm so sorry, Katie, but we don't have a choice. We won't last much longer on the streets. Look at you." She was nearly crying now. "There's no other way."

Katie shook her head as if she could dispel this nightmare. A thousand memories ran through her mind of all the times Mama had said that no Turner would ever end up in the workhouse. She had spoken of the workhouse as though it was some kind of prison, a place full of shame and suffering, where one only went if one had failed completely. The thought had always frightened Katie. Now, it strangled her in terror.

"Mama said—" she began.

"Mama's not here!"

Molly's yell snapped across Katie's soul as though her big sister had struck her. She stared up at Molly, every part of her stinging in agony. She was trembling.

Molly was right. Mama wasn't here. Nor was Papa. It was only them, and she'd always thought that Molly could do anything, could keep everything together. Molly was the great stone pillar who supported Katie's world, but looking at her pale face and the tears trickling down her cheeks, Katie knew that her sister had finally cracked. The pillar was crumbling.

Katie's world was falling apart.

"I'm sorry, love." Molly roughly seized her hand. "There's no other way."

"Names, please!" The woman at the desk made the word *please* sound like a curse.

Katie clung to Molly's hand as her sister plodded across the room. This was what Molly had meant when she'd talked about breakfast. There must be food here in the workhouse. Her trembling hands steadied as she stayed close by Molly's side. Even without James, perhaps this would be tolerable. She would have Molly with her, after all.

Molly told the woman her name and birthday.

"And the little one?" The woman jerked her head at Katie.

Katie thought it so strange that the woman would call her that. She was thirteen, after all, practically a woman.

"Katie... Katie Turner," said Molly.

The woman jabbed her pen at the ledger as though this offended her somehow. Then she stood, and something frightened Katie about the way she straightened, like a monstrous predator about to pounce.

"Anise!" she roared. "That one's for the girls, this one's for the women. You take the little one. I think she'll put up a fight."

One for the girls, one for the women. The horrible truth met Katie with a terrible impact, as though someone had struck her in the chest with a sledgehammer.

They were going to take her away from Molly.

"What?" she screamed. "What are they talking about?" She prayed that someone would say it wasn't true, that her fears were all foolish, that it would be all right.

But of course, no one did.

The woman prowled from behind her desk. Another, younger lady detached herself from the shadows at the edge of the room and stalked nearer. Katie couldn't watch them both at the same time.

Katie clung to Molly's hand with all her strength. "What's happening?"

"I'm so sorry, Katie." Molly sounded like she was choking. "I'm so very, very sorry."

"No! No, don't take me away from her!" Katie stumbled backward, trying to escape both of the women. "I want to be with my sister! I want to be with my sister!"

"It'll be all right, Katie." Molly clutched her in a trembling embrace, tears flowing freely down her cheeks now, and that terrified Katie more than anything else. "Go with these people. They'll take care of you."

"No! I want *you*, Molly!" Katie cried the words so loudly that her throat burned with the impact.

Molly twisted out of Katie's grasp. "Go on, now. Go on."

Katie was screaming. She couldn't tell if she was screaming words, only that she clawed at Molly's clothes, that she would do anything, anything, to stay with her sister, the only person who had always been with her since she was a baby.

The younger lady's fingers closed on Katie's arms like a claw. "It's time to go."

"Let go of me!"

"*Enough!*"

The woman from the desk bellowed the word. Katie's knees buckled; she almost fell to the ground in terror. The woman loomed over Katie, her eyes ablaze, and Katie knew suddenly that this woman would do terrible things to her if she didn't comply.

"Stop that fuss at once," she said. "Go with her, or you

will be cast onto the streets alone, and no workhouse in London will take you in!"

Alone. The word resounded around the inside of Katie's soul, barbed and jagged, tearing her apart. She could not be alone on the streets. She knew, with the fearful certainty of the starving, that she would not survive.

She turned to Molly a last time, and her sister was broken, sobbing, tears pouring down her cheeks. Katie had never seen Molly like this before—not when Papa sent them to London, not when she pulled Tessie from the cotton mill fire and almost lost her own life in the process, not when Tessie ultimately expired, nor when Mama died. Not even when James was deathly ill.

She'd never seen Molly cry. But now her older sister wept with shattered abandon.

It made it difficult to feel angry. Perhaps anger would have been better; anger, at least, would have propelled her forward. Instead, Katie felt her world collapsing, as though the ground beneath her feet had crumbled into ash. She felt her body crying, but in her heart, all she felt was numb and trembling shock as she turned away and walked into a cold, dark future with no family at all.

THE WORKHOUSE WAS everything Katie had feared.

She had not known, specifically, exactly what made this place so horrifying. Her mother had not described to her the fact that there were not enough beds for all the girls in the room, so that the older ones lay like queens upon real beds with straw mattresses and the littler ones piled into heaps on the pallets. No one had told her of the unique horrors of sleeping tucked against a mass of utter strangers who might kick or punch in their sleep; she had never heard of how it would feel as the clammy sweat of a sickly young girl soaked against her own skin while her scalp crawled with the writhing of new lice. Nor had Mama said what mealtimes were truly like: mad scrambles for survival more than orderly times of repast, with the bigger girls elbowing the little ones aside, ready to snatch up away their meagre rations. Even when Katie succeeded in keeping her bowl, the sustenance within proved little better than the streets: watery soups with no salt, chunks of dry bread and hard cheese, or gruel that stuck to the roof of her mouth like glue.

No, Mama had not known the horrors well enough to tell Katie what exactly to fear about the workhouse, but the gleam of terror in her eyes had been real. She had feared isolation, physical pain, hunger, and constant, unending humiliation. She had been right to fear this. All this became Katie's new reality in the workhouse, and over the next few days, she became intimately acquainted with all of these.

Worst of all, cruelly, was the lessons.

Katie had heard whispers about the lessons on that first evening as she huddled in a corner with her bowl of gruel. They had given her a sudden pang of hope at the time. Molly could read and write, skills Katie had always envied. In the better years when they were working as costermongers, Molly had taught her a few basic letters, but that all ended when they became homeless.

The thought of learning to read was a tiny speck of cheer that she clung to through that long, cold first night. But she soon learned that those "lessons" meant nothing.

By the third day, Katie had learned exactly how to behave at the lessons. She kept her head low as the bell summoned her and the dozens upon dozens of other girls from the dining hall down the long, cold, windowless hallway to the classroom. Katie made sure to stay near the back, where the littlest girls were; they were too miserable and scared to push or trip her, unlike the other girls her age.

Their progress down the hall grew steadily slower. They were crawling when they reached the narrow door that led into the classroom, all because of the big girls in front. These were Katie's age or a little older, yet to her they seemed like titans. They dawdled along the hallway, pausing to inspect their nails or stare at nothing.

One of them stood a head taller than everyone else. Her fine, black hair was like a shadow on her shoulders, making her an apparition of darkness to Katie's frightened eyes.

Their teacher waited at the door. She was herself a slender little woman, looking hardly any older than Molly.

"Hurry up, girls," she shouted. "Hurry up."

The big girls at the front ignored her. Maggie Granger, the shadow-haired one, even walked a little slower.

The teacher said nothing to them as they dawdled into her classroom. Instead, her sharp grey eyes landed on Katie.

"Hurry up!" she barked. "How often must I tell you to be punctual?"

Katie cowered. "Yes, miss. Sorry, miss."

"Get inside," the teacher snapped, clutching her wooden ruler in one hand like a weapon. Katie had often seen it applied to young hands and heads, but never to Maggie Granger and her cronies.

She slunk into the classroom. It was, she thought, the most bare room in all the workhouse, containing nothing but a few rows of steel benches securely bolted to the floor and a blackboard little bigger than a poster at the front. Maggie and the rest took the prime seats at the back of the room. The little ones flocked in a frightened stampede to the front row, and Katie strove to hide somewhere in the middle, trying her best to be invisible.

Their teacher, Miss Dawson, strode to the front of the room. Maggie's group never stopped laughing. One of them threw her head back and laughed, a raucous, cawing sound, like the ravens who used to roost in the trees at the graveyard where Mama was buried.

"Quiet," said Miss Dawson.

Her voice was a tiny, ineffectual piping against the hubbub of conversation from the bigger girls. The little ones fidgeted and whispered to one another. Katie tried to sit still and stared earnestly at the blackboard, where the same row of letters were written out as had been there since the first day.

"Quiet, I said!" Miss Dawson called.

Her cry had no effect on the crowd. Maggie Granger kicked the little girl sitting in front of her. The child fell to her knees against the next bench and sobbed.

"Clementine, stop that at once," Miss Dawson ordered.

"But it wasn't her, miss," Katie cried.

Miss Dawson stared at her for a moment during which she failed to remember Katie's name. "Quiet—you! Or you'll go to the refractory ward!"

Katie shrank back. *What is that?*

Maggie leaned closer to her. "Be careful, new girl," she hissed, "you'll be without company, food, and light for days and days if you're not."

Katie stared at her in horror. Surely no such punishment could exist even in this place, could it?

Miss Dawson had given up on getting the class to be quiet. She turned to the blackboard. "Get out your slates," she ordered, "and copy these letters after me."

Katie looked around for her slate, which Miss Dawson

had said was supposed to remain underneath her seat. A few children half-heartedly retrieved theirs from beneath their benches, but Katie couldn't find hers. Her hands trembled as she searched.

Something hard jabbed into her back. "Looking for this, new girl?"

Katie looked up. Maggie leaned between the rows, holding out a cracked slate, its pencil worn to nothing but a nub.

She froze in the face of Maggie's baleful glare.

"Well?" the bigger girl barked.

"Pay attention, girls!" Miss Dawson pleaded as another small girl burst into tears.

"Y-yes," Katie managed. "Yes, that's mine."

"Take it, then."

Katie slowly extended her hand. At the last moment, Maggie slapped her fingers on the back of the bench with the slate, resulting in a pang of agony. Katie cried out and snatched her hand back.

"That's enough!" Miss Dawson bellowed. "You! New girl! Where is your slate?"

Katie clutched her aching hand to her chest. "It— it— it —" She thought of the long, cold night in the dormitory she had to share with Maggie Granger. "I don't know where it is, miss." The lie came easily compared with the consequences of the truth.

Miss Dawson gripped her wooden ruler. "Then you'll have three strikes, as the workhouse rules say, and you'll find that slate or sit alone in the refractory ward for the next class. Come here at once."

Shivering, Katie dragged herself across the room. The other children laughed and booed; the loudest, raucous laughter came from the back, led by Maggie. Miss Dawson's thin face was puckered into pale harshness as Katie reached her.

"Hold out your hand," she commanded.

Katie knew what came next. Her supervisor at the cotton mill had struck her hands many times for tiny transgressions like moving too slowly beneath the cotton mule and losing a few hairs when the hideous machine came too close. She slowly extended her hand and braced herself.

As the ruler thudded over her palm with burning agony, Katie dared not look at the teacher. She looked at Maggie Granger instead. Her grin was so wide that Katie knew at once this was exactly what Maggie had planned.

Why? Katie wondered. What had she done to deserve this hatred?

Tears filled her eyes. They could not dull the pain in her hand, but at least they veiled the horrible glee on Maggie's face.

CHAPTER 3

CHAPTER THREE

Few times in Katie's day were as desperate and frightening as standing in line for breakfast, such as it was.

Years ago, Molly used to tell stories of the breakfasts they had enjoyed on the farm in Yorkshire: eggs and sausages and thick slices of fresh bread and butter. Sometimes there were even kippers or oranges, she said. Katie wondered if anyone in the world really could eat that well even once a day. In the workhouse, breakfast was a glob of cold gruel in the bottom of a tin plate, and perhaps it would have disgusted her a few years ago in better times.

Now, she trembled in anticipation of that clammy grey substance.

She could feel Maggie Granger's breath on the back of her neck. The bigger girl was so close behind her that goosebumps prickled Katie's arms.

Please, she prayed silently, *please let me get to eat this time.*

The line shuffled forward, nearing a long table where a hollow-eyed woman scooped gruel from the great cast-iron cauldron into the bowls that the girls offered. The woman's face was grey, her cheeks hollowed out by some disease that left her lips faintly blue as well. Katie wondered if she would look this way, too, if she lived to be a grown woman in this terrible place.

Finally, she reached the table's end and grasped a spoon and bowl with shaky hands. She approached the woman with the gruel. Her stomach rumbled painfully at the smell of food, even if this was the plainest, most miserable food imaginable.

"Hold still," the woman rasped.

Katie fought with her shaking hands and quickly glanced over her shoulder. Maggie was right behind her, gathering up her own spoon and bowl.

The woman dumped a spoonful of gruel into Katie's bowl. Katie ducked her head and scrambled off.

"Oi," Maggie barked. "You! Where are *you* going?"

"No raising voices in the dining hall," a matron bellowed.

The same matron wouldn't stop Maggie from stealing Katie's breakfast. Katie hugged the bowl to her chest and scanned the room, searching for an empty seat, but only one table remained open: the one where Maggie and her cronies always sat.

Her head swivelled around. Maggie waited impatiently for the woman to fill her bowl with gruel.

"Pssst!"

The small sound came from somewhere near Katie's knees. She looked around, panicking.

"Down here," someone whispered.

Katie looked down as the tablecloth twitched aside, revealing a young and smiling face tucked beneath the table.

"Quick!" said the face. "Before she sees."

Maggie had turned her attention, if only for a moment, to the woman with the ladle. Katie dived beneath the table.

"Shhh now." The girl under the table gave her a blinding grin, her teeth white in the shadows. "She'll walk right past."

Katie held her breath, clutching the bowl to her chest. To her frightened mind, Maggie's footsteps thudded like those of a giant, but the other girl was right. Maggie walked right past their table.

Katie turned, wide-eyed, to stare at the smiling girl. "How...?"

"I've been here a while. I've learned a few tricks," said the girl.

Katie stared into her bowl for a breathless second, awed by the idea of having her entire meal to herself, before a nasty thought struck her. What if this girl—with her pretty blonde hair and big brown eyes—had merely lured Katie down here to steal her gruel herself? She looked Katie's age; she was big enough to be a bully.

Panic gripped her. Katie seized her spoon and bolted a mouthful of gruel in a frightened gulp, then almost choked.

"Hush, hush!" the other girl hissed. "They'll find us!"

Katie struggled to stop herself from coughing. She swallowed the mouthful with an effort.

"I shan't steal from you, you know," said the girl with a sudden, radiant smile. "I'm not like that."

Katie stared at her. She hadn't known that there were girls in this workhouse who were simply "not like that"; to her, they were all predators or prey, bullies or the bullied. It struck her, looking into those peaceful brown eyes, that this girl existed somewhere beyond those realms.

"I'm Hannah," the girl added. "What's your name?"

"K-Katie."

"Glad to meet you, Katie." Hannah returned her attention to her own bowl of gruel.

Katie kept a wary eye on her, but she ate slowly, and Hannah never looked twice at her bowl. The portion seemed pitiful compared to the pit of hunger in her stomach, but her hands had stopped trembling when she'd scared up every tiny morsel left in the bottom of the bowl.

"Don't mind Maggie," said Hannah.

"She's so frightening."

"Oh, I know. But it's all right. She'll soon move to the women's section," said Hannah. "Everyone does, the month when they turn fourteen."

"I know," Katie murmured. "That's why they took me away from my sister. I'll only be fourteen in February."

Hannah tilted her head. "You have a sister in the workhouse, too?"

"Molly." Katie hadn't said her name aloud in—what—weeks? Time seemed meaningless in the workhouse; she might have been here for days or years. "She's seventeen."

"I had a big sister, too." Hannah's smile turned wistful. "She died."

"I'm sorry."

"It was a long time ago, before Papa's business failed."

Katie looked up. "Your family was well-off, too?"

"Well, much better off than now, I suppose. Papa used to have a shop; Everett Haberdashery, he called it. Then thieves robbed our shop and took so much money that Papa had to borrow some, and it only got worse and worse after that."

"My papa had a farm," said Katie, "but then the drought came. My mama died and my brother went away. It was only Molly and her beau and me." She paused. "Is your papa in the workhouse?"

"No." Hannah spoke steadily. "Papa and Mama died the same time as my sister. It was the cholera."

Katie reached out a hand. "My mama died of cholera, too."

The movement was reflexive; she did not expect anything from it, but nonetheless, Hannah reached out and gripped her hand tightly in response.

"It's hard to be alone," Hannah whispered.

"Yes," said Katie; but she had the feeling that she was not alone anymore.

KATIE SQUINTED at the letters on the blackboard. Small as it was, she had to look closely to see the figures on it from her position at the very back of the classroom, wedged between the chest of drawers where the slates were stored and the corner of the back wall.

This was the only disadvantage of the spot Hannah had showed her months ago when they first became friends. With Katie and Hannah out of sight for most lessons, Maggie had chosen other children to pick on. Miss Dawson was too busy shouting at the little ones for crying when Maggie kicked them to pay much attention to two girls tucked into a corner, slates in hand, quietly paying attention.

D-O-G. Katie carefully copied the letters onto her slate,

the pencil digging into the hard surface with a scratchy sound. "Dog," she whispered.

Hannah grinned. "You're learning." She had covered her slate in fine, careful scribbles; Hannah had been able to read and write long before coming to the workhouse.

"What does yours say?" Katie whispered.

Hannah turned the slate over. "See if you can read it."

Katie looked at the letters carefully and sounded them out one by one. "I, am, hopey?"

"Happy," Hannah corrected.

"Happy, to, have, a..." Katie stopped. "F-r-eye-ee-nd."

"Friend," said Hannah.

Katie looked up.

Hannah smiled, lighting up the world. "I really am happy to have a friend."

"Me too," Katie whispered.

Miss Dawson scribbled something new on the board. Katie eagerly copied the next word down: *R-U-G*. "Rug," she read.

"You're coming on well. You'll be writing letters before you know it," said Hannah.

Letters. Molly used to write letters to Papa, once. She'd stopped after Mama died and never wanted to talk about it when Katie asked why. If only Katie could write to Papa herself and beg him to rescue her from this place... But it wasn't allowed, and where would she find ink, paper, and stamps, even if she knew his address?

A bell clanged deep inside the workhouse, announcing that it was supper time.

Katie and Hannah put their slates away in the drawers and moved on before the other children had finished rising from their benches. They were the first children to reach the dining hall, ignoring Miss Dawson's ineffectual cries to slow down. By the time Maggie and the other bullies reached the hall, Katie and Hannah were safely in their hiding place under the table, eating their stringy fish soup in peace.

It was still hot enough to burn. Katie blew on her spoon for a minute and relished the hot, if watery, mouthful.

"Will we get soup more often, do you think, all the way until spring?" she wondered.

Hannah nodded. "We usually get bread and cheese more often in summer, but we get soup for winter."

"I like soup better. Sometimes they put real meat in it."

"Or beans. Beans are nice, too."

Katie wasn't sure she would use the word *nice* to describe the gummy mess of mashed beans with hardly any salt, but it was food, and with Hannah by her side she ate three times a day.

"Molly was right about one thing," she murmured.

"What's that?"

"We do eat every day in the workhouse. In that way, I suppose it's better than the streets. In the last few weeks on the street I think we ate once every two or three days most of the time."

"I was never on the streets." Hannah splashed her spoon in her bowl. "When my mama died after my papa and sister, the vicar came to bury her, and after the funeral he brought me straight here. I'm glad he did. The streets sound horrid."

"It's horrid here, too."

"I think it's even more horrid for you than for me, because you know your sister is still alive and you can't go to her."

The words tugged Katie's heart. She paused, feeling a

sudden, queasy wave of longing that allayed her hunger for a brief moment.

Hannah touched her hand. "I'm sorry. I didn't mean to make you sad."

"It's all right. You don't make me sad." Katie moved a little closer to her on the cold stone floor. "You... you're the only thing here that makes me *not* sad."

Hannah smiled. "You, too."

"I'll find Molly." Katie cleared her throat. "I know I will. It's only a little while until February, when we'll both be fourteen and we'll have to go work with the women. And then Molly will be there."

"Yes!" Hannah smiled. "I was so afraid to move, but if Molly's there, I know we'll be all right."

"Yes, we will. We'll be more than all right. Oh, Hannah, I can't wait for you to meet Molly. She's wonderful. She can do anything—anything in the whole world—and she always knows what to do next. Even... even though she brought me here, I know she did it to save me. She knew we would be separated for a few months, but she did it to keep me from starving on the streets."

"She must have been terribly brave to give you up and come to the workhouse. It sounds as though Molly would do anything for you, no matter how much it hurt her heart."

"She would," said Katie confidently. "I know it. Even before Mama died, Molly was the one who looked after all of us."

"She was?"

"Yes. Even the grown ups used to rely on her. She was... she was the one who took care of us, but Michael was the one who took care of *me*."

"Michael?" said Hannah softly. "Who is he?"

Katie was quiet for a moment, a small smile crossing her face. "Someone I knew when I was little. We were... we were very close. His family lived with ours for a time."

"He was a friend?"

"More than that," Katie said softly. "We cared for each other very much. I suppose you could say we were sweethearts, though we were just children." She stirred her soup thoughtfully. "He was kind to me when I was frightened and alone. When I was seven and everything was falling apart, he made me feel safe."

Hannah leaned closer. "What was he like?"

"Gentle. Protective. He used to share his food with me when I was hungry, and he'd tell me stories when I couldn't sleep." Katie's voice grew wistful. "We even made promises to each other before his family had to leave. That we'd find each other again someday."

"Do you think you will?"

Katie was quiet for a long moment. "I hope so. But we were children then, and that was eight years ago. People change so much from childhood." She managed a realistic smile. "He'd be a man now, probably with his own life, his own path. I wonder sometimes if he even remembers those promises. They felt so important when we were small, but..."

"But you still think of him."

"I do," Katie admitted. "Not every day like I used to, but when I think about happier times, he's always there in those memories. I suppose I'd like to know he's well and happy, wherever he is. When I knew him, he was kind, but always sad... especially after his sister Tessie died."

"You've told me a little about Tessie before. She died even though Molly saved her from a fire."

"She had brown lung. It was all just too much for her...

It broke Michael's heart. For a long time after that, I used to give him half of my milk every night, because I thought it could make him feel better." Katie touched her chest. "Now I know nothing can make you feel better after your sister went away, but he always talked about it and thanked me for it, even years later."

Hannah rested a hand on Katie's knee. "Where is he now?"

"I don't know." Katie stirred her soup, her expression growing wistful. "His family had to leave during the cholera outbreak. That was eight years ago now." She was quiet for a moment. "We made promises to each other before he left. That we'd find each other again someday, that we'd always be together."

"Do you think you'll ever see him again?"

Katie's smile was both hopeful and sad. She shrugged. "Those promises felt so real when we were children, and what we had was real. But I was seven and he was eleven. We're different people now." She looked down at her hands. "Sometimes I wonder if he even thinks about those promises anymore. They might seem like children's games to him now."

"But they weren't games to you?"

"No, they weren't games," Katie said softly. "We loved each other, in the way children can love. It was innocent but it was genuine." She paused. "I suppose I hope that if we did meet again, there might be something there to build on. But I also know that childhood love doesn't automatically become adult love. That would have to grow between who we are now, not who we were then."

Hannah leaned closer. "You still care about him."

"I do," Katie admitted. "I probably always will. But caring about someone and having a future with them are different things, aren't they? I try to be realistic about that, even though..." She trailed off.

"Even though what?"

"Even though part of me still hopes," Katie finished quietly. "Do you really think we aren't stuck here forever?"

"I know we aren't. Your Molly will have a plan, won't she? She'll be able to get us out someday."

Katie's tears cleared. She sipped her soup and nodded. "Molly will have a plan. Molly *always* has a plan."

Katie smiled again, softer this time, as a future began to take shape in her mind—one with warmth, and friendship, and Molly's sure hand leading the way. Maybe, just maybe, there'd be room in it to look for people lost to her. Maybe even Michael.

"I believe in Molly. Everything is going to be all right."

The last few weeks in the girls' section at the workhouse was a vast improvement on the previous months, all for one reason: Maggie turned fourteen the month before Katie and Hannah did, and she was suddenly, blissfully, gone.

It seemed as though a communal breath of relief ran through the girls' dormitory on the first night without Maggie. Hannah said there would be a new bully eventually—there had been an older girl before Maggie, and another one before that—but for that first night, everyone slept in peace, fearing no elbows to the face or trodden fingers. Katie and Hannah no longer had to hide beside the closet during lessons. They could sit at the table at mealtimes, which eased the ever-present chilblains on Katie's fingers.

Sleeping through every night was a glorious luxury, but Katie woke early on the morning of the first day of February with a little sting of excitement deep in her stomach. She kept her eyes closed, curled on her side with her back to Hannah's, and listened to her friend's slow breathing for what felt like an eternity until the bell finally rang.

Katie was up before the matron could bang on their door and tell them to get dressed. She shook Hannah gently.

"Hannah, Hannah, wake up," she cried. "It's today. We're moving today. We'll finally get to see Molly!"

Hannah sat up, her hair in her eyes, her voice bleary. "Wh-what?"

"It's the first of February, Hannah. Today is the day!"

"Breakfast in a quarter hour!" The matron hammered on the dormitory door. "Every bed had better be spotless when I go in there!"

A mad rush of activity filled the dormitory as the girls scrambled out of bed and hastened to fold their blankets on their straw mattresses or sleeping pallets, lest they anger the matron and earn reduced food or a stint in the dreaded refractory ward. Hannah and Katie worked together to fold their two blankets and place them neatly at the foot of the sleeping pallet they shared.

"Do you think Molly knows?" Hannah asked.

"Oh, of course she does. She knows my birthday is this month. By now she must have seen, like we did, that they move people around on the first day of each month in this workhouse." Katie laughed. "She must be as excited as we are. I know she can't wait to hug me—I just know it!"

Hannah's eyes sparkled as they led the crowd of girls to the dining hall, where the usual gruel awaited them for breakfast. To Katie, it might as well have been eggs and sausages and kipper and buttered bread, so high was her excitement for this glorious day.

Her longing for Molly had never felt so fierce. She ached to see her sister's soft eyes, to feel those steady arms wrap around her and remind her what safety felt like. Everything would be all right once they were together. Molly would know what to do.

She always did.

"Easy, Katie." Hannah laughed. "No one's going to take that from you."

Katie realized that she was bolting her gruel as quickly as she could eat. She slowed, grinning. "I know! But I want breakfast to be over as quickly as we can. I want to go and see Mol."

"I can't wait, either. She sounds so—so—I don't know; so much like someone who is a protector."

"That's exactly what Molly is. She'll protect us too, Hannah, and everything will be all right when we're with her. Molly took care of me through everything that happened. James, too. She'll take care of you as well."

Though it seemed to take a hundred years, breakfast finally came to an end, and the sour-faced matron from the women's section came into the dining hall. It was the same woman who had been at the intake desk on that awful day when Molly, Katie, and James first came to the workhouse, and the sight of her still contrived to send a shudder through Katie's spine. Mrs. Crowe had cold, hard, unforgiving eyes, and if it wasn't for the fact that Molly was waiting for her, Katie would have been terrified to go to the women's section with her instead of staying here with insipid little Miss Dawson.

"Silence!" she screamed.

The girls in the dining hall cowered as one. Katie kept her head down, shaking. The woman's shriek reminded her so painfully of the day when she had cried *Enough!* in that dreaded intake room.

Mrs. Crowe consulted the piece of paper she held in her hand. "Katie Turner and Hannah Everrett, come with me," she ordered.

Katie ducked her head and hurried to rise. She scuttled toward Mrs. Crowe, whose face twisted with fury.

"What are you doing, you stupid girl?" she yelled. "Take your dishes to their place! Do you think they wash themselves, you ungrateful swine?"

"Sorry, Mrs Crowe," Katie croaked.

"Don't speak! Do it!" Mrs. Crowe barked.

Katie rushed to grasp her empty bowl and spoon and took them to the basket on the table. The stories all said that the women who lived in the workhouse did the washing-up, but the matrons always made it sound as though they did it themselves, even though they had smooth, clean hands that looked like they had never seen a day's work in hot water and lye.

Hannah's breathing was harsh on her neck as they scurried to Mrs. Crowe's side. The matron swept them with a harsh, piercing eye, her expression filled with disdain, then turned on her heel and marched away without explanation.

Katie held out her hand as she followed the matron into the hallway. Hannah's fingers tangled with hers and gripped them tightly.

They seemed to go along the hallway for a terribly long way, taking all sorts of twists and turns and staircases within the cold bowels of the workhouse. Katie clung to Hannah's hand even though their fingers grew slippery with a sweat of excitement. She could hardly wait to come around the corner and see Molly's dear face light up with joy.

Her soul longed for the moment when Molly's arms would wrap around her. Everything would be all right then. Molly had a way of making everything all right, even when the entire world was falling to bits.

At last, the matron reached a narrow door. "No more lessons for you," she said with cruel relish. "It's time you began to do real work."

The door swung open, and Katie stared into a great, quiet, semi-dark room with only a few small windows that allowed greyish sunlight to piece the gloom. Fabric lay everywhere, the same ugly grey and white stripes as Katie and Hannah wore, and women bent over rough tables to sew.

Katie eagerly stepped through the door and looked up and down the rows of women, searching, searching. Any minute now, she would spot Molly. She would have to hold in her excitement until Mrs. Crowe left, but she thought she could manage. It would be hard not to scream Molly's name and run across the room at once—but just meeting Molly's eyes and seeing her smile would be enough for her in this moment.

Katie turned her head left and right. Dozens of women sat in this room with their heads bent over that unattractive fabric. Her eye skipped over the grey heads, searching for a girl with warm brown hair. Her heart throbbed faster and faster, sending fresh pulses of hope agonizingly through her limbs. There—a brown-haired young woman with her back to Katie! But when she turned to ask her neighbour for a pair of scissors, her face was all wrong, her nose too pert, her eyes the wrong colour.

"What are you just standing here staring for?" Mrs. Crowe barked. "Get to your workstations at once!"

Katie wanted to protest, but Hannah pulled her forward.

"A dress each day," Mrs. Crowe ordered, "or you'll go to bed without any supper, do you hear me? None!"

"Yes, Mrs. Crowe," Hannah whimpered.

"Turner, speak," Mrs. Crowe commanded.

Hannah gave Katie's arm a little jiggle, and Katie abruptly realized that the matron was talking to her. "Yes, Mrs. Crowe."

The matron stumped off to a large armchair at the front of the room near the fire. Hannah towed Katie toward an empty desk, but Katie barely saw it. She couldn't stop looking from one row of women to the next.

Surely, surely, Molly must have seen her by now. Her face would be turned up toward Katie. She couldn't miss her.

Unless—

The possibility had never occurred to Katie, but now it grew like a cancer in her belly.

Unless Molly was not here at all.

She quickly dismissed the thought. Of course Molly was here. They had only been in the workhouse for a few months; where else would she have gone? She would never leave Katie here. Never.

"Katie, sit." Hannah tugged at her.

Katie sank onto a bare wooden stool and stared at the heap of fabric in front of her. Their lessons in the girls' section had included sewing, of course, but she barely glanced at the fabric, pins, pattern, needles, and thread before her. Instead she quickly looked up and down the rows again.

"You! Turner! Everett! Get to work," Mrs. Crowe barked.

"Katie, please," Hannah whispered. "We'll get in trouble."

Katie picked up the pattern and pretended to look it over, but in reality, she was hiding her face as she took one more look at the women around them.

She was shaking. Sickness rose in her belly as the appalling, unthinkable truth became undeniable.

"Where is she?" Hannah whispered.

Katie picked up a pair of scissors with a hand that would not stop shaking. "She's— she's— she's not here."

Hannah stared at her.

"She's gone, Hannah." Katie's tears spilled over. "She must be dead."

"No, no, Katie, don't say that." Hannah touched her arm. "They would tell you. She has to be alive."

Katie remembered Mrs. Crowe coming into the dining hall one day to tell a little girl that her mother had died. Hannah was right; Katie had received no news.

"But where can she be?" Katie whispered.

"She must have gone out to look for work."

Katie shook her head, her heart fluttering in her veins. "No. No, Molly would never leave me, never. She wouldn't do such a thing. Oh, Hannah, she wouldn't. She *wouldn't*!"

"Hush, Katie. Mrs. Crowe will notice if you make a fuss."

"But Hannah... she wouldn't. She would never leave me here. *Never*!"

But even as she said it, Katie knew that Hannah was right. If Molly wasn't here, it was because she had left her.

Perhaps she had never gone into the workhouse herself, after all. The workhouse considered her an adult. She could have left whenever she wanted.

Perhaps she had never even seen these dormitories, but

waited only until Miss Dawson led Katie away before she turned and left.

Perhaps she had abandoned her here in this place. Never to return.

CHAPTER 4

CHAPTER FOUR

A tear splashed on the wet floor. It vanished with the next stroke of Katie's brush as she scrubbed the stone, but more kept falling, mingling with the cold, soapy water.

She struggled to hold in her sobs as she worked the brush into the corners of the men's dormitory. If possible, this place reeked even more than the girls' did. The stench of old sweat and unwashed bodies was so pervasive here that it seemed to have seeped into the stone. But the reek was nothing compared to the smell of the Thames the previous summer, and Katie's heart was so heavy that she barely noticed anything as unremarkable as a smell.

"Oh, Katie," said Hannah softly. "Don't cry."

The words only made Katie's tears burn her eyes all the more. "Why would she leave me, Hannah?"

"Maybe she's in the infirmary," said Hannah.

She had repeated the same comforting line a dozen

times over the week since they had joined the women's section.

"She can't be. Not anymore. She would be dead or better by now. They never let anyone stay in the infirmary too long. She's left me, Hannah, I know it."

Hannah reached out to touch her shoulder. "It'll be all right."

Katie knew that Hannah said the words because they were the only ones she could think of, but she could not believe them. How could anything be all right now that Katie was alone in the world? She had clung with all her heart to the thought that Molly was only a few walls away.

She had never imagined that her sister might abandon her.

The clang of a pail and a whimper of terror caught Katie's attention. She looked up, over the labouring bodies of the women all around the dormitory, and saw a pool of dirty water spreading over the floor by the door.

An older woman scrambled with her brush, trying with futility to sweep the water back into the pail. And Maggie Granger stood over her.

A mutual shudder ran through Katie and Hannah.

"Mrs. Crowe!" Maggie called. "Look at this! Elsa threw her pail out on the floor. You'd swear she was trying to make this floor dirtier, not cleaner."

"Johnson!" Mrs. Crowe rapped. She stormed into the dormitory from her post in the hallway. "What in heaven's name do you think you're playing at, throwing this water everywhere?"

"I didn't!" Elsa cried. "It was this Granger girl. She knocked it over!"

Maggie whirled around and fixed Mrs. Crowe with a frigid glare. Mrs. Crowe had to tip her head back to look her in the eye. The girl towered over everyone in the room, and a breathless silence hung over the women as they waited to see what would happen next.

There was only the faintest flicker in Mrs. Crowe's eye. She stepped backward.

"Clean up your mess, Johnson, and it's half rations for you tonight," she said.

"What?" Elsa cried. "This is nonsense!"

Mrs. Crowe rounded on her. "Be silent and go back to work, or you'll have no rations at all!"

Elsa ducked her head, a scowl of fury on her face, and returned to her scrubbing. Maggie gave a heartless laugh and strolled away as Mrs. Crowe went back outside to the hallway.

Maggie sat on the largest bed, folded her hands in her lap, and watched. None of the working women dared to say a word to her. Katie lowered her head and stared down at her brush, determined not to catch Maggie's attention again.

"I thought that being here with the women would take her down a notch," Hannah whispered.

Katie gulped. "It hasn't."

She glanced at Maggie, who pushed her scrubbing brush around with her foot, putting up only the faintest pretence of work.

"If anything," said Katie, "I think she's getting worse."

The only good thing about the move to the women's section was that Maggie couldn't be bothered with Katie and Hannah.

They sat at the far end of the dining hall, well away

from the trouble, and hastily ate bowls of gritty vegetable soup. Nearer the front of the room, Maggie slapped bowls from other women's hands or simply stole their food from them. Elsa was trying to fight back that evening, but her two terrifying friends—Daphne and Clementine—seemed to have already given up. They sat meekly beside Maggie, heads hanging low, submissive. It seemed that they knew they would be given peace once more when they acknowledged Maggie as the queen of the workhouse.

They sounded like snapping, snarling wolves to Katie. She slurped a last mouthful of watery broth with turnips that had boiled rather too soft.

"It's only a matter of time," she mumbled.

Hannah scraped up the last droplets of food from her bowl. "Until what?"

"Until Elsa gives up too, and Maggie can start stealing food from *us* again."

"I suppose." Hannah sighed. "At least they're too busy fighting each other to bother with us... for now."

"We'll have to hide under the table again, I suppose."

Hannah shook her head. "One of the other women tried it at lunch. It didn't work. Mrs. Crowe sent her to the refractory ward."

"Maggie should be in the refractory ward."

"They're too afraid of her. You know it'll never be so."

The bell clanged. Katie and Hannah jumped up and hurried to put their bowls in the great washing-up bins, then scrambled down the long hallway to bed. Their life was a race once more—a constant quest to avoid Maggie and the other bullies so that they could eat enough food, avoid being hurt during work, and snatch a few hours of uncomfortable sleep.

The bunks of the girls' dormitories were only a memory

now. Even the sleeping pallets here in the women's section were all taken, especially with Maggie sprawling across the biggest bed in the room. Instead, Katie and Hannah had the worst sleeping spot in the dormitory: a pallet with two broken slats, which poked them in the ribs at night despite the straw that they had stuffed beneath it in a bid to make it more level.

They washed quickly and miserably in cold water before tucking themselves between two threadbare blankets on the pallet. Washing Katie's hands stung all of the blisters on her fingers from a full day of sewing, and the soap burned all the places where she had pricked herself with a needle. Even with all that, Katie still struggled to finish a dress every day.

Her stomach still growled with hunger even on full rations. The thought of not finishing a dress and going to bed without any supper was horrific.

Molly brought me here because we were starving on the streets. Why has she left me here to starve alone in this place instead?

The thought plagued her all day and all night. It trapped her like a coffin, wrapping around her arms and legs, making it difficult to move and breathe at times. While she was busy trying to stay away from Maggie, trying to sew, and trying simply to survive, there were times when she could almost forget about it. But thought always returned when she lay on the sleeping pallet at night before exhaustion could carry her off to sleep. Molly's abandonment pinned her to the ground, made her feel as though there was not quite enough air in the dormitory.

Without Molly, she was alone in the world, and that knowledge made her breathe in frightened little gasps.

Then, a soft, warm hand touched her shoulder in the dark. "Katie?"

Katie pulled the blankets over her head and struggled not to cry.

"Oh, Katie." Hannah rolled closer and wrapped an arm around her. "It'll be all right."

"It—it's not all right," Katie whispered between sobs. "Mama's gone. Henry's gone. Tessie, Joan, Peter... Michael... and now Molly. Everyone went away, Hannah. Everyone left me."

"I'm here," said Hannah quietly.

Katie's sobs slowed. "Please... please, don't go."

"I'm not going anywhere," Hannah whispered.

She wasn't the first person to make Katie that promise. Michael had done the same thing with his gentle eyes and kind voice. She trembled, terrified. How long would it be before Hannah left her, too?

Quietly, Hannah began to sing. She sang under her breath so that no one would hear, and her voice was a quiet rasp, holding no beauty. But Katie closed her eyes and listened to the little tune anyway.

"Lavender blue, diddle-diddle, lavender green. When I am king, diddle-diddle, you shall be queen..."

And peaceful, quiet sleep came to her at last.

Coughing was not an unfamiliar sound in the women's dormitory early in the morning, but this sound was new and different. It was a horrible, bubbling, wrenching sound that made Katie's chest ache just to listen to it.

She looked around nervously, but Hannah was close by

her side as they dressed for the day, and the coughing hadn't come from her.

"Who's ill?" Hannah wondered aloud.

"I don't know."

"She sounds terrible. I hope Mrs. Crowe will help her, whoever she is."

Katie shrugged. It mattered little to her.

They smoothed their plain pinafores over their striped dresses, pinned them up, and then carefully folded the blankets on their broken pallet to avoid trouble from Mrs. Crowe. Hannah and Katie tucked themselves into a corner near the front of the room to avoid Maggie's prying eyes.

The terrible cough came again.

"Oh, Katie." Hannah grabbed her arm. "It's Maggie!"

"What?" Katie looked up.

Hannah was right. Maggie cupped a hand over her mouth and coughed, her great body twitching and jerking with the force of each one. Daphne and Clementine were staring at her with wide, uncertain eyes.

"Well, maybe she won't give us such a hard time today, then," said Katie.

"Oh, poor thing. She looks awful."

"Poor thing!" said Katie. "How can you say that after all the terrible things she's done to us?"

"Mama always said that all people are people."

Katie didn't know what that meant, but the clang of the breakfast bell spared her from trying to find out. The women hung back, waiting for Maggie to move. No one dared step toward the door until the coughing fit was over, but even then, Maggie didn't walk into the hallway. She stood with her hands on her knees, breathing hard, as if exhausted.

"Move!" Elsa barked.

Several women scattered, bumping into Katie and Hannah, who joined the nervous flow of women drawing away from the door.

Elsa pushed through the crowd, ignoring Maggie completely. "Come on, Daphne, Clementine," she ordered.

The two bullies gave Maggie a last, wide-eyed look, then hurried to join Elsa. They led the way from the dormitory, and the other women followed.

Katie soon lost Maggie in the crowd. She clung to Hannah's hand, and they held onto each other tightly as they followed the mass of women to the cold and bare dining hall. The usual, nauseating smell of watery gruel filled the air as the women formed a line, with Elsa, Daphne, and Clementine at the very front. Maggie was somewhere near the middle, and Hannah and Katie patiently waited at the back.

The coughing reverberated around the dining hall. Mrs. Crowe came in and stalked over to Maggie, her eyes dangerous.

"What's the matter with you?" she demanded. Her voice rang through the hall and brought a hush on the assembled women.

"Nothing," Maggie rasped. Her voice sounded raw and painful.

"I'll send you to the infirmary if you can't keep up with the work."

Hannah gave a tiny gasp. They had learned, in their few weeks in the women's section, that few people ever came back from the infirmary.

"I don't need the infirmary," Maggie spat.

Mrs. Crowe laughed. "We'll see about that. One dress each day, Granger, or you can choose between the infirmary and the refractory ward."

She stalked away, and Maggie glared after her, but did not yell like she might have done only the day before.

The line moved on. Katie and Hannah received their gruel at last and stuck together as they shuffled across the dining hall to the tables near the back, where the unnoticed younger women could sit and eat in comparative safety.

"Oh, Katie," Hannah whispered. "Look."

Katie dragged her gaze away from the blob of gruel in her bowl. Elsa, Daphne, and Clementine had finished their gruel, and they now prowled like hungry lions around the dining hall, seeking more.

"We'd better hurry," Katie hissed.

They ate as they walked, gulping down the gluey bites as quickly as they could. The gruel was tasteless and stuck in Katie's throat, but her stomach welcomed the sustenance with ravenous grumbles.

She had finished half the bowl before she reached her table, and she and Hannah huddled over their food, shovelling it down as quickly as they could. Katie braced herself to feel Daphne or Elsa's hard hand descend on her shoulder, but she reached the bottom of her bowl without incident.

"Thank goodness." She scraped up the last mouthful and swallowed it. "I can't believe they've left us alone."

"They've left us alone because they've found someone else to steal from," said Hannah softly.

Katie looked up. Elsa and her traitorous cronies had congregated around the same table where they usually sat, but their bowls stood forgotten in their places. Instead, they had fixed their attention upon Maggie.

The sickly girl had only eaten a few bites of her gruel. Her coughs echoed around the dining room as she bent over her bowl. The fit passed slowly, and she breathed hard for a few moments before reaching for her spoon to take another bite.

"Poor, poor Maggie." Elsa's voice was syrupy sweet as she leaned on the table beside Maggie. "You must be feeling so very ill."

"Perhaps not so hungry," said Clementine, behind her.

"Perhaps you won't even finish that," said Daphne, opposite her.

Maggie cupped her hands around her bowl and drew it protectively closer to her chest. "Leave me alone," she snarled, but her voice held none of its usual fire. She sounded weak and exhausted, and Elsa's eyes gleamed, knowing that Maggie was already beaten.

"We should do something," said Hannah.

Katie stared at her. "Why?"

"She needs help. They'll take her gruel away, Katie."

"I know that, but why should we do anything? She's taken food from us a hundred times. Let her feel how it feels."

Hannah's jaw tightened. "It's not right. She's ill."

"I said, leave me—" Maggie began, but her words dissolved into another coughing fit. She hugged her bowl as Elsa, Daphne, and Clementine all moved a little closer.

Suddenly, the tall girl seemed much smaller than before, and Katie felt a pang of empathy. Maggie looked so unwell... and so afraid.

"There's nothing we can do." Katie returned her attention to her bowl and hopefully ran her spoon around the inside, looking for the last scraps of food.

"Of course there is, Katie. We have to help her." Hannah swung her legs over the bench.

"Where are you going?" Katie cried.

"To distract Elsa and the others. You can help Maggie while they're not paying attention."

"Hannah!" Katie hissed, but her friend had already set off across the dining room, her skinny shoulders squared with resolve.

Katie scrambled to her feet. Maggie had recovered from her coughs, and she glared at Elsa, hugging her bowl.

"Get away from me," she hissed.

"Hand it over, Maggie." Clementine held out a hand. "We know you're not going to eat it."

"Where's your sense of charity?" Elsa growled.

Maggie glanced at Elsa's fingers, then returned her gaze to the woman's face, but she was pale. Katie, too, had seen the bruises Elsa could leave when she pinched anyone in her way.

Clementine's shoulders tightened. From long practice dodging Maggie herself, Katie knew that Clementine was about to snatch Maggie's bowl away the moment Mrs. Crowe wasn't looking—but her chance never came. Instead, Hannah brushed past Daphne, lightly knocking against her with her elbow.

Daphne whipped around. "How dare you!"

Hannah jumped backward, wide-eyed. "Oh, I'm s-so sorry,. I... I... I didn't see you there."

"Didn't *see* me? Are you blind as well as stupid, girl?"

Clementine and Else abandoned Maggie and rounded on Hannah as well. Katie stood frozen in terror, watching, until Hannah met her eyes under Daphne's upraised arm and gave her a sharp nod.

Elsa lunged at Hannah, who bolted. Daphne and Clementine gave chase while Hannah emitted a blood-curdling scream.

"Stop! Stop that at once!" Mrs. Crowe yelled.

In the resulting pandemonium, Katie jogged across the dining hall to Maggie. She couldn't very well refuse to help Maggie now—not after Hannah had caused such trouble for herself.

She snatched up Maggie's bowl. "Come on!"

Maggie spun. "Give that back!"

"That's what I'm going to do, you fool," Katie snapped, "but you have to come with me if you want to keep your breakfast."

Maggie sneered.

"I can give it back, if you like." Katie held out the bowl. "But you know they'll just take it again."

Mrs. Crowe's yells had finally stopped the bullies. Through the corner of her eye, Katie watched Hannah slip into the crowd while Elsa and her cronies turned on Mrs. Crowe and shouted at her until even the matron looked pale and shaky.

"Are you coming or not?" Katie demanded.

"Oh, all right." Maggie seized the bowl.

Another coughing fit bent her double as they walked across the hall, but Katie more or less dragged her to the sanctuary of the table at the back, where Hannah was already waiting. Maggie glared at them both as she sat down, but she said nothing. She merely ate, slowly and painfully, each gulp clearly hurting her throat.

Elsa, Daphne, and Clementine returned to their table with thunderous expressions on their faces, but they didn't come looking for Maggie. They merely turned to the next woman unlucky enough to sit near them and tried to take her bowl instead.

Maggie finished her gruel in relative peace. She lowered her spoon and stared at Katie and Hannah over the rim of her bowl.

"What do you want?" she rasped.

Katie folded her arms. "We want you to stop being so unkind to us."

"Katie!" said Hannah. "That's not why we helped you, Maggie."

"Why, then?" said Maggie.

Katie didn't know, but Hannah's smile held the warmth that had kept hope aflame in her heart for these long and weary months in the workhouse.

"Because all people are people," said Hannah, "and that means we should care about everyone. That's what my mama always said."

Maggie stared at her for a long, tense moment.

Then, to Katie's amazement, the big girl's face crumpled like a crushed flower.

It was as she wept that Katie realized exactly what Hannah meant. *All people* are *people*, she thought, *even this one*.

CHAPTER 5

CHAPTER FIVE

Katie strolled easily down the workhouse hallway, arms swinging. Her dress was tighter around her shoulders these days, and with the rise of spring, slats of sunlight made their way into the hallway from the narrow windows high up on one wall. They struck the grey stone with what had to pass for warmth in the workhouse. It barely warmed the hallway enough that their breath no longer steamed as it did in winter, but Katie closed her eyes as she passed beneath a scrap of sunlight, enjoying its brief kiss on her skin.

Her steps slowed. A few months ago, an infringement such as this would have resulted in a slap from Mrs. Crowe or a rough shove from one of the other women. Instead, the line of paupers slowed, maintaining a careful few feet of space from Katie.

One woman tripped and stumbled, accidentally brushing Katie with her arm.

Maggie whirled around. "Hey!" she barked. "Stay away!"

The woman scrambled back, wide-eyed. "S-sorry. Sorry."

"You don't lay a hand on her, do you hear me?" Maggie barked. "Not a hand!"

The woman cringed. "Y-yes."

Mrs. Crowe shot them an irate glare from the door to the dining hall, but she said nothing. Katie didn't enjoy the glitter of fear in her eyes or share the bitter hatred with which Maggie stared at her, but she appreciated the fact that the woman didn't come near her or Hannah as they comfortably wandered into the dining hall.

No one did. Though Elsa, Daphne, and Clementine now led the row of women to the serving table, a bubble of space remained around Maggie, Katie, and Hannah somewhere in the middle. The aura of menace that always seemed to shimmer around Maggie like a mirage kept them secluded and relaxed in the line with no one to push them around.

"What is it this afternoon?" Hannah wondered. "Is it fish?"

"It's Thursday, isn't it?" said Maggie. "Then it'll be pie."

"I like pie, even if the pies here always seem to have nothing but potatoes in them, and maybe a few bits of grisly pork."

"We used to have rabbit pie when the Coster mongering business was going well," said Katie. "When I found out it was made of rabbits, Michael and Henry had to convince me that the rabbit had died of old age."

Hannah giggled. "That sounds like you."

"They called me Katie-pie ever since."

"Aww." Maggie chortled. "Katie-pie. That's a funny little name."

"You know, you need a pet name, too," said Hannah.

"I don't. Do I look like a pet to you?"

"You're our pet," Katie teased. "Our mastiff."

Maggie barked, making Katie jump. Hannah giggled. Mrs. Crowe seethed, but dared not say a word.

It was pie indeed, and Maggie eyed her slice as a disinterested woman slopped it onto her plate. The mealy filling leaked out from underneath a pale crust.

"What did you mean," Maggie asked as they crossed the room to their tables, "when you said 'even if' these pies are full of potatoes? Aren't all pies full of potatoes?"

"Well, no," said Katie. "When we made rabbit pie, they were mostly full of rabbit, with only a few little bits of potato in them."

"That's very strange." Maggie slammed her plate on the table and slid onto the bench. "What else did you eat outside the workhouse?"

Hannah rubbed her chin. "All sorts of things, really." She ate in leisurely bites, unafraid of losing her meal. "You know the oranges we get at Christmas? We used to get them all winter. There were candied peels, too."

"What are those?"

"You've never had a candied peel?" Katie asked.

Maggie shook her head. "I've never been outside this place. My mother left me here when I was born, they told me."

"Oh Maggie! One day," said Hannah, "when we all get out of here, I'll find some money, and I'll buy us a big bag of candied peels so that you can taste them."

"When we all get out of here!" Maggie threw back her head and laughed. "Oh, Hannah, you are funny."

Katie stared at her pie, suddenly struggling to find her appetite.

Hannah frowned. "I'm not trying to be funny, Maggie."

"How would we ever 'get out of here?' We have nowhere to go, Hannah, and no one outside these walls who loves us."

Katie was quiet for a moment. "That's... mostly true," she said carefully.

"What about Molly?" Hannah asked.

"Molly left me here." Katie's voice was flat. "So did Henry and James. I understand why—they had their own survival to think about. But it still hurts."

"But what about Michael?" Hannah asked gently. "The boy you told me about?"

Katie's expression softened. "Michael didn't choose to leave me. His family had to go during the cholera." She was quiet for a moment. "I do think about him sometimes. Wonder if he remembers the promises we made. But Hannah, that was eight years ago. He'd be a man now, probably with his own life."

"The boy you last saw when you were only a child?" Maggie gaped. "And you think he remembers you?"

"I think he might," Katie said quietly, ignoring Maggie's scorn. "What we had was real, even if we were young. But whether he remembers and whether he could still care about me now... those are different things." She looked down at her hands. "People grow and change. The man he's become might have no room in his life for childhood promises."

"So you've given up on him?"

"No," Katie said softly. "But I've learned not to stake my entire future on maybes. If I ever saw him again..." She paused. "Well, I'd want to find out who he's become. See if there's anything left to build on."

"Seems a fool thing to me," Maggie grunted. "Men are fickle. I doubt he remembers your name."

"Oh, Maggie, have a little faith," said Hannah. "Things might not be all bad, you know. What do we have except hope for the future?"

"Hope for the future?" Maggie shook her head. "We don't have even that, Hannah. All we can do is survive here and now."

"What do you think, Katie?" Hannah asked. "What is your hope for the future?"

Katie considered this carefully. "I hope someday I'll be strong enough to make my own way in the world. To find honest work and support myself." She managed a small smile. "And I hope that if Michael and I ever do meet again, I'll be someone worth remembering—not just a helpless girl he once protected, but a woman who can stand beside him as an equal."

MAKING dresses had slowly become easier. Though Mrs. Crowe dared not beat Katie anymore, she still felt a pang of relief as she ran the last stitch through the newly finished dress and tied it off as neatly as she could. It still didn't look as nice as the things Mama and Molly used to sew, but it would keep some poor pauper woman in this workhouse warm, at least.

Katie snipped off the thread and returned the needle to the pincushion. Around her, the other women did the same, putting away their sewing things and smoothing out the dresses they had completed.

Mrs. Crowe went to the door as the lunch bell rang. "Pick up all of your pins," she loudly ordered, as she always did. "I won't have you leaving them lying about on the floor. They're far too expensive."

The women shuffled to the door. Elsa, Daphne, and Clementine went first, of course, thumping other people out of their way if they were slow to move aside.

Maggie followed, with Katie and Hannah following closely in her wake.

"Today is Tuesday, isn't it?" said Hannah. "I believe it'll be fish and potatoes today."

"Perhaps they'll roast the potatoes this time instead of mashing them," Maggie proposed.

"Ooh, I hope so," said Katie, "and maybe even give us a little salt."

Mrs. Crowe stepped forward as they approached the doorway. "Katie Turner," she barked.

Katie slowed, but Maggie did not. The big girl squared her shoulders and strode toward Mrs. Crowe, looming over her.

"What do you want with Katie?" she demanded.

Fear flickered in Mrs. Crowe's eyes, but she held her ground. "This is none of your business, Granger, and I suggest you watch your tone."

Katie grabbed Maggie's arm. "Maggie..."

She felt the big girl stiffen as she spotted him, too: a muscular porter standing in the hallway behind Mrs. Crowe. He was a tall man with high cheekbones, and Katie knew by looking at him that he would knock Maggie to the ground like a bowling pin.

Maggie slowly stepped back.

"Turner, are you listening?" Mrs. Crowe snapped.

"Yes, ma'am." Katie hastily nodded.

"Very well. Come with me." Mrs. Crowe turned away.

Maggie seized Katie's hand. "Where are you taking her?"

"Once again, Granger, I suggest you be quiet and mind your manners." Mrs. Crowe wheeled around. "Or I will have Laurence here teach you the lesson that you should have learned long ago."

The porter stepped forward, hands bunching into fists. His face looked like it had been carved from granite, and Katie noticed cuts and bruises on his knuckles, but none on his face.

"It's all right, Maggie." She disentangled her hand from Maggie's.

"Katie..." Hannah reached for her sleeve.

Mrs. Crowe's eyes narrowed.

"Don't," said Katie. "You'll get in trouble. It's all right. I'll—I'll come back in a minute, I'm sure."

She knew where she was going, and she could tell from the terror on Hannah and Maggie's faces that they did, too. She could think of only one destination for her: the refractory ward.

Katie had never been there, but she heard that there were no windows, only silence.

She hadn't done anything wrong, except for being friends with Maggie. That would be enough reason for Mrs. Crowe to throw her in the refractory ward.

"Katie," Hannah begged.

Mrs. Crowe stepped forward. "Do you wish to spend the night in the refractory ward, Everrett?"

"Let me go." Katie pulled away. "It's all right. I'll be back. Let me go." The only thought more unbearable than going into solitary confinement was the thought of Hannah or Maggie being punished for trying to protect her.

The two girls watched helplessly as Katie followed Mrs.

Crowe down the hallway. She paused at the end to look back, and tears were sparkling on Hannah's cheeks. The girl covered her mouth with her hands, her eyes alight with fear. Maggie, too, looked troubled, but she kept a steady hand on Hannah's back.

"How many times must I tell you to come, girl?" Mrs. Crowe snapped.

"Yes, ma'am." Katie ducked her head and followed her.

Her blood pounded in her ears as Mrs. Crowe marched down the hallway, her shoes ringing on the stone floor. She didn't know where the refractory ward was, but it seemed like a terribly long walk as they followed twists and turns of the hallways that Katie had never seen before. Each step made dread grow in her belly.

Then, suddenly, there was daylight. Katie blinked, confused. They were in a large room with several doors, and one of them opened to the outside, allowing a cascade of bright sunshine to pour into the room.

The sunshine was so glorious that it was a moment before Katie's eyes cleared and she saw the street beyond. She had not seen anything beyond the workhouse and its bleak courtyards in almost a year, and the sight of a wild thistle blooming in a pavement crack seemed the most colourful thing in the world. It struck her silent for a moment.

"Here you are, Mrs. Cromwell," said Mrs. Crowe.

The matron's voice sounded suddenly very different. It had lost its harshness, and held instead a strange sweetness that was, to Katie, somehow more terrifying.

She dragged her eyes away from the thistle and realized with a horrible shock that she was in that same intake room where Molly had left her; the one where her sister had lied to her, telling her that it would all be all right, and then abandoned her in this place of pain and starvation. Mrs. Crowe stood behind the desk, Katie near her, and a thin woman with a hook nose faced them both. She wore a magnificent dress—grey and black, but strikingly decorated with feathers and ribbons and fabric roses that dotted the stern lines of the bodice. A fascinator perched on her steel-grey hair, adorned with more feathers and roses, and she held a lorgnette with silver frames encircling the glasses.

Panic spread through Katie's limbs.

"Wh-who are you?" she stammered.

Mrs. Crowe slapped her hand. Katie gasped at the painful blow.

The woman in the beautiful dress stepped back. "You told me you had compliant, well-mannered young ladies here."

"Oh, I do, Mrs. Cromwell, I surely do," Mrs. Crowe simpered. "Katie here is a lovely girl, she really is. She was a little startled by your beauty, that's all."

"Ah." Mrs. Cromwell smiled, a cold and cruel expression that never reached her slate-grey eyes. "Of course. One can hardly blame anyone for such a mistake. She has hardly seen a single lovely thing in this place, I suppose. I must leave her dumbstruck."

"Indeed, you do," said Mrs. Crowe, shooting Katie a sharp look.

Katie could not have spoken at that moment even if she wanted to. She felt numb fear spread through her body. She had no idea what was happening, but she felt a terrible suspicion that it could not be good—not with that cruel look in Mrs. Crowe's eyes.

"She's been working in our sewing room for the past three months and proven herself an able seamstress. You won't need to do much training," Mrs. Crowe added. "She can go right to work for you."

Katie's breath froze. *Work for Mrs. Cromwell?*

"Yes, yes. Of course she will require training." Mrs. Cromwell sniffed. "Sewing ballgowns in my millinery is a very different task to cobbling together these pathetic things you call dresses. Fit only for paupers, indeed!" She gestured at Katie's grey-and-white dress with her lorgnette. "Despicable. It is a start, however. Come closer, girl, and let me look at you."

Katie stared at her. *Sewing ballgowns in my millinery.* She knew, then, with terrible certainty, that she would not return to Hannah and Maggie as she'd promised.

"Are you deaf as well as stupid?" Mrs. Cromwell barked. "Come closer!"

Katie found it in her to shuffle forward a few steps. Mrs. Cromwell raised her lorgnette to her eyes and peered at Katie through it, her gaze unrelentingly sharp as it travelled over her bony body.

"Yes, well, you seem healthy enough." Mrs. Cromwell lowered the lorgnette. "She'll do."

"Excellent. I'm sure she'll be a credit to you," said Mrs. Crowe.

"If she's not, I'll bring her right back, and you had better have my money waiting for me." Mrs. Cromwell spun on her heel. "What is your name, girl?"

The grey eyes pierced her. Disobedience was unthinkable. "K-Katie."

"Katie. Terrible. Such a common name. Well, it hardly matters—no one much will hear it." Mrs. Cromwell's skirts rustled as she strode to the door. "Come on, then."

"Please." Katie gulped. "Mrs. Crowe, let me—"

Mrs. Crowe rose, her eyes afire. Katie knew her well

enough then to know that the woman would scream at her with that horrifying whip-crack of a voice if she did not comply.

Tears burned her eyes. There was no going back, she realized, no saying goodbye to Hannah or Maggie, and Mrs. Crowe would never explain what had happened.

They would think she had left them, as she thought Molly had left her.

"Come on," said Mrs. Cromwell again.

CHAPTER 6

"No," Mrs. Crowe said firmly. "Come along now."

Katie realized with dawning horror that there truly was no going back, no saying goodbye. They would think she had left them, as she thought Molly had left her.

PART II

CHAPTER 7

CHAPTER SIX

*F*our Years Later

THE CANDLE STUB flickered in the tiny, dark room.

Katie paused briefly, a forbidden break, to flex her aching hands in a bid to urge a little blood back to her numb and tired fingers. A thin draft blew through the crack alongside the narrow window of her garret. She adjusted the bit of paper she'd stuffed into the crack, and the draft faded, but the tiny room was no less cold.

It could hardly be called a room; perhaps the word "closet" would be more appropriate. Tucked at the back of the attic where Mrs. Cromwell stored bolts of extra fabric, the garret was so narrow that Katie had to turn sideways to fit between the cot and the wall. There was nowhere near enough room on the sewing table that faced the little window, but that window was the only mercy in Katie's life. The grimy glass—cracked, but miraculously still holding—offered at least a glimpse of the outside world.

It was more than she had received in the workhouse; yet over the four long, cold years since she had left the workhouse, Katie had often found herself longing for its small comforts, especially Hannah's arm around her in the night.

The candle flame steadied. The light grew only a little better. Its yellow glow made Katie's eyes hurt as she bent over the next row of stitches on the silken sleeve of the extravagant blue ballgown she was making for Lady Ashton. In the first few days at the millinery, she remembered the many colours and textures enchanting her, giving her hope that perhaps life would be a little better here.

It had been a foolish hope.

Katie winced as the needle caught the tip of her index finger, right below the metal rim of the thimble she wore. She carefully dabbed away the droplet of blood—Mrs. Cromwell would be irate if any of it landed on the silk—and returned to her sewing, finishing the long seam up the underside of the sleeve. Her hands, back, and arms all cramped steadily.

The church bell tolled a quarter to seven. Katie sewed faster. She had been up at her desk since five that morning, and she knew Mrs. Cromwell expected her to have the shop open and ready at eight, but first she had to finish this dress. There was no telling when Lady Ashton might come in for her final fitting.

Anxiety clenched in Katie's belly as she tied off the last stitch. If this dress fit anything other than perfectly, she would be to blame, and Mrs. Cromwell would make sure she knew it.

She brought the dress downstairs and hung it up ready for its fitting, then swept out the millinery. It was a small shop and utterly crowded with mannequins, racks of clothes, and great bolts of fabric behind the counter. A book of designs rested on the counter and Katie made sure it was always open to a different page, enticing visitors to choose new styles and patterns. She turned a few pages, displaying a striking ball gown with long sleeves, and was carefully arranging the fitting area when Mrs. Cromwell came in.

The old woman had not slept well, judging by the redness around her eyes, and Katie knew she was in for an even worse day than usual.

"Where's that gown, girl?" she demanded without saying good morning.

"It's hanging right over here, ma'am. It's all ready."

Mrs. Cromwell eyed the dress as Katie held her breath.

"You've left a piece of thread on it." Mrs. Cromwell picked it off the sleeve. "What will Lady Ashton think? You stupid girl! Go over the whole dress, thoroughly this time, and make sure you haven't made any more of a mess."

Katie ducked her head. "Yes, ma'am. Of course, ma'am."

"Don't you remember the time you left in a pin in the dress and it struck Lady Huntingdon?"

Katie rubbed the back of her hand. It still ached in cold weather at times thanks to the blow Mrs. Cromwell had given her for that mistake. "I do, ma'am."

"Then you know not to do such foolish things. Hurry, girl, hurry! You don't know when Lady Ashton is coming in."

"Yes, ma'am."

Katie checked the dress over, but found no more thread pieces. Her heart still thumped uncomfortably as she returned it to its rack.

"What are you still doing here?" Mrs. Cromwell demanded. "You have other gowns to sew. Get back to work. And make sure you're down here to assist Lady Ashton when she comes in, do you hear me? I don't want her to wait one minute, girl, not one single minute!"

Katie scurried upstairs and returned to her sewing, piecing together another gown for yet another wealthy lady. As she worked the needle through the silk, she wondered if any of these ladies paused to consider the feeble hands that had sewn the dresses they wore with such pride and glee. Did they think that seamstresses were well paid and worked in warm rooms with plenty of light? Or did they simply never consider them at all?

The clatter of hooves caught Katie's attention. She peered through the tiny window and spotted a carriage drawn by a beautiful grey pair. The crest on the door was the Ashtons', and Katie rushed downstairs, making it just as Lady Ashton came into the millinery with her companion by her side.

"Good morning, Mrs. Cromwell," she called.

The milliner scrambled from behind the counter, cooing and fawning. "Oh, Lady Ashton, you *are* beautiful today. Why, look at you! You're simply glowing. It is an honour to have you here, a great honour."

Most of the millinery clients enjoyed Mrs. Cromwell's simpering, but Lady Ashton was one of the rare exceptions. She was a young lady—recently married and only a little older than Katie's eighteen years—and raised an elegant eyebrow at Mrs. Cromwell's flattery. Her lip twitched as though she found it amusing.

"I look forward to fitting my dress," she said.

"Ah, of course, of course. Straight to business." Mrs. Cromwell took the dress from the rack. "A most magnificent design, this gown, although challenging to sew. I believe I have undertaken the challenge with aplomb, my lady."

Lady Ashton's gaze flickered to Katie. "Of course you have."

"Allow me to show you the features we added to the bodice."

While Mrs. Cromwell waxed lyrical about the dress, Katie hung back. Lady Ashton's companion, a pert-nosed young lady with a kind face, was flipping through the book of designs.

"My, my," she remarked. "What beautiful ideas you have here, Mrs. Cromwell."

The milliner preened. "I do enjoy making interesting new gowns."

"Of course," said the companion dryly. "I'm sure you work your fingers to the bone, sewing all these dresses yourself."

"Millie," Lady Ashton chided.

The companion cleared her throat. "Would you like to fit your dress now, my lady?"

"I would indeed," said Lady Ashton.

Katie stepped forward.

"Where is that stupid girl?" Mrs. Cromwell snapped.

"Right here, ma'am," said Katie.

"Oh. Well, don't just stand there. Help her ladyship with the gown," Mrs. Cromwell barked.

Katie took it and led Lady Ashton and Millie to the fitting area, then drew a screen carefully over it. Millie was quick and capable at helping her mistress to undress, and Katie stood to the side, holding the dress. Some fittings could be awful—new tirades of abuse often came from the clients.

"Oh, my!" Lady Ashton gasped as Millie fastened the last strings of the dress. She turned left and right, admiring the rustle of her petticoats and the sparkle of the silk. "Well, this is simply beautiful, and so very comfortable. It fits perfectly."

Katie reached for the screen.

"Wait—wait a moment." Lady Ashton held out a hand. "It was you, was it not?"

Katie froze. "I beg your pardon, ma'am?"

"Hush, hush. Not so loud. You are the one who sewed this dress, were you?"

Katie hesitated.

"Of course she was," Millie whispered. "Look at her fingers, all cut up from sewing."

Lady Ashton's lips turned down at the corners.

"Lady Ashton?" Mrs. Cromwell called. "How does it fit?"

"You know what to do," said Lady Ashton to Millie. She swept the screen aside and twirled in the light, making Mrs. Cromwell laugh with glee.

Millie swung a fist toward Katie. She cowered until she realized that the older girl wasn't trying to strike her; instead, her clenched hand held something.

"Take it quickly," Millie hissed, "before Mrs. Cromwell sees."

Katie held out a hand. Millie dropped something silvery and shiny into it. Katie gasped at the sight of an entire shilling.

"But—" she began.

"Hide it. Quickly!" Millie whispered.

Katie whisked the shilling into her pinafore pocket. Its weight hung there, filled with promise, until Lady Ashton concluded her business with Mrs. Cromwell.

She held the door open when they left. Lady Ashton

paused on the threshold for a moment. Her sparkling eyes met Katie's, and she winked.

"Thank you," Katie mouthed.

Millie patted her on the hand, and then they and all their kindness were gone.

KATIE WONDERED if Lady Ashton knew what a single shilling could mean to a mere seamstress like her.

Such a wealthy lady must think in pounds, not shillings, but to Katie the single coin seemed like all the money in the world. She had not held her own money in her hands for years; Mrs. Cromwell considered her an apprentice, barely worthy of room and board. As a result, Katie had spent four long years trapped in that millinery, unable to go anywhere at all.

Katie stared at the shilling in her palm. It was more than enough for cab fare to the workhouse and back. Mrs. Cromwell would be furious if she was even a minute late returning from her Sunday break, but this might be her only chance to learn what happened to Hannah and Maggie. After four years of wondering, she had to know - even if it meant facing Mrs. Cromwell's cane.

Her heart was in her mouth as the hansom-cab rattled through London's streets, accelerating in nervous spurts as the horse sprang forward at the sharp touch of the cabbie's whip. Her destination was two miles away from the millinery. It was no great distance to walk, Katie knew, yet the only time she was allowed to leave the shop was during her Sunday morning break—and that was but two hours long, from eight until ten.

She could not walk four miles in that time, and so, for

four long years, she had longed and longed for the friends she lost, but been unable to go in search of them—until Lady Ashton had given her exactly the fare she needed to take a cab.

The cabbie yanked the horse to a halt. "Here we are, then," he barked, "at the workhouse."

Katie scrambled from the seat she shared with an old man who smelled of vinegar. He snored on as she handed a sixpence to the cabbie, and the man drove away with a clatter of wheels.

Her heart throbbed in her mouth as she stared up at the workhouse. Though it had been four years, somehow it felt like only yesterday since she left here with Mrs. Cromwell. Nothing had changed; the same young man sulked in his guardhouse, the walls still rose with the same imposing sternness, and the iron spikes still shone dully on their edges.

She had to be quick if she would make it back to the millinery in time to avoid a slap on the hand with Mrs. Cromwell's cane. Katie hurried around the workhouse's edge, searching for the tiny gap in the wall she had seen many times in the women's exercise yard. Sometimes, when Maggie was in the mood, they would take turns to peer through it and watch the world go by on the street.

Her heart fluttered. Had they repaired the gap? Did they still use the same yards for exercise? There were a thousand reasons why she might not be able to speak to Hannah, even today, even after the miraculous shilling, but she allowed none of them to stop her. She had to try.

Then, she saw it—the dark gap in the wall. Hope leaped in her. She hurried to it and crouched beside it, her mind racing. It was a quarter to nine in the morning, right in the middle of exercise hour, and there was no rain. They were in here. They had to be in here.

Katie crouched and peered through the gap at a mass of grey -and-white striped dresses. Women wandered aimlessly around the yard or sat in little knots, talking. For a horrible moment, she recognized no one, and it reminded her painfully of the day she had so hoped she would see Molly again, only to learn that her sister had left her.

"Hannah?" she whispered. "Maggie?"

Nothing happened. Katie's heart trembled; she feared it would shatter.

Then, a gruff voice spoke. "Katie? Is that you?"

"Maggie!" Katie cried.

Maggie's face appeared in the gap. What little Katie could see of it was pale, and the eye that squinted through the gap was red.

"Oh, Maggie, it's so good to see you!" Katie whispered. She wished the gap was big enough to reach through.

"What are *you* doing here?" Maggie demanded.

"I want to see you and Hannah. Where is she?" Katie eagerly asked. "Can I talk to her?"

"No." All the warmth had left Maggie's tone; she sounded cold and hard again, the bully she always used to be. "No one can talk to her anymore."

Katie's heart froze. "What?"

"She's dead, Katie."

Katie's knees buckled. They slammed painfully into the paving, but the jolt of agony could not compare with the ripping sensation inside her chest.

"No," she moaned. "No, no, no. What... how?"

"Consumption, they said it was. She was never the same after they took you away."

"I didn't want to go." Katie struggled to speak through her tears. "I didn't want to. They made me go."

"I know. That's how it works. But she missed you anyway, and then she grew sicker and sicker, and now she's dead." Maggie stepped away from the wall. "Wish it was different. Goodbye, Katie."

"Wait!" Katie begged.

Maggie stopped, but said nothing.

"Do you... do you know where they buried her?"

Maggie sighed. "I do, but you shouldn't go there."

"Maggie, please. I have to... to... to see her headstone... to say goodbye."

Maggie's voice hardened. "Whatever you wish. The church on the corner—they buried her in its graveyard."

"Thank you," Katie called, but Maggie had already walked away.

Katie would be back at the millinery late, no matter how fast the cab she found to take her home, but she no longer cared.

The church loomed behind her, its spire tall against the grey sky, as she plodded through the mud of the graveyard. Its lofty height and elegant architecture spoke of hope, but here where Katie slogged through the filth, she felt that there was none.

Some of the graves here had pretty headstones: carved granite with names and dates and short but kind epitaphs in memory of the souls that once colonized the bones that lay beneath. But there were others... great tracts of empty space, the earth still damp and fresh, where no headstones stood.

The smell appalled her. It held not the magnitude of the Great Stink of 1858, but it was somehow more poignant, more personal. The sharp reek of burning straw could do little to cover the horrific smell of decay.

Of decomposition. Of death.

Katie was shaking as she approached the corner where the groundskeeper had said the workhouse girls were buried. The way he'd said it had somehow convinced her that every woman who died in the workhouse lay quietly in a wood coffin, as Mama had lain when they lowered her into the ground on that horrific day. She had imagined a headstone at every grave. She had imagined kneeling beside Hannah's to pay homage to the girl who had loved her when she had no hope left.

That image, in itself, had been heartbreaking enough. It could not begin to prepare her for the awfulness that truly lay ahead.

She reached the edge of the pauper's grave before the smell made her steps slow to a frightened shuffle. As she neared it, she saw that it was a vast, yawning hole consuming this entire corner of the graveyard. Heaps of straw burned at intervals around and inside it, attempting to drown out the reek. But it could do nothing for the stink of death.

It was not the smell, however, that ultimately stopped Katie in her tracks. It was the sight of the bodies.

There were dozens of them. Each wrapped in a stained sheet, they lay in rows at the bottom of the pauper's grave, anonymous forever. Some were tall, some shrivelled, some heartbreakingly small.

Hannah could have been any one of them.

Katie's knees buckled. She landed on the wet earth with

a broken sob, unable, once again, even to say goodbye to her best friend in the world.

And as she wept, the terrible knowledge wrapped around her like a wet towel:

Papa had sent her away. Mama was dead. Michael had been dragged away. Molly and Henry had left her. Hannah had died.

She was completely alone in the world now. But she would not give up. Tomorrow, she would begin asking every customer about the Turner name, about Yorkshire. Someone, somewhere, would know something about her family. She had survived this long - she could find them.

CHAPTER 8

CHAPTER SEVEN

*K*atie walked to the bakery, although she hardly knew why.

It was the one great question with which she had wrestled the most since last Sunday when she found the mass grave that contained Hannah's body. The single word had resounded through her mind while Mrs. Cromwell applied her ruler with vicious force to Katie's hand for getting back late. It had echoed through her soul for that long, dreary week as she bowed her head over her sewing and struggled to handle the needle with a blistered and bloodied hand. It had been so loud inside her mind that Katie hardly heard the milliner's constant jibes and savage remarks.

Why? Why? Why?

She did not wonder why Hannah—a shining light in the darkness—had been snuffed out, why her family had left her, why cholera had taken Mama, why the drought had driven dear Papa to send his family to London in the hope that they would have a chance of survival there. It never occurred to her to question these things. This was how life was, how it had always been. It was cold and hard.

As Katie trudged across the cobbles, her hands tucked into the threadbare coat, she asked herself not why she had suffered this fate, but why she bothered to go on.

The single penny rolled between her fingers. Mrs. Cromwell had given it to her with an evil glare earlier that day, as though she thought Katie might somehow use it for herself instead of buying the loaf of bread that was to sustain her for the next several days. This was her Sunday afternoon errand now, a last piece of freedom stolen from her after she returned late last Sunday.

A shiver ran through Katie at the thought of what might happen to her if she angered Mrs. Cromwell a second time. She had never seen the milliner so angry.

The thought brought her back to the question: why go on? It seemed utterly pointless. Her existence was a desperate scrabble in this cold, rainy city, and whether she lived or died would affect no one. No one at all.

The sound drifted from somewhere to Katie's left, shocking her to a halt. It was a human voice, but it said no words.

Instead, it was laughing. Not the cold laughter of the harsh men who ganged up on others in dark alleyways or the hysterical cackle of the women who drank opium in abandoned doorways at the slum's edge. This was warm, hearty laughter, filled with real joy, and it had been so long since Katie last heard such a thing that the sound made her pause.

"Oh, you are silly, my love," said the laughing voice.

The rhythmic clink of a hammer against metal punctuated the voices as two other people—men, by the sound of it—joined the laughter.

"I'm telling you, Mama, it's true," said a young man's voice. It was deep and melodic, and something about the accent seemed familiar. It reminded Katie of Molly's broad Yorkshire. "I saw it with my own eyes when I went out for bread—a dancing monkey, wearing a little hat. The old man with him was with the circus."

"Why, I'd love to see that," said the woman's voice.

"Oh, my darling." Another man, sounding older, sighed. "If I could only take you to see the circus, I would."

"Someday you will, my dear. Someday we'll all go to see the circus together. All them dancin' monkeys will dance just for us."

Their laughter joined again, the hammer ringing without a break.

Katie found herself drawn toward the sound of genuine happiness. In her bleak world, such joy seemed almost impossible. She wandered toward it, her footsteps carrying her from the cobbled street into a grimy alley.

She had to walk many blocks to find a baker who would sell her a half-decent loaf of bread for a penny, and none of Mrs. Cromwell's ever-respectable clients would ever set foot in this part of London. Here, tiny cottages with no gardens huddled against each other as if for warmth. Great cracks ran through the sagging walls, stuffed with newspaper to keep out the drafts. Many windows were missing, replaced by boards or bits of wood. The crooked chimneys leaked anaemic tendrils of acrid smoke. Bits of string drooped from house to house, supporting washing all faded to the same shade of blue-grey, great holes yawning in many of the damp garments.

In a place like this, the laughter seemed even more

precious. It led Katie to one of the cottages. The building could not have contained more than two or three tiny rooms, and the voices came from a lean-to built against one side, little more than a canvas roof draped between precarious brick walls.

Inside, a tiny forge struggled against the harsh wind. Its smoke whipped away from red sparks as metal warmed within. The anvil beside it was puny and beaten down with years of use, but the family gathered around it seemed cheerful despite their circumstances.

The woman, bent and worn but moving with purpose, was heating rods of iron in the forge. She used tongs to pass them one by one to the two men, each equipped with a hammer, who bent over the anvil and shaped the warmed metal into nails and dropped them into a waiting bucket. The younger man and the woman had their backs to Katie, but their voices carried clearly in the crisp air.

"How many do you believe we've done for today, Papa?" the young man asked. "Almost enough?"

"What—half a bucketful? Aye, perhaps, but let's not stop. You know how the man who gives us the iron is. If we don't give him more than that value in nails, he won't be happy."

"And that'll leave us with nothing to eat," the woman added matter-of-factly.

"Aye. I know you're tired, son, but—"

"I'm not tired," said the young man quickly, even though his hand trembled slightly with exhaustion on the hammer. "I was only asking. Don't worry about me, Papa."

"I'm glad you're not tired, son, because I am. Would you pass us that cup of water?"

The young man turned, and that was when he spotted

Katie standing uncertainly at the edge of their makeshift workspace.

For a moment, they simply stared at each other. Katie felt a strange flicker of recognition, but she couldn't place it. There was something familiar about his eyes, his build, the way he held his head...

The bread tumbled from her hands and bounced on the grimy floor in its paper bag as understanding dawned slowly.

"I... I beg your pardon," Katie stammered, suddenly aware she was staring at strangers. "I heard voices and... I didn't mean to intrude."

The young man set down his hammer, studying her face with growing amazement. "Wait," he said slowly. "I know you. Don't I?"

Katie's heart began to race. That voice, deeper now but with the same gentle cadence...

"Michael?" she whispered, hardly daring to believe it.

"Son, what are you—" Peter began at the anvil behind him, then stopped mid-sentence. "Wait... can it be?"

"Katie?" Michael said, wonder filling his voice. "Katie Turner?"

"Oh my word!" The woman—Joan—dropped her tongs and spun around. "It IS you! Katie!"

Katie stood frozen, overwhelmed by the impossibility of it. "Joan? Peter? But how...?"

Michael stepped toward her carefully, as if she might disappear. "We only moved to this street this week. I can't believe... Katie, is it really you?"

"I... yes." Katie felt tears spring to her eyes. "I can't believe you're here. All of you."

Joan rushed forward and enveloped Katie in a warm

embrace. The familiar scent of her—soap and herbs and the faintest trace of Yorkshire countryside—brought back a flood of childhood memories.

"Oh, my dear girl," Joan murmured, holding her tight. "Look at you. All grown up."

When Joan released her, Peter approached with a broad smile, his eyes bright with unshed tears. "Little Katie Turner. Though not so little anymore, eh?"

Katie looked between the three of them, hardly able to process what was happening. These people who had known her as a child, who had been part of her family before everything fell apart—they were here, alive, together.

"I thought... I never thought I'd see any of you again," she managed.

"Nor did we think we'd see you," Michael said softly. "Katie, where is your family? Molly and Henry?"

The question brought Katie back to her present reality. "I... I don't know," she said, her voice catching. "Mama died of the cholera, and Molly and Henry... they left me at the workhouse years ago. I haven't seen them since."

Joan's face crumpled with sympathy. "Oh, you poor lamb. How long have you been on your own?"

"Since I was fourteen. Four years now." Katie wiped at her eyes with the back of her hand. "I work for a milliner in the better part of town. It's... it's not easy, but I manage."

Peter's expression grew troubled. "That's no life for a young woman, especially not alone."

"Where are you living?" Joan asked with maternal concern.

"Above the millinery. Mrs. Cromwell—my employer—she provides lodging in exchange for work."

Michael frowned. "Is she good to you?"

Katie hesitated, then forced a smile. "She's... strict. But I have a roof over my head and food enough."

The three of them exchanged glances, clearly not fooled by her attempt to downplay her situation.

"Well," Joan said firmly, "you're not alone anymore. You've found us again, haven't you?"

Katie felt something loosen in her chest—a knot of loneliness she'd carried for so long she'd forgotten it was there. "I suppose I have."

"How often can you get away from this milliner?" Peter asked. "Surely she gives you some time to yourself?"

"Sunday mornings. Two hours, from eight until ten."

"Then you'll come see us next Sunday," Joan declared. "We'll catch up properly, won't we? I want to hear everything that's happened to you, dear."

"I'd like that," Katie said, and meant it. For the first time in years, she had something to look forward to.

Michael picked up her fallen bread and brushed it off before handing it to her. "Will you be all right getting home? It's getting dark."

"Yes, I know the way." Katie clutched the bread to her chest, reluctant to leave but knowing she had to return before Mrs. Cromwell grew suspicious.

"Next Sunday then," Joan said, squeezing Katie's hand. "Eight o'clock sharp. We'll be here."

As Katie walked away, she turned back once to see the three of them watching her go, their faces full of warmth and concern. The familiar ache of loneliness was still there, but for the first time in four years, it wasn't quite so sharp.

She had found them again. Michael, Joan, and Peter—the people who had known her when she was loved and cared for. They remembered her, wanted to see her again.

Maybe that was reason enough to keep going.

KATIE'S EYES darted to the clock on the wall.

It was ten minutes to eight. Sunday morning meant two precious hours of freedom, and more importantly, for the past few months, it meant seeing Michael.

She swept the shop floor quickly, though she'd done it the night before. Mrs. Cromwell insisted on daily sweeping, Sunday or not. Katie didn't mind—she was too focused on the morning ahead to care about extra work.

She put away the broom and hurried upstairs. Her plain black dress hung ready—the only respectable outfit Mrs. Cromwell allowed her. Katie smoothed her hair and pinned her bonnet, trying not to look too eager.

At eight o'clock sharp, the church bell chimed. Katie made her way downstairs, forcing herself to move calmly.

"Good heavens, child!" Mrs. Cromwell appeared suddenly. "Where are you rushing off to?"

Katie's heart skipped, but she kept her voice steady. "I thought I'd take a walk, ma'am. The weather's nice today."

Mrs. Cromwell studied her with suspicious eyes. "Very well. Be back at ten o'clock sharp, or you'll work until midnight."

"Yes, ma'am. Thank you, ma'am."

Katie left the millinery, walking sedately until she was out of sight. Then she quickened her pace toward the lamppost where Michael would be waiting.

He was there, leaning casually against the post, his fair hair catching the morning light. When he saw her, his face brightened with genuine pleasure.

"Good morning, Katie," he said warmly.

"Hello, Michael." She felt the week's tension ease from her shoulders.

"How have you been?" He fell into step beside her, his voice concerned. "You look tired."

"I'm better now," she said honestly. "How was your week?"

"Long. But worth it, knowing I'd see you today." He glanced at her sideways. "I brought something for you."

From his pocket, he produced a small, slightly bruised apple. "It's not much, but I thought you might enjoy it."

Katie's eyes lit up. Fresh fruit was a rare luxury. "Michael, you shouldn't spend your money on me."

"It didn't cost anything. The grocer was throwing out the bruised ones. I thought this one still looked perfectly good."

Katie accepted it gratefully. "Thank you. That's very thoughtful."

They walked toward the small park, talking easily. Katie found herself watching Michael as he spoke—the way his eyes crinkled when he smiled, how he gestured with his hands when explaining something about his work. She felt a warmth in her chest that had nothing to do with the sunshine.

"Katie?" Michael's voice brought her back to the present.

"Sorry, I was daydreaming."

"I was asking if you'd like to sit by the pond. The ducks are out today."

"That sounds lovely."

They found a bench facing the water. Katie bit into her apple, savouring the sweet tartness. "This is delicious. Thank you again."

"I'm glad you like it." Michael watched the ducks paddling about. "I've been thinking about what you said last week. About feeling trapped at the millinery."

Katie's stomach tightened. "Michael, I didn't mean to worry you—"

"You should worry me. I care about you, Katie. I hate seeing you unhappy."

There was something different in his voice—a tenderness that made Katie's pulse quicken. "I manage well enough."

"You shouldn't have to just manage. You deserve better than that."

Their eyes met, and Katie felt that fluttering sensation again. "Do you really think so?"

"I know so." His voice was gentle but certain. "You're kind and clever and—" He paused, colour rising in his cheeks. "You're special, Katie. Very special."

Katie felt her own cheeks warm. "You're special too, Michael."

For a moment, they simply looked at each other. Something was shifting between them—a recognition that their friendship was growing into something deeper.

"Katie," Michael said softly, "I need to tell you something."

"What is it?"

"I..." He hesitated, then took a breath. "I look forward to these Sunday mornings all week. Not just because I enjoy your company, but because... because I care about you. More than I probably should."

Katie's heart began to race. "What do you mean?"

"I mean I think about you every day. I worry about whether Mrs. Cromwell is treating you well. I save up little stories to tell you, things I see during the week that I think might make you smile." He looked down at his hands. "I think I'm falling in love with you, Katie."

The words hung in the air between them. Katie felt dizzy with surprise and joy.

"I know I shouldn't say such things," Michael continued quickly. "You're in a difficult situation, and I don't want to make it worse by—"

"Michael." Katie reached out and touched his hand. "I care about you too. More than I knew how to say."

He looked up, hope flickering in his eyes. "Really?"

"Really. I think... I think I'm falling in love with you too."

Michael's face lit up with wonder and relief. Very carefully, he took her hand in both of his. "Katie..."

"I know it's complicated," she said softly. "With Mrs. Cromwell, and your work, and everything else. But what I feel for you—it's real."

"It's real for me too." Michael squeezed her hand gently. "I don't know what we can do about it yet, but Katie, I want you to know—I'm going to find a way for us to be together properly. Not just stolen Sunday mornings, but a real life together."

"How?" Katie whispered.

"I don't know yet. But I will. I promise you that."

A church bell chimed in the distance—half past nine.

"We should head back to meet Mama and Papa," Michael said reluctantly. "They'll be waiting at the market square."

Katie nodded, though she was disappointed to end their private conversation. As they walked back through the park, Michael kept glancing at her, a new warmth in his expression.

"Are you all right?" he asked quietly. "With what I said, I mean."

"More than all right," Katie replied, feeling shy but

happy. "Though I'm not sure how to act around your parents now."

Michael smiled. "Just be yourself. They adore you already."

* * *

They found Peter and Joan by the produce stand, just as Michael had predicted. Joan was sorting through potatoes while Peter held a loaf of bread, beaming at something the baker had said.

"There you are!" Peter called out when he spotted them. "We were starting to wonder if you'd gotten lost."

"Just enjoying the sunshine," Michael replied, his cheeks slightly pink.

Joan looked up from the potatoes, her keen eyes moving between Michael and Katie. "You both look well. How was your walk, dear?" she asked Katie.

"Lovely, thank you. The daffodils are blooming beautifully."

"Ah, spring at last," Joan said with satisfaction. "Michael, help your father with those vegetables. I want to have a word with Katie."

Michael shot Katie an apologetic look but obediently moved to help Peter. Joan linked her arm through Katie's and drew her a few steps away.

"You look different today," Joan observed quietly. "Happy, but nervous. Has something happened?"

Katie felt heat rise in her cheeks. Joan had always been perceptive, even when Katie was a child. "I... that is..."

"Oh, my dear girl." Joan's eyes crinkled with understanding and joy. "He told you, didn't he?"

"Told me what?" Katie whispered.

"How he feels about you, of course. I've been watching that boy pine for weeks, working up the courage."

Katie looked over at Michael, who was examining cabbages with exaggerated interest while clearly trying to overhear their conversation. "How did you know?"

"A mother knows her child's heart," Joan said fondly. "Besides, he's been impossible to live with lately—distracted, sighing, asking me what girls like to hear." She squeezed Katie's arm. "I take it you share his feelings?"

"I do," Katie admitted softly. "But Joan, is it right? With everything being so complicated..."

"Love is never simple, dear one. But it's not always complicated either." Joan's voice grew serious. "Katie, there's something I want you to know. Something that might set your mind at ease."

"What is it?"

Joan glanced around to make sure Peter and Michael were still occupied. "How long were you and Michael apart, after we had to leave the tenement?"

"Eight years," Katie said, her throat tightening at the memory.

"Eight years is a lifetime at your age. And in all that time, when other young men his age were chasing after every pretty girl who walked by, Michael never even looked."

Katie stared at her. "He didn't?"

"Not once. Even when his father and I suggested he might want to court someone, he refused. Said he wasn't interested in anyone."

"But why?"

"There were girls over the years, of course," Joan said, folding her hands. "Pretty ones, clever ones. But Michael never seemed to take to any of them. I used to ask him why, and he'd just smile and say, *'None of them remind me of her.'*"

She looked gently at Katie.

"He always spoke of you with such warmth, even when he was just a boy. Not like someone pining, mind—but like someone who remembered where he felt most at home. You were part of our family, Katie. You still are."

She gave Katie's hand a little squeeze.

"And when he saw you again, after all these years... well, I think his heart simply remembered you before his head caught up."

Tears pricked Katie's eyes. "I had no idea he felt that way for so long."

"Well, now you do." Joan patted her arm kindly. "That boy has carried the memory of you for eight years, Katie Turner. Even when he didn't know if he'd ever see you again, he never forgot the little girl whose hand he held through the darkest days. You were the one he looked after when everything else was falling apart—and I don't think he ever stopped wanting to."

Katie looked over at Michael again, seeing him with new eyes. He was laughing at something Peter had said, but when he caught her looking, his expression grew soft and wondering.

"So you see," Joan continued, "Whatever complications you're facing, you can be certain of one thing—Michael's feelings for you are true. What he remembered of you was never forgotten, but what he feels now has grown from who you are today. That kind of affection, born of memory, tested by time, and renewed in truth—is the rarest kind of all.

"Thank you," Katie whispered. "For telling me that. I... I needed to hear it."

"I know you did, dear. Now, shall we rejoin the men? Michael looks like he's about to burst from curiosity."

They walked back to Peter and Michael, who were now pretending to have an intense discussion about turnips.

"Find everything you need?" Katie asked lightly.

"Oh yes," Peter said with twinkling eyes. "And apparently Michael has developed very strong opinions about root vegetables."

Michael shot his father a look that clearly meant 'please stop talking,' which made Peter chuckle.

"Well," Joan said diplomatically, "I should get home and start preparing Sunday dinner. Katie, you're welcome to join us if Mrs. Cromwell would allow it."

"That's very kind, but she expects me back by ten," Katie replied, though she longed to accept.

"Another time then," Joan said warmly. "Michael, walk Katie back to the millinery."

"Yes, Mama." Michael's relief at having an excuse for more private time with Katie was obvious.

As they said their goodbyes, Joan squeezed Katie's hand meaningfully. "Remember what we talked about, dear."

Katie nodded, feeling lighter than she had in months.

* * *

The very streets seemed brighter for the day's revelations. Katie felt as though the sunshine was warmer than it had ever been before; as though her feet barely touched the ground as Michael walked her back to the millinery.

Katie smiled, remembering something. "You made me a promise once before. Do you remember?"

"Which one?"

"On the bridge, when we were children. You shared a

sticky bun with me and promised we'd find each other again."

Michael's expression grew tender. "I remember. You were so little, and so frightened. I wanted to give you hope."

"You did. That promise kept me going through some very dark times."

"What exactly did I promise? I remember the feeling more than the words."

Katie closed her eyes, thinking back. "We were both scared about Mama being sick, and what would happen to all of us. I asked if we'd always be friends, and you said yes. You promised that no matter what happened, we'd find each other again. That friends look out for each other."

"And we did find each other," Michael said softly. "Though I have to admit, what I feel for you now is quite different from friendship."

"For me too." Katie opened her eyes to find him watching her intently. "When we were children, you were my dearest friend. Now... now you're so much more."

"Katie," Michael said carefully, "I want to court you properly. But given your situation with Mrs. Cromwell, I don't know how—"

A church bell chimed in the distance.

"A quarter to ten already," Michael said with disappointment. "We shouldn't dawdle."

Katie's heart sank. These Sunday mornings always seemed too short. "I wish we had more time."

"So do I. But Katie—" He offered her his hand. "What I said about finding a way for us to be together—I meant it. I'm going to work toward that every day."

As they walked back toward the millinery, Katie felt a mixture of happiness and uncertainty. Michael's confession had filled her with joy, but the practical realities of their situation loomed large.

"Michael," she said as they approached the shop, "what if Mrs. Cromwell finds out about us? She barely tolerates my Sunday walks as it is."

"Then we'll be careful. And I'll work even harder to find a solution." Michael stopped just around the corner from the millinery. "Katie, I know this isn't easy. If you want to wait, to think about this—"

"No," Katie said firmly. "I don't want to wait. I want to be with you, Michael. Whatever it takes."

Michael's face broke into a smile that made Katie's heart sing. "Then we'll figure it out together."

He squeezed her hand once, quickly, before she walked the final few steps to Mrs. Cromwell's door alone.

***

The past three weeks had been like a dream. Every Sunday, Katie would meet Michael, and they would walk together, talking and laughing, growing closer with each passing week. Then they would meet Joan and Peter at the market, and Katie would feel herself becoming part of their little family again.

Joan had taken to giving Katie small gifts—a flower from her windowsill, a sweet biscuit she'd baked, a pretty ribbon she'd found at the market. "Just because," she'd say with a warm smile. Peter would regale them with stories from his work, making them all laugh with his impressions of difficult customers.

But this Wednesday, as Katie worked in the millinery, she spotted Michael across the street from her window, she knew immediately that something was terribly wrong.

Instead of his usual cheerful wave, he was beckoning urgently, his face creased with worry and sorrow.

Katie's stomach dropped. Michael knew Mrs. Cromwell would be furious if she left her work. He'd only call her down for something serious.

She hurried across the street, her heart pounding. "Michael! What's wrong?"

"Katie, I'm so sorry." His voice was strained, broken. "I didn't want to tell you like this, but... we have to leave London."

"What?" Katie felt the world tilt beneath her feet.

"Our landlord evicted us yesterday morning. We couldn't make the rent." Michael's hands trembled as he reached for her. "Papa heard of work in Birmingham—a nail maker who needs help. It's our only chance to stay together as a family."

"No," Katie whispered. "Michael, no."

"I'm sorry, my love. I'm so, so sorry." Tears filled his eyes. "Mama and Papa are heartbroken too. Mama cried when we had to tell her we'd be leaving you behind again."

"When?" Katie managed to ask.

"This afternoon. We're taking the four o'clock train."

Katie stared at him in shock. Just three weeks ago, he'd promised to find a way for them to be together. Now he was leaving London entirely.

"Where are your parents now?" Katie asked, her voice hollow.

"At the train station, watching our belongings. They... they wanted to come say goodbye, but there wasn't time. Mama asked me to give you this." Michael reached into his pocket and pulled out a small cloth bundle. "She made it for you."

With shaking hands, Katie unwrapped the cloth to find

a delicate handkerchief embroidered with tiny flowers. In the corner, Joan had stitched "K.T." in careful letters.

"She worked on it every evening this week," Michael said quietly. "She said every girl should have something beautiful that's just hers."

Katie pressed the handkerchief to her chest, tears streaming down her face. "Oh, Joan..."

"She also wanted me to tell you that you'll always be her daughter, no matter what happens. That the family that chose you when you were small hasn't stopped choosing you now."

"Come with me," Michael said suddenly. "Katie, come with us."

"I can't," Katie said, though her heart ached to say yes. "I have no money, nowhere to go if things don't work out—"

"My parents would welcome you with open arms. You know they would. Mama said as much before I left to find you."

Katie was tempted, desperately tempted. Joan and Peter had always made her feel like family. But the practical side of her mind, the part that had learned caution through years of hardship, held her back.

"Michael, what if there's no work for me in Birmingham? What if your family can't afford another mouth to feed? I'd be stranded there with nothing."

Michael's face crumpled. "Then what do we do?"

"You go," Katie said, though it felt like tearing her heart out. "You go, and you take care of your parents. Joan and Peter need you, Michael. You can't let them face this alone."

"But I can't leave you alone either," Michael said desperately.

"I won't be alone forever," Katie said, trying to convince

herself as much as him. "We found each other once. We can do it again."

"Katie..."

"Listen to me," Katie said, taking his hands in hers. "When Joan talked to me that first Sunday, she told me how faithful you'd been. How you waited eight years without looking at anyone else. If you could do that then, we can do this now. But this time, we'll know where each other is. This time, we can write letters."

Michael pulled her into his arms, not caring who might see. "I love you," he whispered into her hair. "I love you so much. And I love my parents for trying to include you in this, even when they have so little themselves."

"I love you too. And I love them." Katie clung to him, memorizing the feel of his embrace. "Promise me you'll take care of them. Promise me you'll write when you can."

"I promise. And Katie—promise me you won't give up hope. Promise me you'll wait for me."

Katie pulled back to look into his eyes. "I promise. But Michael, if you meet someone else, if your life takes a different direction—"

"It won't," he said firmly. "Katie, you're the only one for me. There will never be anyone else. Mama and Papa feel the same way about you—you're the daughter they always wanted for me."

"I feel the same way. But if circumstances change—"

"They won't." Michael cupped her face in his hands. "When I'm established in Birmingham, when Papa's settled in the new work and Mama's found her place, I'm coming back for you. And then I'm going to marry you, if you'll have me."

Katie's breath caught. "Michael..."

"I mean it. I want to spend my life with you, Katie

Turner. Do you remember what I said on the bridge?" Michael murmured. "That no matter what happened, I'd find you again?"

Katie nodded, her voice caught in her throat. "I didn't know what love was then," he said, "not truly. I only knew I didn't want a world where you weren't in it. And now that I've found you again—now that we're grown—I finally understand what it is I was looking for.. Will you marry me? Not now, but someday, when we can make it work?"

Through her tears, Katie smiled. "Yes. Yes, I'll marry you."

Michael kissed her forehead gently. "Then this isn't goodbye. It's just... a temporary separation. And when I come back, I'll have both my parents' blessing and a proper future to offer you."

They held each other for another precious moment before the reality of his departure forced them apart.

"I have to go," Michael said reluctantly. "The train won't wait."

"I know." Katie straightened her shoulders, trying to be brave. "Go. Build a life for us."

"I will. I swear to you, I will."

Katie watched him walk away, her heart breaking and soaring at the same time. He was leaving, but he loved her. He'd promised to come back, to marry her. It would have to be enough to sustain her through whatever came next.

* * *

The weeks that followed Michael's departure were some of the loneliest of Katie's life. She threw herself into her work, partly to keep busy and partly because Mrs. Cromwell seemed to sense her distress and was even more demanding than usual.

"You're slower than molasses these days," the milliner snapped one afternoon. "What's gotten into you?"

"Nothing, ma'am. I'll work faster."

"See that you do. I'm not paying you to daydream."

Katie bent over her sewing, trying to focus on the intricate beadwork. But her mind kept drifting to Michael, wondering where he was, whether he'd found work, if he was thinking of her.

It had been six weeks since he left, and she'd received no word. She told herself it was too soon, that he'd need time to get settled before he could afford to send a letter. But doubt crept in during the long, quiet evenings.

"Don't just stand there gawking," Mrs. Cromwell's sharp voice cut through her thoughts. "We have customers."

Katie looked up to see a well-dressed woman and her pale daughter entering the shop.

"Mrs. Kensington, how lovely to see you," Mrs. Cromwell simpered. "How may we help you today?"

"We need a traveling dress for my daughter. We're taking a trip to Spain."

Katie helped with the fitting, her mind only half on the work. Spain sounded exotic and wonderful—so different from the grey confines of the millinery.

"The dress is beautiful," the daughter said softly to Katie as her mother discussed details with Mrs. Cromwell. "You do lovely work."

"Thank you," Katie murmured, surprised by the kindness.

"Are you quite well? You look rather sad."

Katie glanced toward Mrs. Cromwell, who was distracted with fabric samples. "I'm fine, miss. Just tired."

The girl studied her with intelligent eyes. "If you ever need help, my name is Sylvia Kensington. We live on Marlborough Street."

Before Katie could respond, Mrs. Kensington called for her daughter, and they were gone, leaving Katie to wonder at the unexpected offer of assistance.

* * *

Two months after Michael's departure, Katie was sweeping the shop when she heard the postman's whistle. Her heart leaped—could it be?

Mrs. Cromwell answered the door and returned with a single letter. She squinted at the address, then looked at Katie suspiciously.

"This is for you. Who do you know in Birmingham?"

Katie tried to keep her voice steady. "A friend of my family's, ma'am. They said they might write."

Mrs. Cromwell handed over the letter reluctantly. "Well, read it quickly and get back to work."

Katie's hands shook as she opened the envelope. Michael's familiar handwriting filled the page:

My dearest Katie,

I hope this letter finds you well. I'm sorry it's taken so long to write—we've had a difficult time getting settled, but I promised I would write as soon as we were able.

The work is hard but steady, and we've found decent lodgings in a boarding house with other families. Papa's leg is much better with the lighter work, and his spirits have improved greatly. Mama has found employment helping a seamstress (she says the woman reminds her of you, always bent over her needle with such concentration).

Mama cries sometimes when she speaks of you. She says losing you again is like losing a daughter, and she makes me promise every day that I'll bring you to Birmingham as soon as we're able. Papa agrees—he says the boarding house would welcome another young woman, especially one who's practically family.

I think of you every day, Katie. Not just because I love you, but because Mama and Papa speak of you so often. "Katie would laugh at that," Mama will say when something amusing happens. Or Papa will see a pretty ribbon at market and say, "That would suit our Katie perfectly."

I haven't forgotten my promise. Not for a single day. I'm saving every penny I can. Mama is too—she says she's putting aside money for your train fare and a proper wedding dress. (She's already planning our wedding, though she tries to hide it!)

Please be patient with me, and please don't lose hope. Mama and Papa send their love and ask me to tell you that you're in their prayers every night.

Write to me if you can. The address is at the top of this letter. Mama is desperate for word from you.

All our love, Michael (and Joan and Peter)

Katie pressed the letter to her chest, tears of relief streaming down her face. He hadn't forgotten her. They hadn't forgotten her. Joan was planning their wedding and saving money for her train fare.

"Well?" Mrs. Cromwell demanded. "What news from Birmingham?"

"They're well, ma'am. They've found work and settled in."

"Good. Now get back to your sewing. That dress won't finish itself."

But as Katie climbed the stairs to her garret, the letter tucked safely in her pocket along with Joan's handkerchief, she felt lighter than she had in months. Michael loved her, Joan was planning their wedding, and Peter was looking out for them all. She wasn't just waiting for a sweetheart—she was waiting for a whole family who loved her.

* * *

That evening, by candlelight, Katie penned her reply:

Dear Michael, Joan, and Peter,

Your letter brought me more joy than you can imagine. I was beginning to worry, but I understand now why it took time to get settled.

Please tell Joan that I think of her every day, and I treasure the beautiful handkerchief she made for me. I carry it everywhere. Tell her I would be honoured to wear a wedding dress she helped to make, when that blessed day comes.

And please tell Peter that I remember his kindness and his stories, and I hope his leg continues to improve in the lighter work.

Michael, I'm well, though I miss you all terribly. Mrs. Cromwell keeps me busy, which helps pass the time. I've saved a little money—not much, but something toward our future and perhaps my train fare to Birmingham.

Please don't worry about how long it takes. I'll wait for you, Michael. However long it takes, I'll wait. And I'll wait for Joan and Peter too—they're as much my family as you are.

Until we meet again, All my love, Katie

P.S. Joan, if you're reading this over Michael's shoulder (and

I suspect you are!), please know that I dream of the day I can call you Mother properly, and help you with your sewing again.

She sealed the letter carefully and hid it until she could post it the next day.

As she prepared for bed, Katie felt something she hadn't experienced in months: genuine hope. She wasn't just waiting for Michael to return—she was waiting to rejoin a family who truly wanted her. Joan's handkerchief lay on her pillow, and she touched the carefully embroidered flowers before blowing out her candle.

Michael loved her, but more than that, Joan and Peter loved her too. Whatever obstacles they faced, they would face them as a family. And that made all the difference.

CHAPTER 9

CHAPTER EIGHT

"Lavender blue, diddle-diddle, lavender green." Katie sang the words softly as she worked, hanging the new dress on the rack by the door. "When I am king, diddle-diddle, you shall be queen."

Or at least, she thought, *"when I am able, you shall be my wife."* That was more than enough for her. With Michael by her side, any cottage would be a castle.

She stepped back and smiled at the newly-made dress now hanging in the window. It was emerald green, with delicate red fabric roses on the bodice and beautiful red strings to complement the deep colour of the skirt. Any girl would be lucky to own such a dress.

Mrs. Cromwell, of course, would find fault with it, but there was nothing to be done about that. Mrs. Cromwell always did—and it could not steal the joy that filled Katie's soul more and more with every passing Sunday.

It was Wednesday now, right in the middle of the

week. In just a few more days, Katie would spend her glorious Sunday morning with Michael again. The thought of the coming joy drew her through the drudgery like a golden lifeline to which she clung with all her heart.

"Call up your men, diddle-diddle." Her favourite song came easily to her lips when her heart was so full of joy. "Set them to work."

She left the dress and crossed the shop, daring to sing only because Mrs. Cromwell was having one of her 'little lie-downs'. These had become more and more frequent, related perhaps to the increasing blue around the old milliner's lips. Katie didn't mind. To her, they meant only peace.

She climbed the steps to her garret and tucked herself behind her desk, where yet another bolt of fabric and pattern lay, needing to be done by the next morning. Her heart quailed at the thought of the many hours she would have to spend at this desk before she could sleep, but she dreamed of Michael's smile instead, and was still singing as she lifted the scissors.

She was about to make the first cut when she spotted him. She caught only a glimpse of his tall figure from the corner of her eye, but she thought of him so constantly that she recognized him at once. He stood on the pavement across the street from the millinery, an arm raised, seeking her attention.

Delight bloomed in Katie's heart. She waved to him, grinning widely. He knew she couldn't leave her post; nor could he linger in what must be a quick trip to gather more iron or deliver nails to their client.

But Michael's returning wave was not a merry greeting. Instead, he beckoned to her. She leaned closer to the window, feeling a kick of worry in her chest. Was that a frown on his dear face?

Michael beckoned again.

The worry matured into fear. Michael knew that Mrs. Cromwell would never forgive her for leaving her work. He would only call her down if he had no other choice.

Panic surged in her blood as she ran down the stairs. Mrs. Cromwell was still asleep—a small mercy—and the shop was empty. Katie ran across it without being stopped. Then she was hurrying across the street to Michael, and she knew instantly that something was wrong. His pinched expression and trembling lips told her as much.

"Michael!" she cried. "What is it? What's the matter?"

"Katie, my love." Michael's voice cracked.

She thought he was going to cry, and it terrified her. The last time she had seen him openly weep was at Tessie's funeral.

Or on the awful day when Joan and Peter took him away from her...

"Michael," she managed. "What's wrong?"

"I'm sorry, Katie," he whispered. "I'm so sorry."

She clutched at her chest, feeling the painful thud of her heart against her fingers.

"We have to go," said Michael.

Katie thought she might fall. She seized the hard iron of the nearby lamppost to keep from collapsing to the ground. "No!"

"It's true. I'm sorry. I... I didn't want to tell you. I didn't want you to worry... but... the man who supplies our iron and buys our nails..." Michael bit his lip. "He's stopped paying us. It's been two weeks. We have nothing left, not a penny. We... we've been evicted."

Katie gasped in horror.

"We slept on the street last night. My mama..." Michael shook his head.

"Oh, Michael," Katie croaked.

"We heard of another client, one who can help us, but he lives half a day's walk across the city."

Katie raised a hand to her head, trying to keep it from spinning.

"We have to go there, Katie-pie. If we don't..." He squared his shoulders. "If we don't, then I'll never learn to make shoes. I'll never become a farrier. I'll never be able to save you."

"I don't want you to go," Katie gasped.

"My darling, I don't want to leave you." Michael seized her hands, ignoring the impropriety. "But nor can I watch you suffer like this. I have to go. It's the only way I can bring us together—*really* together—in the end." His eyes searched hers. "It's the only way I can marry you."

Marry! The word made Katie's breath catch in her throat. Oh, of course it had been her hope since the moment she laid eyes on Michael a few months ago. But this was the first time that either of them had dared to say it out loud.

"I want you to marry me," Katie gasped. The words came out on their own, breathless and intent.

"I know, my darling. I want it, too. More than anything." Michael squeezed her hands. "This is the only way."

The tears burned Katie's eyes and throat. She felt too many things all at once—terror, love, and above all, blinding hope.

"My promise stands forever." Michael's hands trembled on hers. "We will always be together in the end."

Katie closed her eyes and inhaled, a shaky breath.

"When I see you again, I will marry you," Michael whispered.

With his hands wrapped around hers, it was easy to hope. It was easy to allow that hope to win over her good sense and her rationality. It was easy to believe in a brighter future, no matter how dark the present.

"All right," she said. "I'll see you again soon."

"I'll write when I can," Michael promised. "It might be a few weeks before we can afford, but I will."

Katie opened her eyes and searched his with hope and fear. "Come back to me, Michael."

"Always, my love."

Then he released her hands, slowly, one finger at a time, and walked away.

Katie knew that Mrs. Cromwell would be awake at any moment and demanding her return, but she could not bear to step away. Her hungry eyes rested on him, drinking him in, until he turned the street corner and was once again gone.

IT HAD BEEN THREE WEEKS, and still no word from Michael.

Katie felt every one of those weeks—every one of those *minutes*—like a leaden weight upon her shoulders. The clock in the corner's slow ticking added to it, making her spine feel crushed, her body drooping as she plodded down the stairs to the millinery with a newly completed dress on its hanger in her hand.

She paused by a small window on the second floor and gazed at the street, but there was no one there except for the usual passing crowd and a new tramp across the street.

Would someone ever come for her? Would Michael

return? Molly had cast her out, but perhaps Henry would come one day, her big brother, and take her somewhere safe and warm. The thought made her throat knot. She missed him so.

"Finally," Mrs. Cromwell barked. "Where have you been all afternoon?"

"Working on this dress, Mrs. Cromwell."

"Well, it doesn't look like it. This must be your shoddiest work yet!" Mrs. Cromwell seized a perfectly acceptable sleeve and squinted at it through runny eyes. "Why, you wretched little beast, you're only growing lazier and lazier."

Katie bowed her head and waited for the tirade to finish, then slowly dragged herself across the room to hang the dress.

"And for heaven's sake, stand up straight," Mrs. Cromwell ordered.

Tears pricked the corners of Katie's eyes as she hung the dress. She took a deep breath, trying to control them, and turned to go back upstairs to her garret.

The tinkle of the doorbell stopped her. Mrs. Cromwell gave her a murderous look, and Katie quickly spun around, plastering on a wide smile. A staid old woman in black entered the millinery, half-dragging with her a girl about Katie's age whose appearance was, in a word, pale. From her ashy blonde hair to her watery green eyes, she appeared to have had all the colour wrung out of her.

"Ah, Mrs. Kensington, how wonderful to see you." Mrs. Cromwell simpered out from behind the counter. "You're wearing such a fine piece today."

"Oh, don't be so silly, Agatha." Mrs. Kensington tittered. "You know full well that this is one of yours."

So did Katie; she'd sewn the garment herself in many long, laborious hours in her garret.

"How may we help today?" Mrs. Cromwell asked.

"I'm taking my dear Sylvia here on holiday in Spain, and we need a nice new dress." Mrs. Kensington wrapped a motherly arm around Sylvia's shoulders.

"Of course, of course. We have a few beautiful pieces ready for you." Mrs. Cromwell rounded on Katie. "Don't just stand there, girl. Bring out what we have at once."

Katie scuttled off and selected three gowns that she thought would fit the skinny Sylvia. Mrs. Cromwell curried favour with Mrs. Kensington as Katie brought them out, keeping her head low, exactly as she'd been taught.

"Aren't they just lovely?" Mrs. Cromwell touched the first one. "This is some of my finest work."

None of the dresses were Mrs. Cromwell's work at all; Katie had sewn every stitch. Of course, she dared not say this. She kept her head down as Sylvia pontificated about the virtues of each dress, eventually asking to try a royal blue one whose bold shades could not possibly work with her pale skin.

"Go ahead, my dear. My girl will help you dress," said Mrs. Cromwell.

Katie felt as though she was barely present in the room as she helped Sylvia out of her gown and slid the new one over her many layers. She was right—the blue was *far* too much for Sylvia—but the girl twirled back and forth before the mirror, giggling, as though she felt like a princess.

Katie stood numbly beside her, unable to feel anything except the dread weight on her shoulders. She stared sightlessly through the window. It was a cold, miserable evening, and the streets were largely empty except for the Kensington's' carriage standing outside and the ragged figure of a tramp huddled over a little fire by the tailor's shop.

"We'll take it, of course," said Mrs. Kensington, "once you've done the adjustments."

"Yes, yes. It'll only be a day or two," said Mrs. Cromwell.

Mrs. Kensington frowned. "I'm afraid it can't be a day or two, Agatha. We're leaving for Spain in the morning. We'll collect the dress first thing."

Katie's belly tightened. She knew she would spend all night working on the dress, and what was more, she didn't have the right colour thread to make the adjustments in the store.

"Of course," said Mrs. Cromwell without missing a beat. "They'll be done first thing in the morning."

"Wonderful." Mrs. Kensington gave a big smile. "I'll send a footman for it in the morning."

They left in a susurrus of petticoats, and Mrs. Cromwell thrust the dress into Katie's hands.

"Why are you standing about like this, girl? Go! Get the adjustments done at once."

Katie gulped. "Yes, Mrs. Cromwell, but—"

"But? But? You're not permitted to say that word!"

Katie knew there would be consequences and had no choice but to push on. "We don't have blue thread, Mrs. Cromwell."

"How can we not have blue thread? You know it's your job to make sure we always have every colour we need!"

Fear swelled in Katie's throat. "I... I'm sorry, Mrs. Cromwell. I don't... I don't know why I didn't think to get more. I just..." *I feel as though I'm being crushed slowly to death, and it makes it so very hard to think.*

The blow startled her. Mrs. Cromwell's hand slapped

across her cheek, more impact than pain, making Katie reel backward a step.

"Well, then, go to the haberdashery and buy more thread at once, before the shop closes!" Mrs. Cromwell thundered.

Katie hastily hung up the dress. "Yes, Mrs. Cromwell. Right away, Mrs. Cromwell."

"Take this!" Mrs. Cromwell thrust a few pennies into her hand. "Now get out of my sight!"

Katie clutched the pennies and scrambled toward the side door. "Yes, Mrs. Cromwell."

The old milliner's yell followed her into the street. "Stupid girl! Hurry, hurry! We need that thread right away."

"Yes, Mrs. Cromwell."

"Go!"

Katie ducked her head and scampered across the street, heading toward the corner. The haberdashery was a block away; she would reach it in good time before it closed, but every minute she wasted now was a minute's sleep she would lose. The thought made her limbs feel leaden. How much rest would she have tonight? Two hours? Three?

Her cheek burned as she paused beneath the lamppost on the corner, the same one where she had bid Michael goodbye, and looked left and right for traffic. No carriages came, so she hurried across the street and kept going down the pavement.

There were many people about this late in the evening. Many were women, carrying shopping baskets or babies. Children brushed up against Katie as they chased each other down the street. She held the pennies tightly, keeping a wary eye out for pickpockets.

She was only a few steps away from the haberdashery

door when a cry rang out, shattering the normality of her day, tilting the world beneath her feet.

"Katie!"

It was not her name that made her whirl around, but the voice that called out to her. Despite its depth, it held a strange familiar, and the accent—

The accent was Yorkshire. Like Molly's.

For a confusing moment, she stared at a stranger. It was the tramp, she realized, the one who had huddled by the tailor's shop a few minutes before. He was a scruffy creature, his face weather-beaten, his hair sticking out at odd angles from beneath a hat full of holes. For a moment, fear gripped her, until Katie met his eyes.

They arrested her. She knew them so well.

"H-Henry?" she croaked.

Tears pooled in his eyes. "It's me, Katie. It's really me."

In an instant, the intervening years faded. Her anger and sorrow could not stand against the fractured desperation in his voice. He had hurt her, but he was her brother, and there was no denying the love in his eyes.

"Henry!" she cried, and ran to him.

His was the first embrace she had felt since her last night sharing a sleeping pallet with Hannah in the workhouse, and it smelled terrible, but he was warm and real and alive. Katie buried her face in his chest and wept.

"Oh, Henry, oh, Henry, you came! You came just like I thought you would."

He held her for a long few moments, his arms squeezing her tight, and Katie thought she might die of relief. Michael would come back for her—she believed it—but for now, right now, she was not alone in the world after all.

Slowly, Henry let her go. She pulled back and gazed up at him.

Frank tears of joy rolled down his cheeks. "Katie, it's really you."

"It's me!"

His next words astounded her. "But Molly said she'd lost you in the workhouse."

Katie's legs felt suddenly weak. She had to cling to Henry's arms to stay upright. "You know where Molly is?"

"I do. She's doing so well, Katie. She's been looking for you."

Those last few words gushed through the deepest wound in Katie's soul. She realized, with breathtaking force, that she had been wrong about Molly. Her sister hadn't abandoned her after all. Molly had been searching for her.

Molly would be able to make all of this better.

The words boiled up in Katie from a place of deepest woe. "Take me to her. Please."

Henry's face crumpled. He glanced over his shoulder, as though expecting something to launch from the shadows and attack. "I... I can't. It's a long story." He hung his head, not meeting her eyes. "Katie, I'm sorry. I can't do anything for you."

Katie let go of his arms and stepped back, feeling as though an abyss had opened suddenly at her feet. "What do you mean?"

Henry's shoulders shook. Katie realized again how dishevelled and ragged he appeared. His cheekbones jutted against his skin.

"I have no money," he said. "A bad man is after me and I don't want him to realize that you're my sister, so I can't travel back to Molly with you. I can't do anything for you."

She stared into his harrowed face and saw terrible suffering in his eyes, suffering that had carried on for many years and left her fun, playful brother a mere husk of what he once was. Yet at the same time, there was a depth in him she had never seen before. He did not sparkle like he used to; but now there was something more to him than sparkle. There was a heartbreaking nobility in his face that made her love him more than ever before.

The thought of this bad man frightened her and her heart ached with the dashed hope of seeing Molly again soon, but at that moment, none of it mattered as much as the fact that her brother was here, in the flesh, with her.

She grabbed his arms and looked into his eyes, hoping he would see the ferocity of her love somehow.

"Oh, Henry." Her tears broke free. "You don't realize that you're doing so much for me just because—just because you're *here*."

He gave a strangled sob and hugged her close. Katie melted into her brother's arms.

PART III

CHAPTER 10

CHAPTER NINE

One Year Later

"You! Girl!" Mrs. Cromwell bellowed.

Katie leaped up from her desk in the garret. She cast a fleeting glance through the window over the street and saw nothing but rain pouring from the sky, turning grey and brown where it swirled through the gutters.

"Get down here!" Mrs. Cromwell screamed.

Katie scrambled down the stairs. "I'm coming, Mrs. Cromwell!"

She reached the bottom and almost ducked Mrs. Cromwell's hand, but the old woman still managed to seize her arm and give her a shockingly painful pinch that made her gasp with pain.

"What are you playing at, girl?" Mrs. Cromwell hissed. "We have work to do!"

Katie's gaze darted to the two women entering the millinery and then to Mrs. Cromwell's eyes. They were red and watery, with a milky haze covering them, failing to dampen the cruelty within.

She knew then that Mrs. Cromwell could no longer identify her customers by sight. That was why the old woman called for her so impatiently anytime anyone came into the millinery.

Katie felt a brief flicker of compassion. "Yes, Mrs. Cromwell."

"Don't patronize me, you wretched girl." Mrs. Cromwell shoved her away.

The compassion vanished. Katie struggled to hold back her anger and sorrow as she turned to the customers and curtseyed deeply. At least they were two of the nicer people who came into the millinery: dear Lady Ashton and her steadfast companion, Millie. Millie gave Katie a conspiratorial wink.

Perhaps there would be another shilling in it for her today. Millie had given her money from time to time over the past year.

"Good morning, Lady Ashton," Katie said loudly.

"Mrs. Cromwell!" Lady Ashton swept over to the old woman. "How wonderful to see you!"

Mrs. Cromwell's lips twitched into a smile. "Good morning, your ladyship. It's a pleasure to see you today."

"It's always lovely coming into your millinery." Lady Ashton gave a big smile. "I've nothing particular in mind, but I thought you could show me what you happen to have."

"Of course, of course. You, girl—" Mrs. Cromwell began.

"Dearest Mrs. Cromwell." Lady Ashton laid a hand on her arm. "If I may prevail upon you to show me personally, I would be most grateful. It would be my delight to peruse your goods with your own experienced eye."

Mrs. Cromwell's lips wobbled. "Very well, your ladyship, as you wish."

Lady Ashton glanced over her shoulder and gave Millie a pointed look.

The companion seized Katie's arm. "Over here. Quickly, quietly!"

Katie gasped, but didn't resist as Millie steered her into the fitting area, out of Mrs. Cromwell's sight.

"What's all this?" Katie asked.

"Shhh! Not so loud," said Millie. "I must ask you something most important."

Katie nodded, silent.

"Do you know a young man named Henry Turner? Is he, by any chance, your brother?"

Katie stiffened. Henry had told her all about Fred, the violent criminal who was bent on killing him as revenge for a fight years ago when Henry had accidentally pushed him through a window. She couldn't tell his real name to anyone, she knew.

"Katie, please," Millie whispered, "it's about Seraphina. I used to be her companion."

Katie's eyes widened. "Henry's told me you were her companion. Is Seraphina all right?" The girl was the love of Henry's life.

Millie looked away. "No," she murmured, "no, she isn't. Not at all."

Katie clutched her chest. If something had happened to Seraphina, Henry would be utterly devastated.

"It's her father," said Millie. "He's a brute, that man, a

terrible, horrible brute. He might dress like a gentleman, but he's nothing more than a violent ape!" She was shaking with anger. "I left Seraphina's service because of him; I begged her to marry and be done with him, but she feared that any husband would treat her as her father does. And when she met Henry, well, she never had eyes for another."

"She still waits for Henry?"

"She would wait ten thousand years for Henry, but she can wait no longer, Katie. That man will kill her." Millie touched her throat. "I saw her with terrible bruises all over her neck. He aims to murder her, I know he does, in one of his drunken rages."

"What can we do?"

"There is only one place Seraphina can go where she will feel safe, and that is with your brother."

Katie bit her lip. "But Fred is trying to kill Henry. He might hurt Seraphina, too, if he finds him."

"So Seraphina has told me, but whether or not Fred will ever find Henry, we don't know. It is a certainty that Seraphina's father will harm or kill her unless she flees."

Katie blinked. She had few memories of her own papa, except for a vague impression of his deep, booming voice, but she couldn't imagine him ever harming her. The thought that Seraphina feared her father would kill her was shocking.

"I wouldn't ask this if I thought there was any other way," said Millie. "Seraphina's entire family is under her father's sway; she has nowhere to run except to Henry. Believe me, I wish it could be different. Your brother is a good man, but if she goes to him, she will be ruined at once. She will never be able to return to her old life. She will be destitute... and yet I saw the abuse she suffered at her father's hands." Sorrow filled her eyes. "Even a life in poverty would be far preferable. Please, Katie, tell me where your brother is. For Seraphina's sake."

Henry would do anything for Seraphina. If he knew about this, Katie was certain he would want to rescue her.

"All right." She bit her lip. "I'm not sure exactly. I only see him once a fortnight or so, when he's certain Fred isn't after him, but the last time I saw him, he said he was going to find work at the docks nearest here."

Millie nodded. "I know them. I can tell Seraphina the way. Thank you, Katie."

"You! Girl!" Mrs. Cromwell shrieked. "Come here at once!"

"Yes, Mrs. Cromwell!" Katie bolted to her mistress' side.

Mrs. Cromwell scowled down at her, the milky eyes still capable of conveying a frightening depth of fury. "Show Lady Ashton our newest gown at once."

"Yes, Mrs. Cromwell." Katie turned away.

She met Millie's eyes as she took the dress from its hanger for Lady Ashton's polite commentary. The companion smiled, but her expression did little for the fear gathering in Katie's chest.

She could only hope that she had done the right thing.

Katie kept her smarting left hand tucked into the warmth of her coat against the biting wind. She huddled, shortening her neck in a bid to hide her ears behind her scarf. The buildings on either side of her could do little for the wind; it shrieked down the street like a vengeful ghost, plucking at Katie's clothes with spectral hands, running frigid fingers down her spine.

She clutched the penny in her right hand as she

shielded her eyes with her forearm. At least Mrs. Cromwell had still given her the money for the bread, she supposed, despite the three blows of the wooden ruler she'd received on her left palm for the transgression of knocking a cup of milk onto the dress she was working on.

It seemed she could barely take a wrong step without punishment from Mrs. Cromwell these days. But it was not Mrs. Cromwell who caused her heart to feel tied in a knot.

It was the fear of what had happened with Seraphina.

The strange meeting with Millie had taken place more than a week ago, and Katie had not seen Henry since. What if Fred had already known about Seraphina? What if he had followed her right to Henry? What would he do to her brother?

Was she alone once more?

Katie's numb feet carried her to the stall selling stale bread at half price. She paid a penny for two loaves, one so dry that it crunched in the stallholder's fingers as he wrapped it in newspaper. She tucked them both under her arm and turned to go, her feet leaden beneath the weight of her worry.

Then she saw her.

Katie had never met Seraphina. She was a lord's daughter, after all, a real lady, not a wretched little urchin like Katie. But from Henry's description, she knew her at once. She'd thought that Henry was exaggerating when he said that she looked like an angel and moved like one, too, but that was the first thing that flashed through Katie's mind when she saw her: *angelic.*

The girl wore a plain blue dress now, its skirt mended in several places, and a white pinafore that had seen better days. But when she moved, she somehow still had the air of a princess. Her skin was so pale that it almost glowed. The curls peeking from beneath her bonnet were brightest gold, and when she looked up, her eyes were the colour of anemones.

She clutched a basket containing a few carrots and turnips, and her gaze brushed past Katie at first, but she was searching for something. She turned left and right, seeking, until her eyes found Katie's and widened.

Katie stepped forward. She hardly dared say the girl's name in case she was wrong.

It was Seraphina who spoke first. "Katie? Is that you?"

Katie's heart leaped. "Seraphina?"

"Yes!" Seraphina hurried to her, holding out her arm. "Oh, how wonderful to meet you at last! Your brother has told me so very much about you."

Astonished, Katie returned Seraphina's embrace. "How are you here? How do you know me?"

"I live near here now. Henry has rented a room for us." Seraphina kept her voice low. "I recognized you by your eyes. They're just like your brother's."

"Is he all right?" Katie asked urgently.

"He's fine, Katie. He's trying to stay hidden as much as he can, so he barely even lets me go out, but I begged to see you. He knew you come here to buy bread at this time of week. I hoped I might see you so that I could thank you."

"Thank me?"

"Yes. You led me to Henry through Millie. You led me to safety." Seraphine clutched her hand. "Thank you. I know it must have been hard, as you want to keep your brother safe, but believe me—I would not have survived another day in that house." A tremor ran through her.

The look in her eyes made Katie instantly believe her.

"I'm very sorry," Katie said.

Seraphina blinked. "Oh, Katie, why should you be sorry? You've had a much harder time of it than me, I should think, first in the workhouse and then with that dreadful Mrs. Cromwell. She did that to your hand, didn't she?"

Katie tucked it into her jacket.

"Papa did similar things," said Seraphina, "at first." She tugged at her scarf and showed Katie the yellowing bruises around her throat.

Katie touched her own neck. "How awful."

"It's all right now." Seraphina rearranged the scarf and smiled brightly. "Henry would never dream of doing such a thing. He's a marvellous man, Henry. Brave and kind and just—just wonderful."

"He would do better for you if he could," said Katie, "for both of us."

"Of course. It's that cursed Fred who holds him back. But someday, he will make everything better for us both," said Seraphina. "I know he will." Her eyes shone. "I think he can do anything, you know. Anything at all."

Katie smiled. "So do I."

There was a soft bark, and a scruffy little white-and-brown dog trotted across the square to Seraphina.

"Oh! I must introduce you to Soldier," said Seraphina. "Isn't he lovely?"

"He's marvellous!" Katie bent to scratch his ears.

"You like dogs? Henry was a little afraid of him at first."

"I don't know. I've never had the chance to play with a dog before, but he looks lovely."

"Someday, when all this is over, you can play with him all you like," said Seraphina.

"Are you making soup for supper?" Katie asked. "If you are, I can show you which stall sells the cheapest potatoes."

"Thank you. That would be lovely."

Katie led Seraphina across the market place, ignoring the stallholders who cried their wares.

"May I ask you something, Katie?" Seraphina murmured.

"Of course."

"Have you ever been in love?"

The words seized Katie by the heart and squeezed. She touched her chest, troubled by the pain.

"I'm sorry," said Seraphina. "I didn't mean to upset you."

"It's all right. I... I have been in love. I *am* in love." Katie closed her eyes, fighting the tears, as Michael's dear face filled her thoughts. "But he had to go away to find work somewhere else. He said he would write if he could, but he never did."

"I'm sorry."

"He will come back, you know." Katie opened her eyes. "He promised he would. I'll find him again someday, I will. Somehow."

Seraphina took her hand and squeezed it. "Yes," she said with fierce conviction. "You will."

It was then, perhaps more than before, that Katie understood why Henry loved her so much. Hope burned so brightly within her that it was impossible to hold on to dismay in her presence.

Fear pounded in Katie's blood as she stared at the dress on the hanger.

She stood in the shop window, gaping at the sleeve that hung utterly crooked. Panic throbbed in her. How had she failed to notice that she'd sewn the seam in all wrong? She touched the stitches, realizing with terror that Mrs. Hamilworth would be by tomorrow morning to fetch this dress, this utter disaster of a dress.

"Girl!" Mrs. Cromwell barked. "Where are you? Is Mrs. Hamilworth's dress ready?"

Katie couldn't utter a sound.

Mrs. Cromwell stalked through the rows of racks, her grey eyes searching left and right, her cane tapping on the floor. Her hooked nose was like the beak of some great hunting bird. Katie felt like a mouse crouched in the grass, waiting for her to strike.

For a moment she thought Mrs. Cromwell would pass her by. Then the old woman's head turned and found her silhouette against the window.

"There you are," she hissed.

Katie cringed.

"Speak, child," Mrs. Cromwell barked.

She tried, but the words stuck in her throat as though a noose was already drawing tight around it.

"What is it?" Mrs. Cromwell approached. "What have you done?" Her gnarled old hands found the dress, and Katie couldn't draw her eyes away from the wooden ruler jutting from the pocket of Mrs. Cromwell's pinafore. It might as well have been a loaded cannon in her eyes.

Then Mrs. Cromwell's wrinkled old fingers found the sleeve and traced the crooked seam down the dress' length, and her mouth puckered with rage.

"You useless girl!" She rounded on Katie and drew the ruler like a sword. "You useless, useless girl! You'll get six strikes for that---and you'll unpick every stitch and make it right again at once. And don't think you'll be getting any less work for the rest of the day. I don't care if you have to stay up until midnight to finish that dress!"

Outside the window, a tall figure had stopped in the street. Henry pressed himself against the glass, his face dark with rage as he watched Mrs. Cromwell's tirade. His hands clenched into fists.

Tears choked Katie, but the words came out at last. "Yes, Mrs. Cromwell."

Foam flecked the old monstrosity's lips from her angry tirade. She waved the ruler. "Give me your hand!" Katie's body shook, but she knew there was no alternative. She slowly extended her hand, the welts from the last beating still raw on her palm. Henry had seen enough. The door crashed back on its hinges with a terrific bang. Katie's mouth formed his name, but she didn't have the breath to cry it aloud.

"*Stop*!" he thundered.

Mrs. Cromwell recovered her senses swiftly, her eyes flashing despite their milky hue. "Who do you think you are to set foot in my shop? I'll have the police on you!"

"No!" Katie cried.

Henry was shaking with fury, but he kept his hands low. "I'm not here to do you any harm, Mrs. Cromwell. I'm only here for my sister."

Something about the way he said it resounded down to Katie's bones. Something had changed in her brother's face, she realized then, something subtle but critical. She stared into his hazel eyes and saw a new kind of strength there—still haunted by what he'd been through, still shadowed by years of running and hiding, but no longer broken. The hunted look was fading. For the first time in years, Henry looked like he believed he could protect the people he loved.

Movement behind him caught Katie's eye. Seraphina stood in the doorway behind Henry, her eyes shining, twin red spots in her cheeks. Her blonde hair had straggled from beneath her bonnet and drifted like golden mist over her shoulders, but she did not seem to care.

Mrs. Cromwell recovered her voice enough to scream, "Get out!"

Henry held out a hand. "With pleasure. Katie, come on."

A laugh of disbelieving joy escaped Katie. She was free, she realized then. Free to leave this monster to her age and blindness and loneliness. Free to go where she pleased.

Free, at last, to go back to dear Molly.

She ducked under Mrs. Cromwell's arm, squeezed past her, and rushed to Henry. When she turned to Mrs. Cromwell by her brother's side, she saw that the old crone was actually a tiny thing, shrivelled, pathetic. There was nothing fearsome about her.

The milliner's face slackened into a saggy mask of wrinkled surprise. "Where do you think you're going, Katie?"

"I'm going with my brother." Katie slid her hand into his and interlocked her fingers with them, her palm uninjured and flat against the warmth of his.

Mrs. Cromwell's eyes bulged. "You're not going anywhere. You have work to do. Who's going to restitch that gown? Who's going to finish that dress?"

Katie thought of the mountain of fabric in the garret upstairs and almost laughed with joy when she realized that it was no longer her responsibility. Whatever happened next, she would not spend the night bent double and toiling away in that cold and lonely little room. "I suppose you'll have to do it yourself."

Mrs. Cromwell gaped at her.

Katie felt the strong desire never to see the old hag's face again. "Good day to you," she added.

Henry doffed his crumpled hat to the milliner and led Katie out of the shop. They walked into a foggy day, with the choking grey tendrils coiling around the feet of the businesses and roiling through the low sky, but Katie felt as though the sun had broken through. She breathed again, deeply, perhaps for the first time since Molly had taken her to the workhouse.

Every part of her trembled; whether it was with joy, or terror, or exhilaration, Katie could not say.

She clasped both hands around Henry's arm. Seraphina held his other arm, glowing, and he seemed six inches taller in his bearing. Yet as Katie looked up at him, she noticed something in his eyes—a brightness that held shadows, and dried blood still staining his shirt collar.

Katie was so breathless she could barely speak the words. "Henry, tell me we're going home."

Her brother looked down at her, his eyes alight with relief but haunted by something she'd never seen before. "

"Fred's gone, Katie. He's dead." Henry's voice was quiet but certain. "He came after me with a knife tonight, but in the struggle... he accidentally cut his own throat. It's over. It's finally over."

Katie stared up at him, her mind reeling. Fred, the monster who had terrorized their lives for years, who had driven Henry into hiding, who had made them all live in constant fear, was truly gone? "Dead?" The word came out as barely a whisper. "Are you... are you sure? Really sure?" Her voice broke. "What if he's not really dead? What if..."

"I'm sure, Katie." Henry's hands were steady now as he cupped her face. "I saw him die. I closed his eyes myself. He can never hurt any of us again."

Katie felt her knees weaken as the full weight of it hit her. "We're really free?" Tears spilled over her cheeks—tears of relief, disbelief, and overwhelming gratitude. "Henry, we're really free?"

"We're free." Henry pulled her close, and she felt the tension leaving his body as he spoke the words. "We're going home."

CHAPTER 11

CHAPTER TEN

Katie knew that much must have changed on this street since the first time she saw it. That had been more than fifteen years ago; she had been only a mite then, and she remembered very little other than clinging to her mother's skirts and the horrible shriek of the train's whistle.

Now, the whistle was an everyday sound, and her arms swung freely as she walked down the street. But it was her that had changed, not this corner of London. It was all the same: the tenements as ramshackle as ever, the low cloud of smoke hanging over everything from the factories on Mule Street, and, as before, the inn straight ahead. As it had done then, the inn seemed a bright oasis in this tumble-down street. Warm lamplight shone from its windows in the dreary mid-afternoon. A coil of white smoke rose from the chimney. The wooden sign over the door was brilliant with new paint, depicting two sticks of firewood and a red-and-yellow flame below the words, *The Welcome Hearth*.

Fifteen years ago, Katie and her siblings had found help there in the form of Alfred P. Crumble, the innkeeper who had supported them through their hardest times. It hardly seemed possible that Alfie was gone, yet Henry had told Katie that this was the case, and that—even more incredibly—he had left the inn to none other than Molly.

Her sister was in there. Waiting. Searching.

Katie wanted to run across the street to the door, but Henry had stopped. He held Seraphina's hand and gazed into her eyes.

"I haven't been able to give you anything you wanted yet, my love," he said, "and I can't promise that coming here will change all that at once. I must still find work. There are so many things that I must do..."

"Hush, Henry," said Seraphina. "You have already given me the one thing I longed for the most... peace. Whatever happens next, if I'm beside you, I know all will be well."

The smile that lit Henry's face warmed Katie's heart, but she could wait no longer. "Oh, *do* come on!" she cried.

She ran across the street, hoping her brother was close behind her, and hammered on the door.

There was no response at first, though Katie could smell cooking meat and heard the crackle of a fire within.

All of her trembled. The seconds seemed to pass like centuries. Katie realized that she had not felt safe, truly safe, since the moment Molly left her in that workhouse.

Fear and hope choked her. She hammered on the door again.

"I'm here," someone called from within.

Katie clutched her hands to her chest. That voice! Oh, that dear, dear voice! Even all these years in London had not robbed Molly of her Yorkshire accent. She still sounded exactly the same, earthy and comfortable, as she always had.

Then the door swung open, and Katie was facing her.

She had never seen her sister look this well. Molly was clean, her cheeks pink, her hair smoothly drawn back beneath her starched bonnet. Her shoulders filled the sleeves of her sturdy dress, which had hardly any patches.

But there was a weariness in her eyes, the first echoes of which Katie had seen on the long nights when she waited for Henry to come home, that hung like a dark veil over her expression. It had grown black and intense now and made Katie realize that perhaps having a warm home and a full belly was not the only prerequisite to happiness.

All this passed through her mind in a flash, in an instant. Then Molly's dear presence wrenched from Katie a single syllable: "Mol."

Molly's eyes widened. The veil lifted. Light shone in her face. She seemed to age backwards, becoming instantly a girl again. A great laugh escaped her and she flung her arms around Katie's neck at once.

If Katie had ever doubted that Molly had spent all these years searching for her, then her doubts vanished in that moment, in the fiery fervour of that embrace.

"Oh, Katie! Katie, it's you! I can't believe it's you!"

Tears and laughter poured from Katie in unison as she returned Molly's hug and found her sister's body curved and padded with prosperity. It felt glorious. It felt like it should always have been this way. The truth gushed from her, unstoppable. "I missed you so much. I missed you so, so much."

For in that moment, in Molly's arms, Katie could believe that everything was all right.

Molly's shoulders stiffened. She stepped back, holding Katie at arm's length, and tears spilled over her cheeks. "Katie, I'm so sorry. I never meant to leave you in that workhouse. I went back for you."

Katie's joy was too fierce for her to show the suffering she'd endured on her face. She let the white lie slip from her, seeing that Molly had punished herself a thousand times over for any perceived transgression. "I knew you would, Mol." Then she added pure truth: "It's not your fault."

Molly closed her eyes, fresh tears spilling over, and pressed both hands to her chest. Katie wondered how long her sister had been waiting to hear those words. She felt a painful stab of guilt that she had ever doubted the woman who stood before her.

"I tried so hard to find you," Molly said. "I missed you every moment. I did everything I could to find you."

Her voice trembled with sincerity. Katie fought to hold back her own tears as she realized that all that time she'd spent alone in the workhouse or labouring in Mrs. Cromwell's shop, feeling that no one in the world loved her, feeling utterly left behind—none of it had been true. Molly had been out there all this time, seeking her. Loving her.

"It's a big city, Mol. No one blames you because you couldn't find me." Katie grasped Molly's hands and pulled them away from her chest. "But I'm here now. I'm right here now."

Joy and disbelief shone in Molly's eyes. "You're here," she echoed. "How can you be here?"

Happy excitement swelled in Katie like a bubble. "Because Henry brought me."

She stepped aside, and Molly clapped both hands to her face with a strangled gasp of sheer joy as Henry and

Seraphina joined her on the threshold. Katie barely heard any of the words that came next. She was too busy looking at the raw delight in Molly's face, drinking it in.

Katie was on her hands and knees, but she didn't mind. The water in the pail beside her was warm and there was plenty of soap with which to scrub away the dirt on the floorboards. She worked the scrubbing brush back and forth across the wood, making sure to tuck the bristles well into the gaps around the nails.

Nails. The sight of them made her heart sting.

"Lavender blue, diddle diddle, lavender green," Molly warbled behind the bar, the song punctuated by the thump of a knife on a chopping board. "When I am king, diddle diddle, you shall be queen."

Katie joined in the song. "Call up your men, diddle diddle, set them to work. One to the plough, diddle diddle, one to the fork."

"Do you remember Papa singing that to us?" Molly asked, smiling.

"It's my earliest memory. I remember him rocking me in my cradle, singing it."

"So do I. He taught me to sing the words when you were a tiny baby. I loved rocking you and singing to you."

Footsteps clumped on the stairs from the cellar, and James entered the inn, carrying a wine barrel on his shoulder. He swung it into its place on the bar and slapped his hands clean. "What a marvellous, marvellous thing to hear."

Katie smiled up at him. "What is?"

Molly's husband had lost none of his gentleness over

the years. He was sturdier now, and the strengthened lines of his jaw had eased the look of illness that once consumed him, but the soft sparkle in his eyes had never changed. "My beautiful wife singing as she works."

"Oh, hark at you," said Molly, laughing.

James flung his arms around her and swept her off her feet, then kissed her.

"James!" Molly playfully swatted him with a dishcloth. "We're not alone in this inn anymore, you know."

"It's only Katie. She doesn't mind." James winked.

Katie giggled. She'd seen no such displays of affection in the shack; James and Molly had only even held hands once. But the loop of iron on each of their ring fingers, it would seem, had changed everything.

"I don't mind one bit," Katie affirmed.

"Honestly!" said Molly. "You would swear *we* were the newlyweds."

"I feel like a newlywed, with my wife so happy and lit up." James touched a fingertip to Molly's chin and smiled into her eyes. "Seeing you like this is everything I've ever hoped for, my love."

"I have everything I've ever hoped for," said Molly happily.

James kissed her forehead.

"Speaking of the newlyweds," said Katie, "here they come."

Seraphina and Henry swept into the inn, hand-in-hand and bright-eyed. It had been a fortnight since their wedding, yet the glow of it still shone in Seraphina's eyes. She carried a basket piled high with turnips, potatoes, and carrots; Katie wondered if she'd bought them in the same square where she and her family used to hawk vegetables with the Baileys.

Those were the days... days she spent by Michael's side.

The pang of longing that assailed her was so intense that it snatched her breath. She turned away so that the agony in her chest would not spoil the joyous moment.

"They were on sale, Mol," Seraphina said cheerily, "only tuppence for a bunch of carrots! I bought a whole lot of them. I hope you don't mind."

"That... that's wonderful, Seraphina, but did you buy yeast?" Molly asked.

"I didn't have enough for all of the carrots *and* the yeast. But the price was so good, I had to get them all. Now we have plenty of carrots," said Seraphina, beaming.

Henry's face fell. "Mol..." he began.

Molly visibly gathered herself. "That's all right. You know, we can always use carrots. They're good eating. And I can make a carrot cake with baking soda instead of yeast. I'm sure our patrons will love that."

Henry's shoulders sagged with relief. "That's good news."

"I will help," said Seraphina eagerly. "I would love to learn how to make carrot cake."

The gleaming determination in her eyes erased the tension from Molly's shoulders. "Then I'll teach you."

"I'll put these in the pantry." Seraphina scampered off.

"I'm sorry, Mol," said Henry. "I tried to stop her. She doesn't yet understand that when the money is done, it is, well, done. There's no going home to fetch more from a safe or going to the bank to get more."

Molly touched his hand. "She's still learning. It's a big change for her, and I know she'll be just fine, brother."

"You think so?"

"Look at the determination in her. She's making

mistakes, but all she wants is to learn. She's happy with you." Molly touched his cheek next. "I know she is."

Henry closed his eyes and leaned into her touch. "Thank you, Mol. I think we all are."

"Yes," said Katie, as brightly as she could manage. "We all are."

She felt ungrateful that their shining happiness was not hers. Molly and Henry had done so much for her.

Yet how could she feel happiness with a gaping hole in her heart? Only one person could fill it—Michael.

She had to find him somehow.

KATIE INHALED the smell of fresh linens. She carried them, neatly folded, up the stairs to the topmost level of the inn. This space was almost an attic; the ceiling was so low that James had to duck in places. Still, it made for a private set of rooms for the family, even if those rooms were tiny.

Katie's was no bigger than the garret at the millinery, but of course, she found it ten thousand times more pleasing.

She'd already placed the fresh linens on her bed and on Seraphina and Henry's, and now she headed down the tiny passage to the door at the end. Below her, quiet conversation announced that the inn's guests were awake after their post-lunch nap. Molly would be in the kitchen, starting on supper, while James prepared the drinks for the evening.

Katie nudged the door open with her elbow and stepped inside, almost colliding with a figure at the tiny writing-desk behind the door.

"Oh!" She stepped back. "Sorry, Mol. I didn't know you were in here."

Molly looked up, quickly wiping her eyes. "It's quite all right, Katie. Are you done with the linens? That was quick."

Katie slowly placed the linens on the foot of Molly and James' bed. "Are you all right, Mol? You... you're crying."

Molly exhaled. "I'm all right." She sagged back into her chair by the desk. "I'm looking at these, that's all."

Katie looked over her shoulder. The letters spread out on the desk looked old; their ink had faded, and the envelopes' corners were bent and folded. Each bore the same address on the front: *Molly Turner, The Welcome Hearth, Number Fourteen Jenny Street, London, England.*

Molly hadn't been Molly Turner in the several years since she'd married James.

"Who are they from?" Katie asked softly.

Molly cleared her throat as though fighting tears. "They're... they're from our father, Katie-pie."

Katie's heart jumped. "What? Papa knows where we are?"

"Well, no. I don't think so. These are all from the years when you and James and I were mudlarking in the Thames." Molly gently touched them. "Papa sent so many, and Alfie kept them all. He told me about them when I came back to him after the workhouse. He wanted so badly for me to write to Papa, but... but..."

"You stopped when Mama died," said Katie softly, "didn't you?"

"I did. I couldn't bear it, Katie-pie. I couldn't bear the terrible shame of what had happened. How could I tell him that I'd let our mother die?"

"Mol," said Katie, shocked, "you didn't let her die. You tried your best to help her. No one in the world would blame you for her death, let alone Papa."

"But I do. I blame myself. And when I lost you and

Henry..." Molly sighed. "I promised Papa that I would look after you, and for so many years, I didn't."

"You couldn't."

"That's even worse. I broke my promise to Papa. In a way, I can never make it right again, never. You and Henry are safe under my roof now, but Mama..." Molly's voice trailed off.

Katie rested a hand on her shoulder. "You're taking good care of us now, Mol. We all know Henry's barely making any money with his apprenticeship. Certainly not enough for both of their room and board. And me..."

"You're wonderful in the inn, darling. You pull more than your weight."

"I know you have many mouths to feed."

"It's all right, we have enough to do so if we're careful. And It's my honour. It's the promise I made... and I finally feel as though I'm keeping it, at least a little."

"More than a little." Katie touched her arm.

"Thank you, Katie-pie." Molly swept all the envelopes into a heap, and Katie noticed that all of them had been opened.

"You've read them?"

"I have. I..." Molly squared her shoulders. "I want to write to Papa again."

"Oh, Mol!" Katie clapped her hands. "Wouldn't that be wonderful?"

"Don't get too excited, darling. I don't even know if he still lives and works at the same factory as he used to; it was so many years ago. Yet I know I must try."

Katie perched on the edge of the desk, knowing it was unladylike. "What will you say?"

"I hardly know." Molly produced a sheet of paper and a

pen from the drawer. "It's been so long. How do I explain it all to him?"

"Maybe you don't need to explain. If he's the kind Papa I remember, he'll just be happy to hear from you."

"I hope so." Molly raised the pen; her hand was shaking.

Katie rested her palm on Molly's shoulder. "It's all right, Mol. Tell him how you kept your promise. Tell him we're all here with you, together, and well."

Molly's hand steadied. She placed the pen's tip on the paper and began to write.

Papa,

I know it has been much too long. With all my heart, I am sorry.

I pray that this letter will find you. There is so much to tell, yet all I shall say for now is this: Katie, Henry, and I are living at this inn, and we are all well. Henry and I are happily married.

We all miss you terribly.

Please write back.

Please.

Your daughter,

Molly Harrison.

"What do you think?" she asked.

Katie read slowly; she had striven to keep her ability to read after those lessons in the workhouse. "I think it's perfect."

"I hope he gets it." Molly closed the envelope and carefully wrote a Yorkshire address on the back. "Oh, I truly hope so."

"Maybe he will."

Molly gripped the letter tightly. "Maybe." She placed a stamp on the envelope and laid it at the edge of her desk. "I hope so."

"I hope we find them. Both of them."

Molly looked up. "You're thinking of dear Michael, aren't you?" The sound of his name was enough to instantly bring tears to Katie's eyes. She had to fight them back. "I am."

"Did anyone write?" Molly asked.

"No, but I'm still grateful you helped me place that notice in the London papers. I know it cost us both our spare pennies." Katie bit her lip. "I've been thinking—maybe we should try the Yorkshire papers too. He might have gone north looking for work."

"That's a good idea," Molly said gently. "I just... I don't understand why he never wrote to the London address."

"He might not have seen it. Not everyone reads every paper from start to finish each day. But I had to try something, Mol. I couldn't just sit and wait."

"Of course not, darling."

"Every evening, when I go for a walk with Henry and Seraphina, I beg them to go on different routes. I'm mapping out the whole area, checking every smithy, every workshop. And I've been writing to blacksmiths in other Yorkshire towns—maybe his family moved here too." Katie fought the tears with all of her strength. "I keep lists of everywhere I've looked, everyone I've asked. I won't give up."

"We found each other, didn't we, darling? You'll find him too, somehow. I know you will."

Katie felt the familiar ache in her chest but pushed it down. She couldn't do this to Molly—stand here breaking down before her, when Molly had done so much for their family.

Katie forced a smile onto her face. "Thanks, Mol," she said, as brightly as she could. "Shall I change your linens for you?"

"I'll help you." Molly stood.

They did it together, working in sisterly harmony, and though no one said anything, the silence helped to soothe the ragged edges of the great hole Michael's absence tore in Katie's heart.

CHAPTER 12

CHAPTER ELEVEN

Winter rain beat ferociously upon the windows of the Welcome Hearth. The wild weather—a sudden turn in the last week as the seasons marched on—had driven even more patrons than usual to the inn. The hubbub of their conversation filled the inn, with bursts of raucous laughter from the guests who'd had a little more ale than others.

The Harrisons' dining table was in the cellar. An unconventional spot, perhaps, but it afforded both privacy and convenience. The ring of a bell at the bar would send someone scurrying back up the steps to serve their patrons' needs. For now, everyone sat contentedly at the table, enjoying the roast chicken Molly had made for dinner.

"Ahhh, it's so good to have a whole chicken to ourselves again." James indelicately bit into a drumstick.

"All thanks to my clever little brother." Molly beamed.

Henry smiled. "I can't believe the blacksmith already gave me a better wage."

"It's because you work so hard, my love," said Seraphina. "You do wonderful work."

"Well, it's certainly allowed us to loosen our belts." James raised his own mug of ale. "Here's to you, Henry."

Katie held up her milk cup. "To Henry!"

He blushed pleasantly as the family cheered him and Seraphina squeezed his arm, her face alight with pride. Her skin had lost its porcelain whiteness. Perhaps in the circles where she had grown up, this would be seen as a flaw. But Katie liked the new flush beneath her cheeks. Her curves now more thoroughly filled her dress, and judging by the adoring looks her husband gave her, they only made her all the more beautiful to him.

Katie enjoyed a bite of tender chicken. "Delicious. Thank you, Molly."

"There's sticky buns for pudding," Molly told her.

Sticky buns! The memory surged in Katie's heart, and she fought to keep the piercing sorrow off her face.

"Thank you," she managed.

"What's the matter, Katie?" Seraphina asked gently. "Don't you like sticky buns?"

Katie forced a smile. "Oh, no. I love them."

"Then why do you seem about to cry?"

Katie dropped her gaze to her bowl. "I—I don't wish to ruin the mood."

"Katie, tell us," said James softly.

Katie wrestled with her emotions, saying nothing.

"It's Michael, isn't it?" said Molly.

Michael's name, spoken out loud, had the same effect it always did; it set everything behind Katie's eyes on fire. Her hand trembled on her fork.

"Oh, Katie." Seraphina gripped her hand.

"I'm sorry," Katie burst out. "I don't mean to be ungrateful."

"It's not ungrateful," said Molly.

James didn't look quite as convinced.

"I can only imagine what it would be like to be without the person I love, no matter how warm my bed or full my belly," Molly added.

James softened and kissed her hand.

With a manful effort, Katie swallowed her tears. "Never mind about that. Mol, what did you do with these potatoes? They're so wonderful! I love how soft and floury they are on the inside."

"Katie…" Seraphina began, her tone thick with kindness.

Molly saw what she needed. "It's something new I've tried. I boil them a little before I put them in the oven. That's what gives them that wonderful softness on the inside with the crispy skin."

"They're marvellous," said Katie.

"Speaking of marvellous…" James kissed Molly's hand. His eyes were alight with excitement.

A pleasant flush washed over Molly's cheeks.

Henry sat up straighter. "What is it?" he asked.

Molly wrapped her fingers tightly through James'. "There's something we have to tell you."

"We suppose it's not proper for a large audience, but you're our family," James added. "We love you all so very much."

"Well, what is it, then?" Seraphina leaned forward, eyes alight.

Molly and James exchanged a smile full of some happy secret that made Katie's heart beat faster.

"Well," said Molly, "our family is about to grow by one." Everyone stared at her.

"Oh, don't be dullards." Molly laughed. "I'm—in the family way."

The happy scream jumped out of Katie before she could stop it. She jumped to her feet and hopped around the room, her hands clasped around her face.

"Wh-what?" Henry was suddenly ashen. "Molly, do you mean—"

"Don't look so appalled, Henry." Molly laughed. "Yes, you're going to be an uncle."

"An uncle!" The colour rushed back to Henry's face, and he grinned more widely than Katie thought he could.

"Oh, Molly, how perfectly splendid!" Seraphina clapped her hands.

"When?" Henry managed.

Molly laid a hand on her loose dress. How had Katie never noticed the growing curve beneath?

"In four months or so," she said.

"Oh, my!" Seraphina cried. "Molly, you must be confined at once."

"Don't be silly, Sera." Molly laughed. "There's no confinement for us."

"Oh, Mol!" Katie rushed across the room and flung her arms around Molly's shoulders. "This is wonderful—this is just so wonderful!"

"Thank you, Katie-pie." Molly gave a high-pitched little laugh. "We've waited so long for this moment, and yet now that it's here, I'm almost afraid of it."

"Whyever are you afraid, Mol?" Katie asked. "You've been looking after us ever since we were little."

Henry rested a hand on his sister's arm. "Your baby is

the luckiest little one in the whole wide world to have a mother like you," he said.

It was at that moment that Molly dissolved into happy tears, and became the centre of a group embrace, with her husband closest by her side, her siblings wrapping their arms around her, and Seraphina squeezing her hand, all weeping with joy.

Fear, too, Katie admitted—but only to herself.

MAYBE THE TURNER children truly were alone in the world.

Such was the thought swirling through Katie's mind, as cold as the wind over the grave Hannah shared on that awful day, as she looked down at the letter in Molly's hands.

The bright red ink was stamped across it as brilliantly as fresh blood. *Return to Sender.*

"Are—are you sure, Mol?" Katie managed. "Does it really mean they couldn't find him? Maybe he—he simply wasn't at the factory when the postman looked."

Molly's breaths were ragged with grief. "I'm sure, darling. They only return letters to sender when they really couldn't find the recipient."

"It'll be all right," Henry repeated. "After all, we haven't kept the same jobs all this time, have we, then? He must be working at a different factory, that's all. Perhaps he's found a nicer job."

The front door open, and James strolled in, whistling. He stopped sharply when he saw them clustered by the bar.

"I say," he cried, "what's happened?"

"It's Papa," said Molly through her tears. "The postman

just came. The letter I sent him... it's been returned to sender."

James' face grew soft. "Oh, Mol, darling." He crossed the room in what seemed like a single long stride and wrapped his arms around his wife. She buried her face in his chest, and somehow, by some inner strength Katie did not understand, kept herself from weeping.

"I still think we should try the farm," said Katie, not knowing how else to help.

Molly gently stepped away from James. "Oh, darling. Papa won't be at the farm," she said patiently, as she had just done. "I know you remember him being there, but he had to sell it in the drought." She lowered the envelope to the bar, but her hand was shaking. "I tried, at least," she whispered.

"Don't give up now," Katie urged. "There must be another way that we could find him."

Molly raised her eyes to Katie, and her defences had crumbled. They were pits of suffering in her suddenly haggard face, and they frightened Katie. How long had her sister missed her father? How deeply had she loved him? She had devoted her entire life to fulfilling the promise she had given him.

To Katie, Papa was only a warm voice in a distant memory. But Molly had known him, really known him.

"All this time," she whispered, "I told myself that he was all right, that he was out there somewhere, that perhaps he would even find us again. But now... now I know it isn't so. I know that... that that's an end to it." Her lower lip trembled. "Oh, perhaps a foolish part of me longed to see those green hills again."

"Mol, try not to worry about it," said Katie gently.

"I'm not worried." Molly squared her shoulders and fought for control.

"Perhaps you should sit down, darling," said James, touching her shoulder.

"No, no. We'll... we'll soon have guests," said Molly. "I must get ready for them. It's sausages and mash tonight."

"Mol, wait." Henry reached for her arm.

Molly shook him off and marched, stiff-legged, to the pantry. Katie and Henry faced each other over the envelope on the bar.

James quietly took it and tucked it into his coat. "It'll do her no good lying about like this."

"Perhaps Seraphina was right. She looks so pale. She *should* be in confinement," Henry whispered.

"Molly, in confinement? It'll do her no good. I've tried."

Molly stumped from the pantry, carrying two fistfuls of potatoes. She dropped them on the bar and leaned against it, swaying for a moment.

"Molly?" James' voice wobbled.

She raised her head and cleared her throat. "I'm all right."

"Mol, don't you just want to have a little lie down?" Katie suggested.

"Katie, bring me the good sharp knife," said Molly, "and stop saying such foolish things. I'm perfectly... I'm..."

Her head lolled back.

"Catch her!" James bellowed.

They all lunged at the same moment, but Henry was there first, though James heroically seized Molly's arm across the bar and slowed her tumble. Henry flung his arms about her and stopped her from hitting the floor when she collapsed. Her head tipped back over his arm, her face utterly grey, her limbs lifeless.

"Molly!" Katie wailed.

James was on the other side of the bar in a trice. Clattering footsteps announced Seraphina's descent from upstairs, featherduster in hand, her face smeared with dirt.

"What's happened?" she gasped.

James cradled his wife, touching her face, his hands shaking. "Go for the doctor. Someone. Quickly!"

Henry was out of the door before the words were cold.

"Smelling salts," said Seraphina firmly. "She needs smelling salts. I know Mrs. Cooke down the street always has some for her fainting spells." She swung her shawl over her shoulders and rushed away.

Then it was just the three of them again: Molly, James, and Katie, just as they had been in the shack on the Thames. Except it wasn't just the three of them, Katie thought. The way Molly lay made it impossible not to see her growing belly. There was another tiny life with them, one that Katie suddenly was very afraid for.

"What can I do, James?" she whimpered. "What can I do?"

He looked up at her, his faced lined with fear. "Pray."

Katie did, as best as she knew how, but it still seemed like the minutes slipped by as slowly as if time had crystallized in that room. Molly took slow breaths, and her colour seemed to return a little. Or was it merely Katie's imagination? Was her sister slipping away before her eyes, and taking her unborn little niece or nephew with her?

Katie had known many moments of terror in her life. She had faced toothless, yellow-eyed men on the streets, cowered in corners from Maggie Granger and Elsa's cronies, and hidden among the dresses from Mrs. Cromwell's cruelty. But none of those moments could begin to compare with the fear she felt in those long minutes.

Finally, finally, the door crashed open, and Seraphina burst in, holding a little glass bottle triumphantly aloft. "Smelling salts," she announced.

Katie scrambled out of the way, and Seraphina crouched beside Molly. Even from this distance, the smelling salts had a foul stench that made Katie want to retch. Seraphina held them beneath Molly's nose, and her face twitched at once, curling up in revulsion.

"Come on, Mol!" James clung to her hand. "Come on, come on."

The door still stood open, and Henry all but leaped through it with his hair on end. "I found him!" he bellowed.

Dr. Connors followed close behind, looking even older and frailer than before. He leaned heavily now on an ivory-headed cane and moved with difficulty as he shuffled across the room, but his eyes were as keenly piercing as ever. They landed immediately on Molly, who had begun to groan a little.

"Smelling salts!" he said to Seraphina. "Excellent. Move aside, my dear, but you have done very well."

Seraphina withdrew as Dr. Connors stiffly crouched beside Molly and felt her neck, then her forehead. Molly's eyelids fluttered open when he was listening to her belly with something that looked like a strange wooden trumpet.

"Doctor," she whispered. "James... what... what..."

"Hush, darling." James kissed her forehead. "Hush now."

Dr. Connors straightened. "You've given your husband a terrible shock, Mrs. Harrison."

Molly's hand twitched toward her belly. "My baby..."

"He's quite all right in there, for now. His heart is as strong as yours, my dear."

Katie clutched her chest. Seraphina wrapped an arm

around her shoulders, and Henry buried his face in his hands. James somehow clung to his stoic expression as he cradled Molly in his lap.

"Are you in any pain now, Mrs. Harrison?" Dr. Connors asked.

Molly's voice was a little stronger now. "No, sir. None."

"You had some pain before, though, didn't you?" said Katie. "You touched your tummy. It looked like it hurt."

"My feet hurt more than anything else. I felt... I felt a little faint." Molly blinked. "I have to make the mash for supper."

"I'm afraid you will be doing no such thing," said Dr. Connors severely. He put the wooden trumpet back in his bag. "You have hopelessly strained yourself, Mrs. Harrison, and to spend any further time on your feet endangers both you and the baby."

Molly's hand fluttered to her belly, her eyes wide.

"You must rest in your condition, or you risk losing your child," Dr. Connors repeated.

"But... but doctor, how are we to run the inn if I'm in confinement?" Molly whispered.

"None of that, Mol," said James. "It doesn't matter. *You* matter—and our little one, too."

"We'll run the inn," said Katie. "I'm here to help, now."

"Me, too," Seraphina chipped in. "We'll keep it running just as smoothly as you do, Molly."

Katie knew immediately that it wasn't true. No one could run the Welcome Hearth like Molly could, but she resolved that she would do everything she could.

"Straight to bed," said Dr. Connors. "I will help you get her up the stairs, Mr. Harrison."

"Straight to bed," Molly repeated faintly. Her hand

trembled on James' arm as he gently helped her to her feet. "For how long, doctor?"

"Until the baby comes."

"Until the baby comes! That will be months!"

"Yes," said Dr. Connors, "so we hope, Mrs. Harrison, if you don't strain yourself any further. If you do, then it will not be months. It will be weeks—and your child will not survive."

The colour bled from Molly's face, her eyes alight with terror.

"It's all right, Mol." Katie touched her hand as James and Dr. Connors led her past, toward the stairs. "We'll make sure everything goes well here."

"Oh, Katie," said Molly faintly, "if the inn doesn't do well, then..." Her voice trailed off.

Katie knew as well as she did how much they all relied on the inn.

"It'll do well," she said firmly. "I promise."

They led Molly away, and Katie stared at the inn around her, the half-peeled potatoes, the barrels on the bar.

For the first time, she understood a fraction of the weight Molly had carried with her all these years. The weight of a promise.

CHAPTER 13

CHAPTER TWELVE

Katie's feet throbbed fiercely. She ignored them as she walked around the inn, picking up the plates and tankards from the round tables. In the distance, the church bell chimed the half-hour. It would soon be midnight.

The Welcome Hearth was quiet now, blissfully quiet, at last. Katie ached all over. It seemed that the work never stopped; she still had dishes to wash and then the bread dough to knead for the next morning, or their overnight guests wouldn't have fresh toast for breakfast.

Seraphina was in the scullery when she brought the dishes in. Her shoulders drooped with exhaustion and lines marred her pale face, but she tried to give Katie a cheery smile as she entered.

"I can finish these, Katie," she said. "Then you only have to sweep the floor and knead the dough."

Katie had forgotten about the floor. "Thanks."

"Where's James?" Seraphina asked.

"He fell asleep by the fire, poor thing. I can hardly blame him."

"No, I suppose not. He's been on his feet all day. I had to send Henry up to bed, too; he was nodding off where he stood, and he has to shoe at least a dozen horses at the smithy tomorrow, or the blacksmith will dock his pay."

"Poor Henry," said Katie. *Poor me and you,* she thought, *and poor Molly. Poor all of us.*

She punched down the dough, kneaded it, and set it on the windowsill to rise overnight. The first morning sunlight would stir it to life—and she would be here, she thought tiredly, ready to put those loaves in the oven before their guests woke.

When she had finished dragging the broom around the floor, James was snoring in his armchair, and Seraphina was wiping down the sink. They left James to his rest and climbed the stairs to bed.

Katie felt too tired to wash. She would strip off her corset and crinoline and sleep as she was, she thought, so that it would be less effort to get up in the morning. Tiredness pounded like a headache behind her temples.

"James?" someone called softly as she passed Molly's room. "Is that you?"

Katie nudged the door open. Molly lay against her pillows, pale, her arms wrapped around her voluminous belly.

"Are you all right, Mol?" Katie asked. "Are you in pain?"

"No, darling. I was wondering where you all were, that's all. I was listening to the church bell and thinking of how awful it must be for all of you, working these terrible hours."

Katie sat on the edge of the bed. "No more awful than it was for you before you had Seraphina and I to help you."

"Poor Seraphina! I can't imagine working all those hours and then coming in to help in the inn at night." Molly's lips turned down at the corners. "If I could only get up a little…"

"No, Mol. Look at you. You're pale as it is. If you're on your feet too much, you know what could happen." Katie seized her hand and squeezed it. "It would be the worst thing you could do to us after all this."

"I know." Molly sighed, shifting in discomfort. "Hopefully it's only another few weeks."

Katie patted her hand. "Do you need anything?"

"I need to know if James is all right."

"He's asleep by the fire. I hadn't the heart to wake him."

"No," said Molly softly. "Don't. He needs all the sleep he can get. I'll see him at breakfast."

Katie left her looking very alone in their big bed. She went to her own room and pulled off the corset and crinoline that restricted her so much, then sat on the bed in her chemise, drawers, and petticoats.

Her room had a tiny window. It did not overlook the street—only the sky. Katie stared up at the stars and wondered, as she did every night, if Michael was staring at those same stars.

Their brightness reminded her piercingly of his eyes, his smile.

"I haven't forgotten you," she whispered. "I know I haven't searched for you much these past months, but I've never forgotten you. Never. I'll find you someday, my love."

Tears threatened to strangle her. She forced them back.

"I've never stopped loving you," she said.

The words lost themselves in the sky. Katie longed not to say them to the stars, but to him.

The longing made her feel hollow. She curled up on the bed, exhaustion sweeping over her, but it was a very long time before she slept.

KATIE CAREFULLY ARRANGED a little vase of flowers on the breakfast tray. It seemed a pointless and unnecessary thing sometimes, in the face of all the tasks that lay before her, but Molly had always said that the Welcome Hearth could be more than a common inn. It could be a great thing, she said, if they kept trying to put in the little touches that would attract ladies and gentlemen instead of rogues and wanderers to this place.

"There." She turned to Seraphina. "How does it look?"

Seraphina blinked above dark bags, but managed a smile. "It's lovely. I'll take it up to the guests, if you'd like to take Molly her tea and toast."

"All right." Katie left the tray to Seraphina and attended to a simpler plate for her sister.

Seraphina gasped as she lifted the tray and accidentally spilled milk over it.

"It's all right!" Katie grabbed a rag and dabbed the milk away. "Sera, it's all right."

She repeated the words at the sight of the sudden tears in Seraphina's eyes.

"I know... I know." Seraphina gave a brave smile. "It's silly. I just— I'm sorry. It's silly."

"It's not silly at all," said Katie gently. "I know that you have a full day's work at your job ahead of you. We've been overwhelmed for months, but it's any day now."

Seraphina squared her shoulders and nodded. "Any day now, it'll all be worth it."

Katie gave her an encouraging smile. She tried to tell herself the same words as she climbed the stairs with Molly's mug of tea and plate of toast in hand. Molly had done so much for all of them; picking up her work in the inn was her duty, no matter how exhausted she felt by it.

She pushed open the bedroom door and found Molly on all fours on the floor, head bowed, teeth gritted. A long spasm rocked her body, and she did not cry out, but admitted a deep and animal snarl that almost frightened Katie.

"M-Mol?" Katie yelped.

The spasm passed. Molly raised her head, breathing hard.

"He's coming, Katie," she groaned.

Katie almost dropped the mug. She planted her burdens down on the nearest surface. "I'll go for the midwife!"

"No," Molly moaned.

Katie froze.

Her sister dragged her arms onto the bed and dug her fingers into the linens, kneeling. "Send someone else," she begged. "Stay with me."

Katie ran to the door. "*James!*" she shrieked.

The cry brought him running, wide-eyed. "Is it—"

"It's time," said Katie. "Go for the midwife, quickly. Quickly!"

Every vestige of colour left James' face, but he turned and bolted down the steps with greater strength than Katie had seen in him for weeks.

She hurried back into the room and knelt beside Molly, wrapping an arm around her shoulders. "James is going for the midwife, Mol. I'm here. I won't leave."

"Don't leave," Molly quavered.

"I won't. I promise."

Molly bowed her head then, and another pain gripped her with terrifying strength. Katie watched her sister's body heave with shocking power. The pain lasted a long time, but Molly didn't cry out; she gritted her teeth and snarled through it, another angry, animal noise.

"Are you— are you all right, Mol?" Katie timorously enquired.

Molly grabbed her hand in an iron grip. The tiny bones in her hand ground together with frightening intensity as her sister's eyes held hers.

"I *will* bring this child alive into the world," Molly growled. "Do you hear me? I *will*!"

"I don't doubt it," Katie squeaked.

She decided not to remark on her squashed hand, which was crushed even further when another pain ran through Molly's body. This time there was a moan on the end of her growl, but it sounded like a war cry: a rebellion against loss, against sorrow.

The midwife came bustling in, red-cheeked with exertion. Mrs. Connors had learned her trade from her doctor husband, and she was grey-haired and brisk as she put her back on the foot of the bed.

"Get up, Mrs. Harrison," she said cheerfully, "and let's have a look at you."

Katie's hand was finally released when they helped Molly onto the bed. Mrs. Connors bustled about, readjusting pillows. She pulled off Molly's sodden drawers with a businesslike air and flipped her skirts back.

"Draw the curtains, Miss Turner," she ordered, "and lock the door. The men shan't come in here."

"Yes, ma'am," Katie stammered.

Molly braced her hands on her belly, which seemed to bulge at a strange angle beneath her loose shift. Katie tugged on the curtains and returned to Molly's side.

"There's no time for hand-holding, dear," said Mrs. Connors. "Grab those warm towels and stand at the ready. This little one is well on his way."

Katie seized an armful of them and stood at the feet of the bed, shivering.

"Mrs. Connors," said Molly faintly, "I…"

"Don't tell me you don't have the strength, dear, because you do."

Molly's eyes flashed. "I have the strength. This baby will live. You'll do whatever it takes for that to happen."

Mrs. Connors grinned. "Now that's the spirit, Mrs. Harrison."

Molly's face twisted.

"Here comes another pain!" Mrs. Connors knelt on the bed. "Go on! Push! Give it everything you have, dear!"

Katie trembled where she stood as Molly shrieked.

"Good girl, good girl, good girl!" Mrs. Connors cried heartily. "Keep going! *Keep going*!"

Then the baby's face came into the world, pink and squashed from the effort, and Molly fell back against the pillows.

"Molly?" Katie whimpered.

Her sister didn't move. Her face was scarlet with effort, streaked with sweat.

"Molly!" Katie cried.

Mrs. Connors nudged her knee with an elbow. "Mrs. Harrison?"

There was a horrible instant of silence. Then Molly raised her head.

"Mrs. Harrison, you'll need to give me a good push

now," said Mrs. Connors sharply. "Your little one's laid a bit askew. I'll need to give him a bit of help, but you need to push with everything you have. Do you hear me, dear? *Everything.*"

A muscle stood out on Molly's jaw. She looked so exhausted that Katie doubted she had anything at all left, but she nodded.

Katie prayed under her breath, clutching the towels, and another pain came upon Molly like a thunderstorm.

"*Push!*" Mrs. Connors shouted.

Molly drew her knees up to her shoulders and bellowed, a war cry, a sound of defiance against all the world's darkness, and the baby came sliding into Mrs. Connors' hand with a whole-hearted squall of protest. The little voice filled the room with its high-pitched wail and Molly immediately burst into tears.

"The towels, child, the towels!" Mrs. Connors barked.

Katie thrust them at the midwife, who rubbed the baby vigorously. It shrieked and waved its tiny fists, its body turning bright pink from the rubbing.

"It's a boy," said Mrs. Connors joyfully. "A firstborn son, and he's perfect, Mrs. Harrison. Absolutely perfect."

"Give him to me," Molly demanded.

"I have to dry him off first, dear."

Molly's growl came from the same intense and guttural place as her screams. "*Give him to me.*"

Mrs. Connors looked up, surprised, as Molly sat up and held out her hands for the child.

"Now," said Molly.

No one would dare disobey that sound, not even the hard-bitten old midwife. She bundled the baby in a towel and held him out to Molly, who placed him on her chest and hugged him close to her face, weeping. The baby wailed; Molly cried.

"Are they all right?" Katie whispered.

Mrs. Connors laughed. "As perfect a mother and baby as you'd ever hope to see, lass. Go on. Now you can do all the hand-holding you please."

Katie hurried to Molly's side and wrapped her arms around her sister's shoulders. "Oh, Molly, you were magnificent. You were absolutely magnificent."

Mrs. Connors produced two pieces of string, carefully wrapped in a clean cloth, from her bag. She tied them around the whitening cord and cut it with a brisk, unemotional snip of her scissors.

"There you are, dear," she said. "Feed that babe now—it'll warm him up. Where's the father?"

"He was in the hallway outside," said Katie.

"Then I'll go and tell him that he has a beautiful son. I'll be back in a jiff."

The midwife washed her hands in a basin and bustled off. Molly raised her head from her baby and gazed up at Katie, her eyes full of happy tears.

"Isn't he beautiful?" she whispered.

The baby had stopped crying. His eyes were open, though they seemed unseeing, and the same soft shade of brown as his father's.

"He's perfect," said Katie truthfully.

"I can't believe we did it." Molly traced the soft lines of the baby's cheeks.

"Oh, Mol, *you* did it."

"No, darling." Molly leaned her head against Katie's. "He only stayed alive because I rested; and I could only rest because of you. He owes his little life to you, dear little lamb."

Katie hugged Molly close and gazed into the baby's eyes. She would have done anything for that child in that moment. The months of toil and trouble seemed pitiful and distant compared to the radiant little child in Molly's arms.

"What will you name him?" she asked softly.

"James and I already chose a name." Molly pressed her lips delicately to the baby's forehead. "We'll call him Alfred, after dear Alfie who left us the inn and changed everything for us."

"Alfred." Katie sighed with contentment. "It's perfect, Mol."

In that moment, everything was.

PART IV

CHAPTER 14

CHAPTER THIRTEEN

Two Years Later

Molly was down to her last string of onions and her last pumpkin. She stood beside her handcart, its new red paint shining in the unseasonal sun, and held up the former above her head. Its strong smell made her hunger.

"Get your onions!" she shouted. "Lovely fresh onions! No spots, no damp, ready to go into your soup or stew!"

The market square bustled. New paint shone on many of the doors and window frames, and the crowd that moved through this area had warmer clothes and cleaner faces than Katie remembered from their early years costermongering in this square. That had been a long time ago, of course—before the cholera epidemic that claimed so many lives here.

They were saying all sorts of things about that epidemic now; that a doctor had proven that cholera came from water and not from miasma, and that washing one's hands could keep one from becoming ill. Perhaps he was right, and that was why the people around Katie were rosier-cheeked than they had been in those days.

"Wait, wait!" someone shouted. "I'll take them!"

A maid in a starched white apron and collar hurried across the square to Katie, waving a shilling in one hand.

"Don't sell them!" she shouted. "Cook only likes your onions, Miss Katie."

"Hello, Marge," said Katie cheerfully. "Does she say so?"

"It's the truth, Miss Katie. She makes French onion soup with them, and it's the only soup the missus will have. She's awfully fussy, you know that."

"It's so strange to think of my onions being eaten in a fancy big house."

"Well, you deserve it, Miss Katie. You've always got the nicest produce in the city. How much are they?"

Katie glanced at the shilling, then at the girl, and quoted her price. If Marge herself had been here to buy food, she might have offered the onions to her at half that amount, but the girl paid it happily. Her master's coffers ran deep.

"Thanks, Miss Katie. Cook's always telling me to come here if she needs anything. I know she told the Bransons' cook to do the same."

"Oh! Is that Mrs. Partridge?"

"That's right. A frightening old lady."

Katie smiled. "She knows what she wants when it comes to potatoes, that much is certain."

Marge giggled and left with her onions, revealing

another cook from a manor house who wanted the pumpkin. Katie sold it, tucked the money into the growing pouch she carried in her apron pocket, and shut up the handcart.

She wheeled it home through the familiar streets. Once, she'd wandered these streets as an urchin, clinging to Molly's hand. As she passed beneath a tall building, she gazed up at it. It was no longer the old tenement where she'd lived with her family as a child; they had torn it down and rebuilt it, and now there was real glass in the windows and smoke in the chimney. But years ago, this had been where her mother died.

Those were different times. Harsh. Frightening. Katie wondered when last she had missed a meal. Certainly not in the three years since she had come back to the Welcome Hearth with Seraphina and Henry, and yet there was a hollowness in her all the same.

In those different days—when she had been too small to push a handcart—Katie had been hungry and afraid, but Michael had been there. He had danced beside her, made silly faces to coax a smile from her weary soul, and given her hope in the darkest of moments.

Out of habit, as Katie headed through the busy streets to the inn, she gazed at every face that passed her. Her eyes dwelled on every young man who hurried by. None of them had his soft, kind eyes or the half-smile that always lived on his face.

None of them were Michael.

She pushed the handcart into the courtyard behind the inn and stepped through the back door, a deep sigh escaping her.

"My, my, Katie-pie," said Molly. "It's not all bad, you know."

Her sister was in the kitchen, stirring a giant pot of stew for the guests' dinner. Motherhood had added generous curves to her body, each one a testimony to the new beauty of her life. Her eyes sparkled as she blew on a ladle of sauce.

"Hello, Mol," said Katie.

Molly's smile faded. "What's the matter, dear? You sound so despondent."

"Nothing." Katie counted a few coins out of her pouch and slid them across the table. "For my board."

"Rubbish. You more than earn your keep helping me in the inn of a night, you know that." Molly pushed them back. "Save them up for a new coat for the winter, darling."

Katie swept the coins into her pouch. Only a few years ago, they would have felt like all the money in the world, yet there was an ache inside her that nothing could fill. "I'll buy some of that expensive mustard at the show tomorrow. They usually have the very best stuff, from Yorkshire."

"Look at you, Katie." Molly beamed with pride. "You're no ordinary costermonger anymore, not like we used to be. Why, all the fanciest households in London want to buy your wares because they know you select only the best."

"They pay well for them, too. That's why it's worth it to go all the way down to the Aggie to all the fancy fairs. You can buy prize-winning pumpkins and tomatoes and things there—and the fancy folks love them."

"Are you going there on Saturday?"

"That's right. Would you like to come?"

"Aye, I would. Alfred always loves seeing all the cows." Molly's tone softened. "I don't like to think of him growing up not knowing what a cow is."

She returned her money to her pocket as Molly stirred the pot, and a few moments' silence followed.

"Go on, then, Katie-pie." Molly tasted her sauce. "What's the matter?"

Katie forced a smile. "Nothing at all. How can I help? Shall I chop some potatoes for the stew?"

"You're not fooling anyone, dear. You have a thundercloud above your head. Tell me what's the matter."

Katie fetched a cutting board and some potatoes from the pantry. She washed them in a basin of water from the outside pump.

"Katie," said Molly, in a warning tone.

Katie hung her head. "I don't want to be ungrateful."

"Darling, you work harder than anyone in this inn. No one thinks you're ungrateful, but we all know you're unhappy."

Katie bit her lip. "I miss him, Mol."

Molly looked up. "Oh, my dear. Is this still about Michael?"

Katie struggled with a sudden tightness in her chest and nodded.

"My poor lamb." Molly hugged her. "It's been so many years."

"Three years," Katie whispered, but they might as well have been a thousand.

"I'm sorry, my dear. We've tried so hard. Advertisements in the paper, talking to other nailers... And no one knows him."

"I don't know where else to look, Mol. I feel like I've looked everywhere. After a day costermongering, my eyes hurt from strain. I search every face, but he's never there. How can he be? He doesn't know where I am. He could be searching for me by the millinery for all I know. How will I ever find him?"

Molly stirred the stew, her silence contemplative. She spoke slowly, tenderly. "Katie, my dear, have you ever thought that perhaps it's time you stopped looking?"

Katie dropped a potato on the floor. "Wh-what? Stopped looking for Michael?" The very thought was ludicrous.

"I know the idea shocks you, darling, but like you said —it's been five years. You're twenty-four now. You won't be a marriageable young woman forever."

Katie stared at her, open-mouthed.

"Don't look at me like that. There are other young men in the world, good and kind ones, who could make fine husbands for you."

"But they wouldn't be *Michael*," said Katie.

"No, my dear, but they would fill that terrible hole in your heart."

"Nothing can. Nothing but him," Katie cried. "He— he promised he'd find me, Mol. He *promised*. He will, I know he will, I just... I just have to keep on hoping." She fought back tears.

"Katie..." Molly began.

"Mama! Mama!"

The little voice pierced the sorrow in the room, clearing it instantly. Katie's tears dried up as she turned to the door, beaming.

Alfred came running in, giggling, his chubby red cheeks smeared with strawberry jam.

"There's my little sunshine!" Molly dropped her ladle and held out her arms. "My, my! What a lovely piece of toast you've been eating."

Alfred ran into her arms. Molly swept him onto her hip and used a dishcloth to dab at his sticky face.

"Auntie Sera made," he announced.

"Alfred!" Seraphina ran into the kitchen, wheezing slightly, a bluish tinge around her lips. "Sorry, Mol. I turned my back for two minutes and off he went."

"That's my busy boy." Molly adoringly cuddled him. "Have you been a good boy for Auntie Sera?"

"Yes," said Alfred.

"The best." Seraphina coughed. "He's helped Auntie Sera sweep the floor, haven't you, darling?"

"Then jam," said Alfred.

Katie held out her arms. "Does little Alfie want to come to his Auntie Katie?"

"No!" Alfred stuck out his hands to Seraphina. "More jam!"

"Do I hear my baby boy being naughty?" James boomed. He and Henry came in through the back door; James carrying a pile of firewood, Henry smelling of the forge. Seraphina immediately rushed over to hug and kiss her husband. James tickled his baby's cheek and nuzzled Molly's neck.

Katie watched, smiling, knowing that she should join in the buzz of happiness and well-being that filled the room. Yet she felt as though she was watching all this joy through a layer of glass; she was on the outside, looking in.

The thought seemed ungrateful, but it was nonetheless utterly true, boiling up from the deepest swamps of her being like a bubble of noxious gas.

Everyone is living happily ever after except for me.

THE AGRICULTURAL HALL—KNOWN as the Aggie—seemed an incongruous nickname for so stately a building. It loomed above the surrounds of Islington, teeming with people, so densely packed that they seemed like ants swarming in and out of the pillared hall with its splendid glass roof allowing the spring sunshine to pour within.

Katie kept her arm linked through Molly's, determined not to lose her in the crowd, as she pushed her handcart with her free hand. Alfred sat on the cart, swinging his little legs and happily eating a very sticky boiled sweet that Molly had bought from the first vendor they saw in the square outside the hall.

The best produce, however, was inside the hall. Katie steered the cart carefully through the masses of people and into the vast building itself.

Here, the noise was overpowering. There were bursts of music from singers and fiddlers in the corner and an endless drone of conversation, but no hawkers' cries; the folks at these stalls had no need to cry their wares. Their produce spoke for itself. Tomatoes as bright as rubies stood in boxes in front of one farmer's stall. Another stall groaned under the weight of turgid orange pumpkins, one displaying a bright red ribbon on the side.

The produce stalls were all around the edges of the building, while show rings had been roped off in the middle. Katie remembered Molly once saying that Papa had always dreamed of showing his cattle here someday. *Maybe that's why I always feel drawn to this place*, she thought, scanning the crowd. Cows trod carefully over wood shavings spread on the ground. They were beautifully bathed and brushed, looking neater than most of the people on London's streets. Farmers in cloth caps and sturdy coats led them around in circles as serious-looking judges eyed the gentle beasts.

"Cow," Alfred shouted, pointing.

Molly laughed, delighted. "That's right, Alfred—and

they're lovely cows, too. Dairy shorthorns. We used to have them when your Mama was a little girl."

"Cow." Alfred's little fingers flexed toward the nearest one, demanding to touch it.

"Maybe later," said Molly.

Katie smiled at the joy on the little boy's face, reflected so precisely in his mother's eyes. She wondered if she would ever have the chance to cradle a little one like him in her arms. A child she'd borne, with his father's eyes...

Longing swept over her, poignant and impossible to withstand. Katie blinked tears away and turned to inspect a knotted string of onions hanging from the nearest stand.

"Fresh from the farm, miss." A studious young man touched his forelock behind the table. "Got second prize in the show this weekend, so they did."

"Second prize?" said Katie.

"Aye, but they say old Bertram cheats." The boy leaned closer. "Paints his onions with varnish, so he does."

"Is that so?" Katie struggled to hide her grin.

The soft voice floated across the hall to her. She thought it was in her head—a sweet memory. Of course the cows here reminded her of her earliest memory.

Lavender blue, diddle-diddle

Lavender green...

Katie cleared her throat. "How much are they?"

"Sixpence a string, miss."

The price was unthinkable for all but London's upper crust; luckily for Katie, they were her best customers. "I'll take three."

"When I am king, diddle-diddle,

"You shall be queen."

This time, she was sure she heard it. She spun around, searching the crowd, though she didn't know what for.

Yet that voice... It sounded so exactly like her memory.

"Miss? Miss, your onions."

Katie ignored the seller. Molly stood a few yards away, by the show ring. Katie joined her and grabbed her arm.

"Mol, did you hear that?"

"Call up your men, diddle-diddle, set them to work..." the voice sang.

Molly turned to Katie, her eyes brimming with tears. "I hear it. Oh, Katie, I hear it."

"One to the plough, diddle-diddle, one to the fork."

"Where's it coming from?" Katie looked left and right.

Alfred giggled. "*Cow!*"

He pointed. The crowd parted as one group of cattle left the show ring. Another waited nearby, beautiful beasts with gleaming roan and spotted coats. At the front of the group, a gentleman stood with his back to Katie and Molly, running a rag over his cow's back to wipe away some dust.

"Is it— can it— could it—" Katie couldn't form a coherent sentence.

"Here." Molly thrust Alfred into Katie's arms.

Katie clung to the little boy as Molly stumbled forward, her movement disjointed, as though she'd forgotten how legs worked.

The gentleman was only whistling now as he returned his rag to his pocket, but it was the same beloved tune.

"Sir," Molly managed, feet away from him.

Katie tottered nearer, hugging Alfred tight.

"Sir," said Molly again.

The man turned. "Beg pardon, m'lady, but—"

There was a frozen moment. Katie searched the man's face: craggy, with greying dark hair and brown eyes that seemed the same shade as Molly's despite the deep folds around them.

"Papa," said Molly in a very small voice.

The gentleman snatched his cap from his head, revealing thinning hairs.

"Class three, cows under four years of age, please enter the ring," a steward called pompously.

The other cattlemen shifted restlessly, but the gentleman who sang "Lavender Blue" didn't move. He clutched his cow's halter as if for support as he stared down at her.

"Papa, please, tell me you remember me," Molly whispered.

"Can it be?" The gentleman stepped forward. "*Molly*? Molly, pet, is that you, all grown up?"

Molly's face crumpled. She held out her arms like a child. "Papa..."

"Molly!"

Their father, John Turner, abandoned his cow in the middle of the hall and ran to Molly. He flung his arms around her and crushed her against him, shaking, shamelessly weeping.

"Molly, my darling, my love!" Papa pressed her to his chest. "At last! Oh, Molly, at last! How I've searched for you! How I've missed you, my dear, and look at you now!"

He drew back, arms still around her, laughing at her. Molly reached up with shaking hands and touched his stubbly chin, then his broad shoulders. Tears streamed over her cheeks. She was shaking.

"Papa, how can it be? How are you here?" she gasped.

"What does it matter, my love? I'm *here*! I've found you!" He squeezed her arms. "You look so well, pet. You *look so well*! I'd feared— I'd feared—" A shiver ran through him. "I'd feared the worst in a thousand different ways."

"Did you get my letters?"

"Not since—well, it must have been eleven years ago. Eighteen fifty-four, that's right. When the news started coming about the cholera in London. When your letters never came again, I thought..." His voice roughened with sorrow. "I thought that the cholera had taken you all."

"Excuse me, sir, but are you entering the show ring or not?" the steward asked testily.

"Hush!" Another farmer held Papa's cow. "Can't you see there's a great thing happening, you great lummox?"

"Papa, it..." Molly covered her face with her hands. "I'm so sorry."

"Pet, no. No, don't apologize."

"I promised to look after them. I tried. I tried with everything I had—"

"Molly." Papa crouched, gently gripped her hands, and pulled them away from her face. "You fulfilled your promise, even if we lost everyone." He swallowed hard, visibly struggling. "I know you did everything you could. You're here before me, pet, alive and well, and that is a wonderful gift."

Molly stared at him. "Oh, Papa, we didn't lose *everyone*."

His shoulders jerked with shock. "We didn't?"

"No. Mama..." Molly's lip trembled.

Papa squeezed her hands. "I'm sorry, my pet. My three little lambs all on their own without their mother..."

"I tried, Papa, I really tried."

"I know you did! Of course you did. But there was nothing you could have done, Mol."

"You don't know what happened."

"The cholera took her, didn't it?"

Molly nodded.

"So many people died. No one could save them all. But

your brother… your sister… are they…" The hope in Papa's eyes was like a sunrise.

Molly's lips twitched into a smile. She straightened; it seemed to Katie as though a tremendous weight fell away from her in that instant, something she had been carrying since Katie could remember.

"They're alive and well," she said, "in fact, Katie is standing right over there, holding my little boy."

Papa's jaw dropped. He spun around as Molly pointed. Katie didn't remember their father's face, but the joy in his eyes still filled her with delight.

"Katie-pie, my darling, is that you? You've grown so beautiful!" Papa gasped.

Molly strode to her side and scooped Alfred into her arms. Papa held out his hand; Katie gently laid hers in it. It was a callused hand, hard and strong, but he closed it around her fingers with utmost delicacy.

"Hello, Papa," she said softly. "I remember you singing to us."

"I'm surprised you remember anything at all, sweetheart." Papa touched her cheek. "You look so much like your mother, but there's a fire in you."

"Papa, this is Alfred." Molly beamed. "Your grandson."

"Grandson," Papa echoed, looking utterly stunned. He tickled the baby's cheek. "Grandson! You're married?"

"Henry, too."

Papa clutched his chest.

"Ever so much has happened, Papa." Katie laughed.

"You have to come with us to our inn," said Molly, "and we'll tell you everything."

"You're staying in an inn?"

Molly's eyes sparkled. "Oh, no. My husband and I *own* the inn."

Papa looked as though he might faint dead away with joy. Instead, he flung his arms around all three of them, hugging them until Alfred whimpered in uncertainty.

He had no way of knowing that this stranger was his grandfather, the man Katie had long since given up on seeing again, alive, well, and in the flesh.

HENRY WEPT LIKE A CHILD. He kept their father at arm's length at first, stammering out his story, admitting to it all: how he had become a thief, then a leader of one of London's criminal gangs of children, how even the adult gangs had hired him to hurt and intimidate others, how he had killed Fred by accident. Katie knew the story, of course. She knew it ended with redemption, with walking the straight and narrow path even if it almost killed him.

But John Turner didn't seem to care how the story ended. Henry was still telling, still apologizing, when he flung his arms around his son and held him. It was then that Henry broke down and sobbed helplessly into his father's chest.

They sat in the tiny kitchen at the back of the inn. There was hardly enough space for them all, but they squeezed in anyway, leaving the service of the guests to a friend of James who was happy to help for a sixpence. Papa and Henry stood by the stove as forgotten teacups littered the table.

James beamed with his arm around Molly as they sat at the table, Alfred playing contentedly on the floor. Seraphina hovered by the door and Katie perched on a stool, feeling a little forgotten.

Papa had wrung James' hand and called him his son.

Now, he held his son by blood, stroking his hair like he was a little boy.

"I'm sorry, Papa," Henry whimpered. "I'm sorry."

"He's never stolen or harmed anyone again." Seraphina stepped from the doorway, valiance in her blue eyes, her chin held high. "Never. Even when he was still a thief, sir, I saw the love and gentleness in him. Don't think any differently of him, I beg you. He is a wonder. He is—"

"He is my son," said Papa. "I could forgive him anything."

Henry's tears stopped. He pulled back and stared at their father in wonder. "You could?"

"Of course, my boy." Papa cupped a hand on his cheek. "It is I who must beg all of you for forgiveness. I'm the one who sent you away into this city."

"You did what you had to, Papa," said Molly.

"Aye, I did, but I wish I had come up with another way—*any* other way—than being separated from you for so long."

"You're here now," said Henry, "you're with us at last."

Papa smiled. "Molly told me you were married, Henry. Tell me, is this vision your wife?"

Henry's face split into a broad grin. "Yes! Look at her, Papa. Have you ever seen something so perfect?" He held out a hand. "This is Seraphina. My darling, this is my father."

"Mr. Turner, sir." Seraphina dropped a perfect curtsey, a relic of her days as a fine lady. "It is my pleasure to meet you."

"Oh, my. I've always prayed for a good wife for my son, and I see all of my prayers have been answered." Papa took the hand Seraphina offered him; when she stiffened, he released it, gentle understanding in his eyes.

There was relief in Seraphina's face. "Henry has told us so much about you. Molly, too."

"We've heard the stories for so long, Papa," said Katie, surprised at how easily the name came to her. "You hardly seem real even now."

Papa touched her cheek. "I'm real, my pet, I promise."

"It's been so many years," said Molly. "What happened, Papa? I wrote to the factory a few years ago, but they sent the letter back."

"I'm not surprised, pet." Papa pulled out a chair facing Molly. "That factory burned down in eighteen fifty-seven." He drew back a sleeve, revealing a waxy scar that traced up to his elbow and vanished beneath his coat.

Molly gasped. Katie wondered if she remembered the flames that consumed the cotton mill, filling Tessie's lungs with the smoke that ultimately killed her.

"The letters that Alfie had..." Molly shook her head. "There were none after eighteen fifty-seven. I thought you'd given up, Papa."

"Molly, pet." Papa's eyes shone with emotion. "I would never have given up on you. Never in a thousand years."

Molly made a choking sound in her throat.

"Tell us everything," Henry begged.

Papa leaned back in his chair and told the story.

"When I heard about the cholera, I feared the worst. I thought perhaps it had taken all of you. If I could, I would have come to London, looking; but my work at the factory barely gave me half a day to myself, and I knew that if I didn't have the job, I would never be able to help you in any real way. So I kept working, kept writing, and kept praying that I would see you again someday.

"Then the fire came. There were too many of us living in that factory. Too many small fires to keep warm, and the chimneys were never swept, and many of us smoked. Who can tell where the fire began? When I woke, it had already burned most of the quarters where we lived, and was spreading to the factory. I tried to help some of my friends outside, but the flames and smoke were too fast. I was within sight of the door when they caught up to me.

"They told me later that some people had pulled me out of the flames before the building collapsed and killed most of the people I worked with. They took me to a hospital, and I suffered there for a very long time. No one ever told me for how long I was in a daze of pain as my burns healed." Papa gestured at his arms and chest, all hidden beneath his unusually thick coat. "The first time my head was truly clear was almost a year later, when they let me out of the hospital. I was more or less well then, but I was utterly destitute. They gave me a dead man's clothes to wear. Those were all I owned.

"For two years, I wandered York, begging. I longed to write, but I hadn't the money to stay alive, let alone to send a letter. It was years before I could finally lay my hands on a pen and paper again. I could remember only one address: Alfred P. Crumble at the Welcome Hearth in London. I wrote, but they returned the letter to sender. They told me that Alfred P. Crumble was dead."

"That must have been shortly after he died, then," said Molly faintly.

"I feared... well, I feared, of course, that the cholera had taken you all. But I knew I had to find you somehow. The Welcome Hearth seemed a dead end, so I realized I had to get to London if I was to find you. For that, I needed money. By then the drought had ended, of course, and the farms in our old village were as lively as ever. I rode in a tinker's cart with him in exchange for walking and watering his horse, and he took me back to the village. There, I found our old farm falling apart. The gentleman who bought it from me had let it fall into ruins. I begged him for work, and at last mended the fences without any payment. I simply couldn't see the place falling to pieces like that. When he saw my work was good, he agreed to let me run the farm again. He paid me well, and let me keep a few of my own stock, besides."

Katie didn't remember the farm, but the light in Molly's eyes said that she certainly did. She clasped her hands over her mouth, eyes aglow.

"I worked for him for only two years before the farm was turning a wonderful profit again. It was easy, with the drought gone. I tracked down offspring from the same cows and goats we used to have and bred them. Providence smiled on me, and our calves were plentiful, and our crops were rich. I offered to buy the farm from the gentleman. He was a good man, but getting old, unable to manage all of his affairs anymore. He let me have the farm back for a song."

"Oh, Papa!" Molly cried. "You mean to tell me that you're back on our old farm?"

"I certainly am, my darling. But don't think that I forgot about you while I was bringing the farm back to its rightful state. Nay, pet, it was all for you. I dreamed always of bringing you all back home. Whenever I could—starting from the first day I worked for this gentleman—I brought stock or produce to the agricultural shows here, knowing that if I had to be at the Aggie for a few days, I might board nearby and spend my spare time walking the streets, looking for you. I never dreamed I would find you right in the Aggie itself."

"That was all Katie." Molly proudly beamed. "She's a

costermonger now, Papa, as well as working in the inn. She's made such a name for herself that all the cooks from the great houses around here come to her for their produce. That's why we go to the Aggie—to get the prizewinning fruits and vegetables she sells."

Papa's smile was a proud echo of Molly's.

CHAPTER 15

CHAPTER FOURTEEN

They ate breakfast in the inn the next morning, pushing together several of the guests' tables end-to-end, and Molly pulled out all the stops to make a fry-up worthy of Papa's return. There were scones, sausages, tomatoes, eggs, potato fritters, and plenty of buttered toast and kippers.

It was a celebration feast, and their laughter filled the place, making their few morning guests smile.

Katie sat opposite Papa, her kippers almost forgotten on her plate despite her growling stomach after a morning's cooking. She wanted to stare at him all the time, as though to make up for their years of separation. He lived up so thoroughly to the stories Molly and Henry had told her. To her, he seemed a glowing giant of a man, a larger-than-life paladin.

"Do you need to get back to the Aggie to water the cattle?" Molly asked as she topped off Papa's teacup.

"No, pet, thank you. I sent a message this morning to ask a friend to care for them. He knows the situation; he's more than happy to look after them."

"That cow you were showing yesterday." Molly sat. "She looks a lot like Evangeline. Do you remember Evangeline, Henry?"

"Oh, yes! She was that cross-looking one with the crooked horns. I hated her. She always wanted to kick when she was being milked."

"She was a lamb once you'd scratched that spot behind her front leg that was always itchy." Molly giggled.

"So that's how you did it, you little rascal!" Papa guffawed. "I always thought you had a magic touch with that cow, but you were bribing her with scratches."

"She was a good old thing. And she milked well, too."

"Of course she did. That's why I bought this cow when I found out she was a granddaughter of old Evangeline."

Molly gasped. "Really?"

"Aye, it's so. I've bought many descendants of the livestock we ran. Brought in some new blood, too. The farm's not like you remember, Mol. It's even better."

There was longing in Molly's sigh as she poured a cup of milk for Alfred. "I suppose you'll need to go back soon, won't you?"

Katie gasped. "Oh, please, not too soon. We've only just found you, Papa."

"He can write, Katie-pie. Don't worry." James patted her shoulder.

"I had something else in mind." Papa cleared his throat, wiped his mouth, and set his napkin aside. "I know you've all built good lives for yourselves here, but I wanted to ask if... well, if you would all come home to the farm with me."

Molly's hands flew to her mouth. She turned to James, her eyes gleaming. "Oh, darling!"

James put his arms around her. They were speechless for a moment, and Katie felt a lump swelling in her throat for them.

"You don't have to," said Papa quickly. "It's all right if you—"

"You don't understand, Papa." Katie smiled. "They've been talking about Yorkshire since were mudlarks on the Thames. They've always wanted to go there, always."

"I never dreamed it could be so," Molly choked out. "I thought I would never see those green hills again!"

"Now you can not only see them, my dear, you can live in them again," said Papa. "There are so many rooms in that great old house. There's room for you, *all* of you. You could raise your boy in the country instead of this reeking old city."

"Papa, I don't know what to say," Molly croaked.

"I don't know anything about farming," said James.

"I'll teach you, my boy. So will Mol and Henry. They remember it, I'm sure."

Henry had an arm around Seraphina. "Oh, Papa, this is too wonderful for words. We were just talking the other day about how we wished we could move to the country."

"Is that so?" Papa smiled. "I thought your beautiful wife might find the city more to her taste, but I'm glad to hear that's not the case."

"It's her lungs," said Henry softly. "The air here is no good for her. She's been through too much; she's too delicate. The doctor says that country air could cure her."

"Then you will have all the country air you can breathe, my dear," said Papa.

"There are so many things I want to show you." Molly

turned to James. "The little church in the village, the river where we played as children, the wonderful country lanes and the hills and fields..."

"I'm a smith," said Henry eagerly. "Is there room for a smith in the village?"

"Henry, lad, you're in luck. Old Bodger's knees are starting to trouble him. I'm sure he'd welcome a new smith at the forge."

"It's perfect," Seraphina cried. "Perfect."

Their happy chatter swamped the kitchen so thoroughly that no one noticed how much Katie struggled to hold back her tears. She slipped from her stool and went into the empty inn, fighting with all of her heart not to cry.

She did not remember Yorkshire. She did not think of it as home.

And it was a very, very long way away from London, the last place where she'd seen Michael.

Leaving London would mean leaving him.

Katie's bones hurt from lack of sleep. The pressure of insomnia built behind her eyes as she trudged down the hallway to Molly's room, struggling with the same knot that had been in her throat since Papa suggested they go home to Yorkshire with him last night.

Molly was singing loudly as Katie approached her room. It was "Lavender Blue," but the old words filled Katie with dread now, not comfort.

She knocked on the door. "Mol, it's me."

"Come in, come in, Katie-pie!"

Katie entered. The room was in disarray, washing and

linens in folded piles everywhere, half-packed canvas bags standing around.

"What do I take? What do I leave? I suppose I can always come back for some things," said Molly. "It's not like I'll ever sell the dear old Hearth."

"Have you found tenants for it yet?"

"I think so. There's a nice couple, the Coopers, who've been looking for a new inn to run after their landlord sold theirs. Henry's smith told me about them. We'll meet them soon. Oh, I hope it works! It'll be so perfect. We'll have the income from the Hearth's rent as well as the farm. We'll never want for anything again, Katie! Alfred will grow up never knowing hunger or—" Molly stopped. "Whatever is the matter?"

Katie couldn't help it. The tears spilled over immediately, and she covered her face with her hands to stop them.

"Oh, Katie, pet." Molly put an arm around her and drew her down to sit on the bed beside her. "You've been quiet all morning. What's wrong? Are you afraid of Papa? He's a good man, dear. He won't—"

"I'm not afraid of him," said Katie. "He's—he's wonderful. I can see that. He'd never hurt any of us. But I... I... Mol, I can't leave London."

"Whyever not?"

Katie raised her head from her hands, tears chilly on her cheeks. "Because Michael is here."

Molly sighed.

"I know you think I should forget him, but I can't. There's never been anyone else for me, Mol. He's *Michael*. He never gave up on me. How can I ever give up on him? If I leave London, I know I'll never see him again. And I know he might not be here anymore— he might be dead—but I know that if he's alive, he's trying to find me. If he's anywhere, he's here. How can I abandon him?"

"Katie…"

"I know you all think I'm a fool, but Michael has always loved me. Ever since we were little children, he would do anything for me. He's the only reason why I didn't go mad in those years with Mrs. Cromwell. He was my light in the deepest darkness of all. I can't leave him. I can't!"

"Katie," said Molly, more sharply.

Katie pressed her lips together and was silent.

Molly brushed a tear from her cheek. "I wasn't going to argue with you, love. I was going to tell you that I understand."

"You do?"

"Of course I do. I didn't until we talked about it the other day. Michael isn't just a friend or a boy who courted you for a while. Michael is your James."

Katie bit her lip.

"I would never leave James," said Molly quietly. "I know I *did*, once. I left him in the workhouse. It was the most terrible mistake I ever made. Everything went wrong for all three of us after that. I should never have left either of you, never."

"Mol, you can't blame yourself for all that."

"I'm grateful it all worked out like it did, but I'll always regret leaving you… and leaving him." Molly squeezed her. "I don't want you to grow up with those same regrets."

"But what do I do? How can I stay?"

"Easily, my love. This isn't like being separated in the workhouse. You can stay here at the inn with the Coopers, earning your room and board and costermongering like you have for the past couple of years. You can write to me every day if you like. I'll always write back. We're not losing one another, Katie-pie, and you can come to Yorkshire to visit whenever you like."

Katie's heart thumped with excitement. "Do you mean it?"

"Of course I do."

"But Papa... what will he think?"

"If you tell him you want to stay at the inn for love, Papa might think you're mad. I would if I hadn't seen you and Michael together all those years as children. But if I tell him that I would like you to stay behind for a little while to keep an eye on the Hearth under the new tenants..." Molly smiled.

Katie stared at her. "Would you?"

"Well, yes, I would. I don't want to leave the Hearth in the hands of near-strangers. If someone stayed a few months to make sure all is well, I would be grateful. Seraphina can't stay—not with her chest—and I'd like to get Alfred to Yorkshire as soon as I can. I know you'll be all right with Ambrose and Gwendolyn. We've met them at church and they seem nice enough."

"Besides, if anything goes wrong, I only have to write to you, and you'll come," said Katie.

"Of course, pet. I would never leave you alone again."

Katie wrapped her arms around her sister and hugged her with all her might.

Molly laughed. "What's that for?"

"For everything you do, Mol. You always understand."

Papa understood, too, or at least, he accepted what Molly and Katie suggested to him the next morning. It was Henry who gave Katie a shrewd look, as though not quite believing her, but he didn't protest.

No one did, and so Katie stood alone on the platform as Papa and Molly loaded their last few things onto the cargo bay of the train. The station was directly across from the Welcome Hearth, and the Turners and Harrisons had caught the last train of the evening to save on the tickets. But this would not be the cramped and airless journey Katie vaguely remembered from Yorkshire. They had second-class tickets, with comfortable seats and cars that had windows.

Molly was glowing as she bounced Alfred on her hip, pointing at the steam billowing from the train. The little boy watched it in wide-eyed fascination.

"All right, that's the last of it." Papa slapped his hands clean. "The cattle were loaded at the Aggie, so we'll unload them when we get home."

"Home," said Molly, smiling.

Papa turned to Katie. "This isn't goodbye, you know. We'll see you again in just a little while. After all, I have cows to show at the Aggie."

Katie hugged him fiercely. "Thanks for letting me stay, Papa."

"Letting you stay! Why, you're doing us a favour."

Henry squeezed her hard and kissed the top of her head. Seraphina made her promise to right every day, and James embraced her for a few seconds longer than normal.

"We'll see you soon, Katie-pie." Molly kissed her cheek. "I'll write the moment we get home."

"I'll answer straight away," said Katie.

Then they all piled into the train and it chuffed off with them, leaving Katie alone on the dark street, shivering in the evening breeze.

She stared after the train until it was out of sight. The breeze seemed to blow right through her hollow chest.

Had she made a mistake?

She closed her eyes and tasted a sticky bun, and knew she had not. Michael would have done the same for her. One way or the other, she had to find him.

She walked across the street slowly and found the inn bustling with regulars. They'd asked many questions about the new couple behind the bar on the first few nights of their training with Molly, but now they seemed content to accept pots of ale and glasses of brandy from the stout old man serving the drinks. Ambrose Cooper was as round as the barrels he poured ale from, with a thinning mop of black hair and small eyes set deep in his fleshy face.

"There you are, Miss Turner," he said. "We were starting to worry about you. You'll catch your death out there, dear."

"Wouldn't want that," said his wife, coming up the cellar steps with a fresh wheel of cheese. Gwendolyn was as rake-thin as her husband was round, with beady little black eyes that darted everywhere, never quite settling on Katie's face.

"How can I help?" Katie asked. "Would you like me to serve the bread?"

"No, no, dear. Don't you worry." Gwendolyn smiled with a mouthful of yellow teeth. "You go up to bed, now. You've had a long day."

Katie stared at them for a second, then remembered that in their eyes, she was the owner's sister-in-law. Perhaps they saw her as something of a landlady.

The thought was reassuring as she climbed the stairs to her little room. She washed, undressed, and curled up between the sheets, feeling tired to her bones.

She missed James' snoring and Alfred's little voice. She even missed Seraphina's occasional cough, followed by Henry's soft voice asking her if she wanted a glass of water.

Most of all, she missed Molly's humming as she finished the last few tasks around the inn for the night.

She had been dozing fitfully for a while when Ambrose's voice jerked her back from the brink of deep sleep, so loud and close that she almost thought he was in her room.

"Oi! Where's my nightcap, woman?"

Katie sat up with a gasp, startled, but her door was shut and her room dark and peaceful. Ambrose was speaking in the hallway outside.

"Gwendolyn!" he barked. "Where is it?"

"On our bed, you great oaf," Gwendolyn snapped.

"No, it isn't. I looked there first. Do you think I'm a fool?"

"Maybe I do."

"Silence, woman, or you'll feel the back of my hand! Now where is my nightcap?"

"How am I meant to tell you if you want me to be silent?"

"Don't give me lip. Tell me where it is!"

"You must have dropped it on the floor, you lummox."

The words were harsh, holding none of the teasing notes that Katie had grown familiar with in Molly and James' banter. Gwendolyn truly meant the names she called Ambrose.

"Watch your tongue, witch!" Ambrose hissed.

Katie had heard enough. She shuffled down in bed and pulled the covers over her head, but even so, she couldn't blot out their strident voices as they argued on.

Those voices carved through the hallways that had been filled with laughter and love only yesterday. They echoed through the Welcome Hearth and filled its beloved rooms with discord.

PART V

CHAPTER 16

CHAPTER FIFTEEN

One Year Later

"Katherine!" Mrs. Cooper shrieked.

Katie jumped, almost knocking her head on one of the heavy racks that held the ale barrels. Her hands ached with cold as soapy water dripped from her fingers and onto the floor.

"*Katherine!*"

"I'm coming, Mrs. Cooper!" Katie shouted.

"Come faster, you lazy wretch!"

Katie dropped the scrubbing brush into the bucket and jogged up the pantry steps, wiping her hands on her apron. She wondered how it had all happened so quickly. Only a year ago, she had called the old woman "Gwendolyn" with kind familiarity. Now, she couldn't imagine using her first name. Mrs. Cooper would slap or pinch her for such insolence.

She scrambled into the main inn, where upside-down chairs stood on the tables and the floor glistened from a fresh scrubbing. Mrs. Cooper stood at the bottom of the stairs to the guest room, scowling, in her nightclothes.

"Haven't you finished scrubbing out the pantry yet?" she barked.

"Almost, Mrs. Cooper."

"'Almost' doesn't count. Go back in there and finish the job."

Katie bit her tongue to stop herself from saying that that was what she'd been doing until Mrs. Cooper interrupted her. "Yes, Mrs. Cooper."

"Not right now, you stupid girl. I called you for a reason. Mr. Blackwell in room four wants a cup of warm milk. Hop to it."

Katie clenched her hands into fists by her sides, grating at Mrs. Cooper's tone. The same words she always imagined boiled up behind her lips. It would be so easy to say them because they were all true.

How dare you talk to me like I'm your servant girl? My brother-in-law owns this inn. One word from me could have you both evicted!

But she knew from experience that saying the words had no effect. The only way to force the Coopers to treat her better would be if James or Molly themselves ordered it.

And they never would, because they would never know.

"Well, are you going to stand there all night? Do it!" Mrs. Cooper barked.

She turned and climbed the stairs back to her warm bed, and Katie said none of the angry words she felt in her chest. Instead, she meekly went to the kitchen, warmed a cup of milk for Mr. Blackwell, and delivered it to the guest's room a polished tray. Then she returned to the pantry's dusty lower shelves and scrubbed away the last few cobwebs, readying the space for another ale delivery.

It was only after she had finished cleaning everything, near midnight, that she at last crawled into the little bunk tucked away in a corner of the scullery. It was cold here, and damp, and Katie lay listening to the drip of the leaky pipe in the corner for a long time before she could fall asleep.

KATIE POISED her pencil over the sheet of paper on the bar before her, missing the writing desk she used to have in her attic room before the Coopers decided that it would be more profitable to use that room for guests. She slept in a corner of the kitchen now. She shifted on the single bar stool, trying to get comfortable, and reread the letter she'd penned.

DEAREST MOLLY,

It's so wonderful to hear about Alfred's new words! I do miss him so. He seems to be growing bigger and cleverer by the day.

Thank you for letting me know how Seraphina's confinement is coming along. I'm pleased that her lungs are so much better and that all is well with her and the baby. How is Henry doing at work now that old Bodger has retired? Is he keeping up with everything all right? I remember in your last letter you said that he had more work than he knew what to do with. That is a good thing, of course, especially with the little one on the way!

I know you're eager for me to join you all in Yorkshire soon, but I've made no progress finding Michael. It seems there is more than one Michael Bailey living in this city. Someone at the produce stand yesterday said that they thought they'd heard of a young apprentice named Michael across the city, but they couldn't remember. I asked them to see if they could find out anything more, but I doubt they will. You know how people are. Not everyone keeps their promises the way you do.

SHE HESITATED. This was the hardest part of writing to Molly: the lying.

I AM VERY WELL, thank you for asking.

KATIE CHEWED the end of her pencil, staring at those untrue words. She could change her life in a single line, she thought. She could say, *The Coopers treat me worse than a servant. They fight all the time. I'm afraid of Ambrose and Gwendolyn slaps me when I do anything she doesn't like. There's no more peace and joy in the Welcome Hearth anymore, only endless fighting.*

But Katie knew she couldn't say that. The moment she did, Molly, James, and her father would be on a train to London, rushing to her rescue, and they would never leave her alone again. They would realize that it had been a mistake to leave her with the Coopers after all.

She would never see Michael again.

Katie finished the letter.

. . .

As soon as I find him, we'll come to you. I can't wait to see Yorkshire with him.

With all my love,
Katie.

KATIE PLACED a penny black on the letter, one of her last; the precious stamp book was running low. Another thing she hadn't old Molly was that the Coopers insisted she work almost full days in the inn. Her costermongering business had buckled as a result. No longer did her vegetables grace the tables of London's nobility.

She could barely afford postage stamps these days.

Katie slipped from the inn and headed into the bustle of London's morning streets to post the letter. A dozen possibilities swirled through her mind. She could find a boarding-house and stay there to search for Michael, supporting herself with her costermongering. But then Molly would know something was afoot...

There was no other way. If she wanted to find Michael, she had to tolerate the Coopers.

And despite a year of this treatment, Katie's hope and longing for him had not changed.

KATIE POURED the ale with care, lifting and lowering the jug exactly as Molly had taught her to achieve the perfect layer of white froth on the top of the mug. She set the jug aside and arranged the mug with a few others on a tray amid the smoky bustle of the Welcome Hearth at its most busy.

The weekday crowds that had once graced this inn every night had thinned, but nothing would keep

Londoners from their pint on a Saturday night. Several ruffians slurped ale and played cards at the tables. Katie had learned to dodge their groping hands as she hurried from one table to the next, dispensing new drinks.

"Hurry up, girl," Mrs. Cooper shouted from the bar. "What are you doing? There's more thirsty folk in this bar!"

Mrs. Cooper sat on a chair behind the bar, near the steps leading down to the cellar. She ate a heel of bread with messy bites, spilling crumbs into her lap.

Katie's stomach growled. It would be a few hours before the guests thinned out and she was allowed to eat.

"Coming, Mrs. Cooper," she called.

She ducked another outstretched hands and approached the bar. Before she could reach it, Mr. Cooper leaned over from the bar stool and snatched a full mug from her tray.

Katie paused. Mr. Cooper raised the mug and slurped, sending foam spilling through the dirty stubble of his lower lip and chin.

"Ambrose!" Mrs. Cooper barked. "Enough of that."

Mr. Cooper planted the empty mug on the tray and mopped his mouth with the back of his arm.

"Oi," an annoyed customer called. "That was my drink."

"I'll bring you another, sir," said Katie quickly.

"You'll bring me another first, wench," Mr. Cooper snapped.

"You'll do no such thing," said Mrs. Cooper from her chair. "He's had enough to drink, the disgusting old drunkard, and he knows it."

Mr. Cooper's bloodshot eyes narrowed. "Hold your tongue, woman."

"I won't," said Mrs. Cooper. "All you do is sit around here and drink while I work my fingers to the bone at this inn. Oooh, you love people calling you the innkeeper, but the only thing you keep is your seat warm!"

Mr. Cooper pushed back his stool and stood, slightly swaying. Katie backed away, but couldn't get far; Mrs. Cooper was in the way on one side, the cellar steps on the other.

"Woman," Mr. Cooper growled, "how dare you give me lip in front of my customers?"

Katie trembled.

"They all know it's true," said Mrs. Cooper, "all of them."

The customers were, indeed, staring. But something told Katie it was Mrs. Cooper's strident tone, not her husband's drinking, that turned their heads.

"Mrs. Cooper—" she began.

"Shut up, you wretched girl. Ambrose, sit back down before you fall down, you're that fuddled."

Mr. Cooper leered. "I told you to hold your tongue, and I'll teach you a lesson, woman, if you don't obey me at once."

"Ha! I've had enough of obeying you, you old fool."

Mr. Cooper lunged around the bar. Katie cried out and instinctively stepped forward, holding out her hand. Mr. Cooper's backhanded slap came out of nowhere, its speed shocking for his level of inebriation. His knuckles rang across her lips and cheekbones with blinding force. She stumbled, dropping the tray, and mugs bounced all around the back of the room.

A regular customer, Sam, scrambled to his feet. "Oi! What's all this, then?"

Katie clutched her throbbing face, but could make no sound. She only watched in horror as Mr. Cooper marched over to his wife. She rose, ready to shout at him, but Mr.

Cooper was no longer in the mood for talking. He slammed both hands into her. Her chair teetered over, and Mrs. Cooper tumbled down the stairs with a terrible cry that ended in a horrid, bony crunch at the bottom.

A gasp rang through the inn. Mr. Cooper swung around, his baleful eyes locked on Katie. She tasted blood from his slap. When he raised his hand as if to deal her another blow, Katie ducked underneath his arm and fled with a cry of terror.

As she bolted through the back door to the kitchen, all she could think of was Mrs. Cromwell and her wooden ruler. The pain of that hard implement upon her palm had been akin to the throbbing soreness now in her face.

It was as though an iron band had been holding her together all this time, like a barrel, holding the planks of her mind in a tight seal so that nothing could escape; not her longing for Michael or how much she missed her family or her increasing rage at the Coopers' injustice. But Mr. Cooper's blow had snapped that band. Now it all spilled through her, raw and uncontrolled and horrifying.

She couldn't stay here. The Welcome Hearth was no longer a home.

She needed Molly.

Sweeping loneliness left her breathless, making her hands tremble as she did what she knew she had to do. She fumbled a canvas bag from underneath her narrow bed and began to stuff her belongings into it: a clean dress, an apron, a coat, an extra bonnet, some books, her pencil and papers, the precious book of stamps, and a small bag of money.

She hugged the bag in her arms as she scampered out of the back door. There were angry voices in the inn, Mrs. Cooper's weeping, a general air of chaos. Katie wanted no part of it anymore. She knew where she could go to be safe and surrounded by love once more.

"I'm sorry, Michael," she sobbed as she stumbled across the street. "I'm so sorry. I failed you. I couldn't do it. I couldn't hold out for you."

Tears splashed over her cheeks as she staggered to the train station where she'd bid her family goodbye only a year ago. A fruitless, heartless, horrible year! Why had she stayed?

She kept the bag close, conscious of the money inside, which should be enough to take her safely to Yorkshire. At this late hour, only a few people gathered on the platform. There was no line for the ticket office even though the late train departed soon. Katie hardly cared; she would rather spend a cold night waiting on this platform than another minute in the Welcome Hearth.

She was still crying too hard to speak to the ticket-seller, so she cast around for a space to sit and compose herself.

A wooden bench stood on the platform. Two older ladies huddled at one end. They paid Katie no mind at all as she sank down onto the other and buried her face in her bag, letting the tears flow, the salt stinging her cheekbone where Mr. Cooper's knuckles had broken the skin.

She was grateful that the two old biddies appeared not to notice her. They could have done nothing to ease her pain.

"I'm so glad you made it in time, Rose. Why, it's so wonderful that we can take this journey together."

"I almost didn't make it at all. Why, I was still halfway across the city from the station when the cabbie's horse lost a shoe. Poor thing was almost on three legs because of it. He couldn't take us another step."

"Oh! But you did make it. Did you catch another cab?"

"I didn't. You know what it's like trying to get a cab at this hour, Dinah. I thought I'd have to send a messenger to tell you I couldn't come. You know I can barely walk at all with this bad leg."

"Of course, of course. You poor thing. How did you manage?"

"Well, it was a wonderful thing. We were down the block from a smithy. It was closed, of course, at that hour, but while the cabbie was unharnessing the horse, a young man came out of the cottage by the smithy. He was a smith's apprentice, he said, having his supper when he heard the horse lose his shoe. He said he would help us at once."

"Oh, Rose, how kind of him."

"He was a terribly sweet young man. Bailey, I think his name was. Yes, that's right, Mr. Bailey. He shod our horse in a jiff and we were back on our way in ten minutes. I wish I'd had more money to give him as a tip, Dinah. He was so lovely."

Katie slowly raised her head, the tears drying on her cheeks as the words resounded through her head. *Bailey. Mr. Bailey.*

"It's good to know there are still kind people in this funny old world," said the old lady called Dinah.

"He's certainly one of them. My son has his own horse for his business, and I'll certainly tell him to use that smithy in the future."

"I beg your pardon," Katie managed.

The two women stared at her as though seeing her for the first time. Rose raised a hand to her own cheekbone at the sight of the bruise on Katie's face.

"I'm sorry," said Katie, "I don't mean to interrupt, but did you say that the young smith's name was Mr. Bailey?"

"Now, young lady," said Dinah, "eavesdropping is hardly—"

"Hush, Dinah. Look at the poor lamb," said Rose. "Who did that to you, dear?"

"Mr. Bailey. Was it Mr. Bailey?" Katie insisted.

"Yes, that's right."

"And his Christian name?" Katie's voice was carefully controlled, though her pulse quickened. "Was it Michael, by any chance?"

Rose considered this for a minute, rubbing her upper lip. "Well, yes, dear, I think it might have been Michael Bailey."

Katie was quiet for a moment, processing this. Michael Bailey. It was probably a common enough name, but still... "Are you quite certain it was Michael Bailey?"

"Yes, yes, now that you say it, quite sure. What's the matter, dear?"

Katie stood up slowly, her mind racing. It could be anyone, of course. Bailey wasn't such an uncommon name, and there must be dozens of Michaels in London. But the timing, the age the old woman described...

"Where was this smithy?" she asked, trying to keep her voice level.

Rose blinked. "The smithy was on Acorn Street, dear, but I don't understand why—"

"Thank you," Katie said quietly. She touched the old woman's shoulder gently. "Thank you very much."

"I say, what's gotten into you?" Dinah demanded.

Katie didn't answer immediately. She picked up her bag and stood there for a moment, weighing her options. It was probably nothing. It was almost certainly nothing. But...

What if it wasn't?

She looked down at the bag in her hands—her ticket to Yorkshire, to safety with Molly. Then she looked back at the old women.

"I used to know someone by that name," she said simply. "A long time ago. I suppose... I suppose it's worth finding out."

She walked—didn't run—toward the platform steps. Her face still hurt, her body was still tired, but there was something else now too. Not wild hope, but a quiet possibility. The first real possibility she'd had in years.

Maybe it was foolish. Probably it was. But sometimes, Katie thought as she hailed a cab with careful deliberation, you had to take a chance on maybe.

"Cabbie!" Katie called, raising her hand.

Getting a cab at this hour was difficult, but Katie walked steadily down the street, scanning for available hansoms. After a few minutes, she spotted one dropping off passengers and managed to hail it before another fare could claim it.

The driver looked her over with mild suspicion—her clothes marked her as working class, and it was late for a woman to be traveling alone.

"It's thruppence a mile," he said, "and payment in advance, if you please."

"I can pay." Katie opened her bag and carefully counted out a sixpence. The weight of that coin in her palm gave her pause—it represented her train fare to Yorkshire, her escape to safety with Molly. But she handed it to him anyway. "The smithy on Acorn Street. Do you know it? The rest when we arrive."

The cabbie examined the sixpence and pocketed it.

"Acorn Street. Bit out of my usual way, but aye, I know the smithy."

Katie climbed into the cab and settled onto the worn seat. As they pulled into the evening traffic, she found herself second-guessing the decision. This was either very sensible or very foolish, and she wouldn't know which until she arrived.

The cab moved at a steady pace through the busy streets. Carriages and wagons jostled for position, drivers calling out warnings and curses, but Katie barely noticed the urban chaos around her. Her mind was occupied with more practical concerns.

What if Rose had misheard the name? Michael Barley instead of Michael Bailey? Or Martin Bailey? What if it was the right name but the wrong person entirely? London must have dozens of Michael Baileys. And even if, by some chance, it was *her* Michael Bailey—what then? Eight years was a long time. People changed, grew, forgot childhood friendships... and perhaps even adult betrothals. Had it truly been a betrothal, or just a wild promise?

The thought that worried her most was what would happen if this proved to be nothing. She wouldn't have enough money left for the train to Yorkshire. She could write to Molly for help, but that would take time—time she'd have to spend on London's streets with nowhere to go and very little money.

You're being reckless, she told herself. *You should have bought that train ticket.*

But even as she thought it, Katie knew she couldn't have lived with herself if she hadn't investigated. The possibility, however slim, was worth the risk. Wasn't it?

He had said they were in love. A corner of her heart told her that love was worth the change.

"Here we are," said the cabbie, pulling up beside a low building with a cottage attached.

Katie looked out at the smithy across the street. A few people walked by, intent on their evening business, but the forge doors were closed and only a single light flickered in the cottage window.

"The smithy on Acorn Street," the cabbie added. "That'll be a shilling and four."

Katie counted out the remaining money and handed it over, her heart sinking slightly at how little remained in her purse. The cabbie touched his cap and drove away, leaving her alone on the pavement.

She stood there for a moment, looking across at the smithy. No wild hope, no terror, no promises of joy. Just a practical decision made by a woman who'd learned to take care of herself. Either this would lead somewhere, or it wouldn't. Either way, she'd manage.

Katie straightened her shoulders and prepared to find out which it would be.

The smithy was the same as all the others in the city; a low building, with a cottage on one side, and a big yard with rails and water troughs and rings in the walls to tie horses to. Its doors were closed on the anvil and forge, but a candle flickered in the cottage window.

Katie knew she should march across the street and knock on the door, but she found herself hesitating. What would she say? *Hello, Michael. Do you remember promising to marry me?* What if he was married now? What if he looked at her and thought her a fool for hanging all of her hopes on those few precious weeks they'd had together as adults?

So much could happen in three years: the length of time they'd spent apart. To Katie, in that moment, it simultaneously felt like the blink of an eye and like a lifetime.

In the end, she was spared gathering her courage. The door opened of its own accord. A fat ginger tom cat trotted out, tail in the air.

"Happy mousing, General," an unseen person called from the half-open door.

Katie's breath caught. The voice was deeper than she remembered, aged by years, but unmistakably familiar. That Yorkshire accent, the gentle cadence—it was him. It was really him.

The door began to close. "Michael!" she called out before she could stop herself.

The door swung open wider. A young man appeared in the doorway—tall, broad-shouldered, work-worn clothes, hands stained with soot. His shoulders were broader than they'd been three years ago.

But his eyes... his eyes were exactly the same.

"Katie?" he said, his voice filled with wonder and disbelief.

"Hello, Michael." Her voice was soft, almost breathless.

For a moment they simply stared at each other. The moment seemed to stretch for years as Katie slowly took in all the ways in which he'd changed: the new strength to his jaw, the width of his frame, the sturdy strength of the bare arms protruding from a sweaty shirt. His cheeks were ruddy, his eyes bright.

He looked well.

Well enough to have moved on from her? To have given up on the girl who kept slipping from his grasp, and chosen another? Her heart stuttered.

"I can't believe it's really you," Michael said, stepping down from the doorway. He moved closer, stopping just an arm's length away. "You were never at the millinery when I went back."

"I left! I didn't have to be there anymore. Oh, Michael, so much has happened." Katie's smile was radiant despite her tiredness. "But Michael, didn't Mrs. Cromwell tell you where I'd gone?"

"When I went to the millinery, she wasn't there anymore. She was dead."

Those words were strangely freeing to hear.

"How did you find me?" Michael asked.

"I heard someone mention your name at the train station. I hoped... I had to find out if it was really you."

"You came looking for me," he said, his voice full of amazement and something deeper—joy, relief, perhaps even gratitude.

"Of course I did." There was no apology in her voice, only simple truth. "I never forgot, Michael. I've never stopped searching for you in all the time since you moved to Birmingham. Did you think I would?"

Something shifted in his expression—a recognition not just of her face, but of what they had meant to each other. "No," he said quietly. "I hoped you wouldn't. I never forgot either, Katie. Not for a single day."

They stood there, drinking in the sight of each other. Katie both longed and feared to ask the question that hovered at the front of her mind and heart: did he remember his promise? Did he still want to marry her?

Was Joan still looking at patterns for wedding dresses?

"Your family—are they well? Are Joan and Peter—?"

"They're here," Michael said, his face lighting up. "Inside. They're going to be so happy to see you, Katie. We've all wondered... we've hoped..."

Before Katie could respond, she became aware of the sound of hoofbeats growing louder behind her.

"Katie, the carriage—" Michael's warning came as he lunged forward, but it was too late.

CHAPTER 17

CHAPTER SIXTEEN

Katie learned afterward that it was seven long days before the haziness in her mind cleared. That period would always be a blur to her, with strange gaps of darkness in her memory. She remembered mostly the pain, but more clearly than that, she remembered gentle hands, soft voices, and the quiet presence of people who cared for her during the long hours.

Once or twice, she managed to open her eyes. She always glimpsed the same little grey room with a cracked window allowing scraps of sunlight to reach the dusty interior. There was always a struggling fire in the stove and the smell of boiling potatoes or gruel. A crack ran through the ceiling, but warm blankets encircled her, and they always helped her to ease back to sleep.

It was sunlight that drew her from her fitful slumber at last: a shaft of brilliance landing on her face. It made her squint, and the action was only a little painful. Even the ache in her chest seemed farther away than before.

"Oh, you poor thing," said Joan. "The sunlight's right on your face."

A curtain hissed, and the light dimmed.

Katie wanted to tell her that she'd enjoyed the sunlight. Instead, only a feeble moan escaped her.

"Steady now, lass. You're all right." Joan's hand wrapped around hers. "Perhaps you need a little more laudanum, poor dear."

"N-no," Katie whispered. She didn't want to go back to sleep, but the single word was almost too much for her energy.

Joan's hand squeezed hers, startled. "Katie? Katie, darling, can you hear me?"

Katie's eyelids fluttered. The light made her wince, but she managed to ease them open.

"Katie?" Joan placed a hand on her cheek. She had aged so much in these past few years. If not for the kindness in her eyes, perhaps Katie would have had trouble recognizing her.

"Hello," Katie whispered.

Joy transformed Joan's face, aging her backward in an instant to the sweet young woman who'd washed Katie and Molly's hair in the Thames all those years ago, and more recently, the kind lady who'd given her the treasured handkerchief she still carried in her sleeve. "Michael!" she shouted. "Peter! Come quickly! She's awake!"

Footsteps hurried in from outside. Michael burst into the room, wearing a blacksmith's apron smeared with soot. Sweat glistened on his forearms, and his face was tight with worry.

"Katie," he breathed, relief flooding his voice.

"Wash your hands," Joan ordered. "You know what the doctor said about cleanliness."

Michael moved quickly to the nearby basin, scrubbing his hands clean, but his eyes never left Katie's face. When he finished, he pulled a chair close to the bed and sat down.

"How do you feel?" he asked, his voice gentle with concern.

"Like I was trampled by horses," Katie managed weakly.

Michael's worried expression eased into a smile—the first real smile she'd seen from him. "Well, you were. So I suppose that's accurate."

"I'm sorry," Katie whispered. "About the accident. I wasn't watching—"

"Don't," Michael said firmly. "Don't apologize. I should have warned you about that corner. Carriages always come around it too fast." His voice grew thick with emotion. "When I saw you go down... Katie, I thought I'd lost you again. I thought I'd found you just to lose you forever."

Peter appeared in the doorway, his weathered face creased with joy and relief. "There's our girl. We were starting to worry you'd sleep through Christmas."

Katie tried to smile. "What day is it?"

"Saturday," Joan said gently. "You've been unconscious for a week."

A week. Katie processed this slowly, grateful for their presence, for being safe and cared for. "I'm sorry to be such trouble."

"You're no trouble at all," Michael said, leaning forward slightly. "Katie, when I saw you standing there in the street... it was like a miracle. I've thought about you so often over the years, wondered where you were, if you were safe." His voice grew quiet, earnest. "I never stopped hoping I'd see you again."

Joan moved to adjust Katie's blankets, her motherly attention warm and familiar. "We all did, dear. Many a night we talked about your family, wondered how you were all getting on."

Michael reached for her hand, holding it gently. "I know we don't have much, but what we have is yours. You belong here with us, Katie. That hasn't changed."

She searched his eyes, her former doubts looming in her mind. Three years, it could feel like a lifetime. Heaven knew it had felt like a lifetime to her. He had waited for her before. Could she expect, could she dare to hope, that he had waited for her again?

"Hasn't it?" she whispered.

He understood the meaning beneath the words, and the tightening of his warm fingers over hers told her everything. "It hasn't," he said.

Her heart swelled within her.

"Is there anything we can fetch from your home for you, Katie?" Joan asked, returning to practical matters. "Do you live nearby?"

Katie managed a small smile. "I live at the Welcome Hearth."

The Baileys exchanged surprised looks.

"Old Alfie Crumble's place?" Peter asked.

"It's not his place anymore. It belongs to Molly and James now."

Michael's eyes lit up. "James—the kind boy who used to help us when we were costermongering?"

"She married him. They have a little boy, and they own the inn."

"Then I'll run to the Hearth this very minute," Peter said, starting to rise.

"Wait," Katie said weakly. "They're not there. Only tenants. Molly went back to Yorkshire with Papa."

Joan gasped, her hand flying to her mouth.

Peter's jaw dropped. "Your father! He's... he's alive?"

"Alive, and owns the farm again." Katie smiled despite the effort it took. "Henry's there, too."

"Henry!" Joan looked as though she might faint from joy.

"Everyone's all right. Everyone's together again."

"But they left you here?" Peter frowned with concern. "Katie, what happened to your face? Michael said you were already bruised before the carriage accident."

Katie's expression darkened. "The tenants at the Hearth. They're... not kind people."

"Why didn't you go to Yorkshire with your family then?" Michael asked gently.

Katie hesitated, then met his eyes. "I wanted to stay in London. I had... reasons."

Michael studied her face, understanding flickering in his expression, but he didn't press her for details in front of his parents.

"Well, you don't have to worry about those awful tenants anymore," Joan said firmly. "You'll stay right here with us until you're completely well."

"And longer, if you want," Peter added. "This is your home now, Katie. For as long as you need it. We don't have much, lass, but everything we have is yours."

Katie felt tears slip down her cheeks—not from pain, but from overwhelming relief and gratitude. She was safe. She was loved. And Michael...

Once again, Michael had proved faithful.

"Thank you," she whispered, her eyes already growing heavy. "All of you. I don't know what I would have done..."

"You don't need to know," Michael said softly. "You're here now. Rest, Katie. We'll be here when you wake up."

As drowsiness began to take effect again, Katie's last coherent thought was wonder at how right this felt—being here, with them, safe at last. It was like finding her way home after being lost for years.

"Katie, darling," Joan said quietly, noticing her growing drowsiness. "Before you sleep—if I write to your family's old address in Yorkshire, will it reach Molly?"

Katie managed to nod weakly before the peaceful darkness wrapped around her. With Michael's gentle presence nearby and the sound of Joan and Peter's quiet voices, she knew everything would truly be all right.

CHAPTER 18

CHAPTER SEVENTEEN

Katie's ribs twinged with every step, but the pain felt distant compared to the sunshine on her face and the warmth of Michael's presence beside her. It would not be proper for him to hold her hand, not even with Joan and Peter as chaperones beside them, not out here on London's bustling streets. Yet they had no need of the physical contact. Simply his smell, his shadow, his footsteps beside her was enough to make her feel anchored in the mad spinning of the world.

The bobby walked along in front of them, whistling briskly and swinging his truncheon, as though in a fine mood to strike somebody with it. Ordinarily, that thought would fill Katie with horror. She'd heard tales of the bobbies' brutality from Henry. But now, she knew that the strong arm of the law was on her side.

She shifted the bag in her hand.

"Katie, darling, *please* let me carry that for you," said Michael.

"It's all right. You have your own things to carry."

Michael shouldered a heavy pack. "Many more things than before, thanks to your sister."

"Poor Molly! I feel so sorry for her. The letter we sent must have given her a terrible shock."

"I can hardly imagine," said Joan. "Poor girl. She thought you were happy and well here in London. To hear that not only had you been misused and mistreated by her tenants, but you were sick and ailing—I can't imagine."

"I think she feels all the worse because she couldn't come to London at once," said Katie, "and I didn't know that she was—" She lowered her voice. "In the family way. Do you think the shock would have harmed her or the little one?"

"Oh, no, of course not, dear," said Joan. "For one thing, she knew at once that you were in safe hands; and for another, Molly's a strong girl."

Katie smiled. "She certainly is that."

"Your poor papa must have been worried sick, too, but he couldn't leave the farm in calving time. No one could. I understand that," said Peter.

"Papa and Molly both knew that I'd be all right because I was with you."

"They needn't have sent us all that money," said Peter quietly. "We would have been all right."

"Nonsense, Pete." Joan touched his arm. "Molly and John were only making sure Katie had all the medicine and doctor's visits she needed."

"She did more than that. All the clothes and food she sent us—"

"She felt guilty because she had to give the tenants a

month's notice to move out," said Katie, "and even worse when the Coopers refused to leave on time."

"Ha! They're lucky Molly can't travel right now." Peter's eyes flashed. "She would have been on them like a thunderstorm, if I know Molly."

"She certainly would." Katie giggled. "I suppose they're lucky it's only a policeman."

"Are you sure we should have packed all of our things?" Joan wondered.

"Don't you worry, ma'am," said the policeman. "Those tenants will be out of your inn in no time. I've got the signed letter from the courts and all. They won't have a choice."

Katie's shoulder had begun to ache sharply by the time they rounded the corner and saw the dear old inn slumbering in the sunshine before them. The sight startled her. It was early afternoon, and a crowd of hungry patrons should have been streaming into it for luncheon, but despite the open windows there was hardly a soul inside.

Instead, strident voices rose from within. The Coopers —arguing, as usual. The sound made Katie's breath hitch.

Michael stepped protectively in front of her. "Don't worry, love. They can't hurt you."

The tension in Katie's belly instantly eased. "I know they can't. Not while you're here."

"Katie? Katie Turner, is that you?"

The sweet little old lady who lived opposite the inn hurried out, clutching a basket full of eggs from the hens she kept in her back garden. Katie had bought many from her when the inn ran out.

"Good heavens, child, it *is* you! Look at you! What on earth happened?"

"It's so good to see you, Mrs. Edwards."

"You've been hurt. Oh, you're so thin! Was it *them*?" Mrs. Edwards hissed.

Katie blinked. "Who?"

"The Coopers, of course. Did *they* do it to you?"

"Oh—no! I was run over by a carriage."

"You poor lamb! But we all know what the Coopers did. They turned you out, didn't they?"

"Something like that."

The old woman sneered. "After Sam told everyone that he didn't see you in the inn anymore, no one could go there. We knew they'd been unkind to you. We've been looking for you, dear, but we couldn't find you. Instead we made sure no one went to the inn anymore. Why, I'm sure they've been losing money, and rightfully so! The old fools!"

"Don't worry, Mrs. Edwards," Katie told her. "We're here to take it back right now."

"I'm coming with you," the old woman declared.

She followed Katie and the others across the street, shouting to everyone she passed that the Turners were taking back their inn. They had amassed a small crowd when they reached the front door, where Katie and the Baileys hung back as the bobby marched up to it.

The policeman knocked. "Ambrose Cooper!"

There was silence within. Katie imagined the frantic glances exchanged inside.

The bobby hammered on the door again. "Ambrose Cooper! Police!"

Mr. Cooper appeared in the doorway, opening it only a fraction. "Ye-ees?"

"You are hereby formally ordered to vacate the premises immediately," the bobby snapped. "Should you fail to comply, you will be removed by force."

Mr. Cooper froze.

The bobby idly swung his truncheon. "Do you understand, Mr. Cooper?"

Mr. Cooper stared up at him for a very long moment. Then he finally said, "Yes," in a small voice.

"Very well," said the bobby, "then there will be no need for force." He sounded vaguely disappointed. "Miss Turner, would you like to supervise their departure to ensure that none of your things are stolen?"

"No," said Katie. "It's all right. I just want them gone."

"Then I shall do the supervision." The bobby marched into the inn, almost shoving Mr. Cooper aside, and shut the door behind him.

The Coopers complied with remarkable speed when a muscular man with a big stick was standing over them. As the crowd thickened around Katie's little crew, with Joan and Peter embracing old friends they hadn't seen in a decade, she leaned against Michael on legs that trembled with weakness. But it was only a few minutes later that the door swung open and the bobby said, with great satisfaction, "They've gone, Miss Turner, Mr. Bailey. The inn is all yours."

The crowd broke into applause, causing dogs to bark up and down the street.

The joyful sound bore them all into the Welcome Hearth. Katie was grinning with triumph, but her smile faded as she beheld the interior. In the month since she had written to Molly and the Coopers had received their notice, they appeared to have done their best to run the beloved inn into the ground. Several of the chairs were broken. A thick layer of dust lay upon the tables. A barrel had burst behind the bar, leaking its fragrant contents all over the floor, and cobwebs drooped in all the corners.

Mrs. Edwards had been right, Katie realized. The people

of this little corner of London—the people who knew and loved her family—had effectively boycotted the Coopers.

Joan trotted upstairs at once as Peter plodded into the wine cellar. Michael helped Katie to a chair, where she sat stunned, staring at the chaos inside the inn.

"Looks as though there's been nobody in the rooms upstairs for weeks," Joan reported, returning.

"Nor is there anything left in the cellar." Peter climbed the stairs. "Only a few barrels of drink, some potatoes, and a hanging bacon."

"They've almost destroyed the Welcome Hearth," said Katie faintly.

Michael crouched beside her. "They're gone now, love."

"That's right," said Joan. "We're here now, and there's nothing here that a broom, a bit of patience, and one good night of business won't fix."

"But we have nothing to serve the guests," said Katie.

"I didn't say nothing." Peter grinned. "Those few barrels of ale will be enough for one merry evening."

"I can make a very good soup with potatoes and bacon," said Joan.

Michael beamed. "And I can fix those chairs in ten minutes with a hammer and some nails."

Katie's heart swelled within her.

"Everything will be all right, love," said Michael.

With all her heart, Katie believed him.

THE INN SHONE WITH FIRELIGHT. A great blaze snapped and leaped joyfully in the fireplace that gave the Welcome Hearth its name, pouring its golden light through the bustling inn, where every table was full and several patrons stood about with pots in their hands, talking and laughing. The air smelled deliciously of rabbit stew and freshly baked bread rolls—and warm, honeyed milk.

Katie looked up hopefully from her book. She sat in the old armchair by the fire, the one that Molly called "Alfie's chair," and watched as Michael crossed the floor to her. He carried a single cup on a little tray with intense concentration. Fragrant steam curled from its interior.

"Here you are, my lady," he said with a playful little bow, holding out the mug.

"Oh, hark at you." Katie giggled.

"Warm milk with honey and a pinch of cinnamon, just as you like it."

"Cinnamon!" Katie gasped. "Could Joan find some?"

"She certainly could, and she's baked it into the sago pudding, too."

"Oh, how wonderful! It's only been a week since we started with nothing but ale, potatoes, and bacon—and now we have *cinnamon*!"

Katie wrapped her hands around the warm mug and raised it to her lips. She inhaled the steam deeply, then winced at the pang of pain in her ribs.

Michael laid a hand on her shoulder. "Are you all right, darling?"

"Still a little sore," Katie confessed, "but that doesn't mean I can't lend a hand in the kitchen."

"Nonsense. You'll sit here and rest until you're all better." Michael pulled up a stool. "I have a moment to sit with you; Papa says that everyone's been served, for now."

They watched the bustle in the inn for a minute, enjoying the merry conversation.

"I haven't seen it like this since Molly left," said Katie softly.

"I don't remember it being this busy when old Alfie was still in charge, but I do remember that it was always warm and safe here, and he always had a crust of bread or half a cup of milk for a hungry child coming home from the cotton mills."

"Ugh! That mill." Katie shuddered, sending a fresh twinge through her shoulder. "I'm relieved they never rebuilt it. What an appalling place it was."

"You and I have seen many of the most horrible corners of London."

"Yes, but now I think we're in the nicest." Katie smiled up at him.

Michael's soft eyes found hers. "I think the nicest part of London—of the whole world—is wherever you are."

With all her heart, Katie agreed.

Dearest Katie,

I'm so happy to hear that Dr. Connors is satisfied your arm is all better! James and I are overjoyed, too, to receive the figures from dear Peter. The Welcome Hearth is thriving under his management. I know he only started running it as a favour to you, but James and I have offered him a contract to lease the inn and run it as the Coopers should have done. It would be nothing but a joy to see him in command of Alfie's beloved inn.

I hope that, now that your arm is all better, you'll be able to come to Yorkshire and see us. We've been so worried for you, dearest Katie. At least we know now that you're in good hands now, but my heart will only settle when I lay my very own eyes upon you, and see that you are truly well.

I miss and love you with all my heart, and though I ache to know what you suffered with the Coopers, I agree with what you say—it has all been worth it now that you're reunited with Michael.

With all my love,
Molly.

KATIE FINISHED READING the letter out loud and replaced it gently in its envelope, then returned it to her apron pocket.

"She loves you desperately, you know," said Michael quietly. "She always has, every minute."

"I've never doubted it," said Katie.

They sat on a wooden bench in the square where Katie used to sell vegetables. There was no need of that now, not with the Welcome Hearth turning a hearty profit, Molly sending home money from the burgeoning farm, and the Baileys treating Katie, in Peter's words, as the "crown princess of the Welcome Hearth." Instead, she and Michael sat resting after one of the walks Dr. Connors had recommended for her constitution. The mingled smells of the marketplace were poignantly familiar to her: salted fish, fresh bread, cheese, and the dusty hessian that made up the sacks in which vendors kept their goods.

A cat stretched out in the sun next to the old lady who sold gruel. The warm light seemed to make everyone a little kinder. All these vendors remembered Katie and Michael from when they were younger; they frequently waved at familiar faces.

"Even all those years ago," said Katie, "when Molly was always angry and worried, and Henry was so furious with her, I always knew it was because she loved us that she was so harsh with us. She was trying to correct Henry. Perhaps she did it the wrong way; but who could blame her? She was only a little girl, doing her best to keep us alive, even before Mama died."

"My mother used to call Molly 'the little general.' Even my parents sometimes looked to her as their leader. I'm glad you know that all that shouting was only because she loved you."

"I did, but I don't think I could have borne it if not for you."

Michael stared at her. "Why do you say that?"

"Because Molly's love was strength, but you... you always showed me softness. Kindness." Katie smiled. "I can still taste the sticky bun you shared with me right over there, on that very bridge, when I felt like there was no hope at all."

"You remember that? So do I. I'll never forget your little face when you tasted that bun."

"I'll never forget it." Katie gazed up at him, her eyes unwavering. "It was the happiest moment I can remember... until now."

Michael's eyes shone.

"Being with you is more wonderful than I dared hope," Katie whispered. "I never stopped missing you, Michael. I never stopped longing for you."

Something changed in Michael's face, as if a flash of determination suddenly ran through him. He stood and held out a hand. "Walk with me, Katie."

She did not question him. She threaded her good arm through his—the injured one still ached a little—and allowed him to lead her across the marketplace. Friendly faces greeted them as they threaded between the stalls. Katie remembered longing desperately for the food that smelled so wonderful at each one: for the fried fish with the delicious, oily chips, for the stew with chunks of nameless meat floating in a hearty broth, for the fresh bread that still steamed in the bakery window. She had never been able to have those things when they scraped out a living as costermongers.

Now it was all so different, and yet none of it truly mattered, not compared with the strong warmth of Michael's arm under her hand.

He stopped on the little humpbacked bridge over the same grimy tributary of the Thames where she'd eaten that delicious sticky bun, overlooking the stretch of dirty water where Joan had washed her hair sometimes on warm Sundays, filling the air with her giggles.

Michael turned to face her, his whole heart shining in his eyes. Katie's breath hitched. She suddenly knew, undoubtedly, what was coming.

He reached into his pocket with one hand as he sank down on one knee, his fingers still gently clasping hers.

"Katie Turner." Michael's voice was husky with emotion. "Will you marry me?"

The answer was so obvious that Katie said nothing for a few moments, staring instead at the carefully forged loop of iron he held up to her; an iron ring, one he'd made with his own hands.

"K-Katie?" Michael managed, terror flashing across his expression.

"Yes!" Katie burst out. "Of course I will. Yes, Michael, yes!"

Michael laughed, a gusting sound of joy and relief. He rose to his feet and threaded the iron ring onto Katie's finger. It fit as though it had always been there; as though it belonged.

THEY WERE MARRIED that very Sunday, simply and joyfully, with Katie wearing a brand-new dress Joan had sewed for her in pale blue. It was a little cold for flowers, but they had bought hothouse lilies from a little flower-seller on the street corner, and Katie clutched that tiny bouquet in one hand and Michael's in the other as they resumed their places in their pews after the ceremony and listened to a sermon that Katie could barely hear. She was too busy listening to the gentle rush of Michael's breathing, feeling his thudding pulse in his wrist as she held his hand. He was hers at last, all hers.

They left the church with the rest of the congregation, and though that congregation consisted of the same dour old faces with whom Katie shared the pews every Sunday, they seemed different to her. Everything seemed differed. She saw them laughing, saw the strange beauty in the folds around gentle eyes or the intertwining of gnarled hands. The sun was brighter than it had ever been when they descended the few steps onto the shabby grounds. The air tasted fresher; the world was alight with hope and possibility.

These church grounds were no longer the sad place where Mama, Alfie, and Tessie lay buried. They were the place where Katie had been married.

Michael's hand trembled upon hers. Their fingers found each other and interlocked. There could be no disapproving glances now, Katie realized with elation, and there was no need for a chaperone. They belonged to one another body as well as soul.

They had exchanged a tentative peck at the altar, but as they now reached the hedge surrounding the church gardens, Michael tugged her into its shelter and pulled her into his arms. Their lips met with a cataclysm of joy and the salty taste of tears as they rolled down Katie's cheeks. She had waited so long for this very moment; all her life, it felt.

Michael drew back, his arms still around her, eyes shining. "Oh, my darling!"

"We've done it." Katie giggled. "We've finally done it."

"We have indeed." He kissed her hand. "Mrs. Bailey."

Mrs. Michael Bailey! What a glorious concept that was.

"What shall we do next?" Michael asked.

Katie blinked. "*Next?*" She had never considered the possibility. As far as she was concerned, all would be well the moment she married him; and so far, that was the case.

"Well, do you want to stay in London, or do you want to go to Yorkshire?"

"I want to go wherever you are. I don't care. What do *you* want to do?"

Michael's arms tightened around her. "I've never stopped missing those soft, green hills. I know you barely remember them, Katie, or even the taste of real fresh air, but they're glorious."

Katie giggled. "Then let's go to Yorkshire."

"Yorkshire it is, my darling." Michael lifted her off her feet. "Yorkshire it is!"

He spun her around until her skirt swirled around her legs and her laughter filled the world.

CHAPTER 19

CHAPTER EIGHTEEN

The prospering Welcome Hearth was responsible for the hired coach that now stood in the street before the old inn, looking to Katie's humble eyes impossibly grandiose with its driver and its big black horses snorting steam into the cold air. She thought of the hansom-cabs that had carried her to her destiny before and felt a flush of relief that this two-horse coach was taking her somewhere very different.

She stood outside the inn, holding a last small case in both hands. Joan's arms were wrapped tight around Michael. They were both shaking a little, and Katie's heart panged with empathy for her husband. She had endured a long parting from her family, and though these circumstances were far better than the horrible separation in the workhouse, she still felt compassion for Michael. He had never truly been separated from his parents before.

Joan's eyes were wet when she pulled away. "Oh, you

silly thing! Don't be sad." She laughed, brushing at her son's cheek. "You're off on the adventure you've always dreamed of, the one you've always deserved."

"Mama, thank you." Michael pecked her on the cheek. "For everything."

He clasped his father's hand for a moment before Peter drew him in for an embrace.

"I'm proud of you, lad," the older man murmured. "So proud."

"Thank you, Papa." Michael's voice cracked.

But when he turned to Katie, his eyes were dry, and a wide smile adorned his features as he gripped her hand. "Are you ready, my love?"

"To follow you anywhere?" Katie smiled. "I always have been."

PETER AND JOAN had apologized profusely that their resources did not extend as far as first-class tickets on the train. The second-class train tickets were far less comfortable than the hired coach, but the train would have reached Yorkshire that very evening, where the coach had to overnight halfway along the road.

Katie, however, had not minded taking the coach at all. It was a chance to see a new place—a different world—and to revel in the company of the man she adored.

They were both giddy and giggling when they disembarked from the coach before the towering inn hunkering by the seaside. Grimsby was a burgeoning port town, with a cluster of tall new buildings by its docks, and the inn they had chosen was several stories high. Its fittings all gleamed with newness.

The day had already been a grand adventure for Katie. She had seen so many things that she'd only ever heard of in books before: stretches of woodland, green fields rolling into the distance, and the breathtaking clarity of the sea away from London. The inn was simply a sequel to the day's glories. The people sounded different and exciting as they crowded around low wooden tables that lurked in the smoky interior. Gas lamps, turned down low, struggled to penetrate the gloom generated by dozens of pipes and cigarettes.

A scrawny fellow stood by the bar, moustache drooping as he wiped the wood. Katie and Michael wandered over to him, laughing. Michael's arm was intoxicating around his wife's waist.

"Evening, good sir," said Michael. "A room for two, if you please."

"Of course." The barkeeper turned away.

An old sailor sitting nearby, swarthy and sweaty, glanced at the pouch hanging from Michael's pocket. "You'll want to put that coin pouch in your pocket, lad. It won't last long like that."

Michael swiftly complied, his face falling. "Why, I didn't expect pickpockets to be so troublesome outside of London."

"Want is everywhere. Pickpockets are everywhere."

"Drunken sailors even more so," said the barkeeper disapprovingly.

"Watch yourself—even in Yorkshire." The sailor sipped a pint.

"In Yorkshire." Katie smiled. "How wonderful to be here at last after all these years!"

"Where are you folks headed?" the sailor asked.

"Bridlington, just up the coast," said Michael. "Her

father has a farm there."

"Ahh, a farm! I grew up on one. I miss them early mornings, the smell of milk, the cows chewin' cud. Those were good days." The sailor waved a mug. "Stay a while, young sir. I'll buy you a pint and you can tell me about your good old days."

"Josie will show you to your room," said the barkeeper, interrupting. "Would you like to take your meal upstairs?"

"Oh, yes please," said Katie. "I'm so tired."

"Go on up, love." Michael kissed her cheek. "I'm all abuzz with excitement. If I go up now, I'll toss and turn and keep you awake. I think I'll eat here and have a pint before bed, but I'll be up in a moment."

Katie yawned and hugged him. "Thank you, love."

Michael kissed her again to the visible disgust of the barkeeper. "Sweet dreams, my love. I'll be with you in a moment."

"In a moment," Katie sleepily echoed.

She followed the serving girl up to a comfortable room. The long day's travel made her limbs feel leaden. She barely had the energy to eat the soup and bread the girl brought her a few minutes later, and after washing and undressing, Katie was asleep the moment her cheek met the pillow.

MORNING LIGHT gently warmed Katie's face. She stirred, sighing with sleepiness. Morning light... She had to hurry! The guests would be wanting their bread fresh-baked in a moment. She had overslept.

Katie sat up with a gasp, but she wasn't in her room at the Welcome Hearth. For a disoriented second, she didn't know where she was. Then the happy truth came back to her: she was at the Grimsby inn, on her way home to the farm with her husband.

Except that her husband wasn't here with her.

She ran a hand over the covers on the other side of the bed. They seemed so undisturbed. Had he come up to bed at all last night?

Fear panged through her, but Katie swiftly muffled it. Of course Michael had slept beside her last night. Why would he not? He must have tidied the covers after rising, then gone downstairs to see about their coach.

She would be beside him again in a minute, Katie told her worrying heart, as she hastily dressed. She was still tying her pinafore as she hurried downstairs.

The inn was quiet and empty, reminding her of the Welcome Hearth in the morning. Only a single old gentleman sat by the window, sipping a cup of tea. The barkeeper was polishing glasses.

The old gentleman looked up as she entered. "Good morning."

"Hello," said Katie hurriedly, glancing around the inn and seeing no one. She rushed to the bar. "Excuse me, sir."

The man's lips pressed together. "Morning, ma'am."

"Did you see where my husband went? Is he outside in the carriage-yard?" Katie tried to keep her voice light.

The barkeeper sighed.

The gentleman at the window stood up.

"Please," said Katie urgently. "Just tell me where he is."

"He left with those sailors last night, ma'am," said the barkeeper.

Everything inside Katie froze. "*What?*"

"They went out to the docks," said the barkeeper.

"And you did nothing to stop them," the gentleman snapped.

Katie didn't listen to the barkeeper's retort. She pushed past the gentleman, who gave a cry of surprise, and rushed through the door. Grimsby was a foreign land to her, but she knew how to find the docks; she knew their smell and the direction of the sea. She set off at a dead run, her entire body burning with panic at the sound of every rattling carriage wheel, but never hesitating, never slowing.

Her panic strengthened her. She was still running at her best speed when she reached the docks and saw the ships lying at anchor.

He had to be here somewhere, he *had to*. He would never leave her.

Michael would never leave her!

"Michael!" she screamed. "*Michael!*"

She spun around, panic swarming her. There were people everywhere, rolling barrels, pushing barrows, carrying sacks. None of them were her husband.

"*Michael!*" she shrieked.

"Who are you lookin' for, then, miss?" said a wobbly old voice.

Katie turned and saw an old woman hunkering beside a stack of barrels. She wore fingerless gloves and a threadbare shawl that hung in tatters over her shoulders. Her shock of white hair was unwashed, and dirt had collected in the deep creases around her face.

Perhaps many women in Katie's position would have recoiled, but she found nothing to despise in the filthy old tramp. She had been a filthier tramp, yet she was still equally human.

"Please," Katie begged, "please, I'm looking for my husband. He... he would never leave me."

"Aye, lass." The old woman shook her head. "Tall young man, is he? Sweet face?"

"Yes! Where did he go?"

"He'll be halfway across the British Channel by now, I'd reckon."

Katie's heart froze. "*What*?"

"He went aboard the *Lucky Jane*."

"No. No, he can't have! Why would he leave me?"

The gentleman running up to her made her jump and scream, but he held out a hand, breathless. It was the same man who'd been sitting at the window of the inn.

"What do you want with me?" Katie cried.

"Dear lady, I have no ill intent," said the gentleman. "I believe I know what happened to your husband."

Hot tears spilled down Katie's cheeks. "I have to find him."

"I'm afraid it's too late for that, and that good-for-nothing barkeeper at the inn knows it."

"They carried him onto the *Lucky Jane*," said the grimy crone. "He was snoring."

"They *took* him?" Katie gasped.

"They shanghaied him," said the gentleman.

"I don't know what that means!"

"It means that they made merry with him, and made friends with him, seeing and knowing that he was a kind and naive young man who did not know the true power of drink," said the gentleman. "They bought him all the ale he could drink, and he thought what lovely people they were, and the more he drank, the more he wanted to stay down in the bar with them, talking and laughing. Let me guess—someone offered him a pint, did they, when you went up to bed on your own? I was sitting in the back. I didn't quite hear."

Katie's tears kept coming. "Yes."

"That would have been one of the sailors. He would

have started it. The others would have joined in, and when your husband fell senseless to the floor, they carried him off to their ship. He'll wake on the *Lucky Jane* miles from home with a splitting head and no choice but to serve aboard their ship."

Katie's knees buckled. The gentleman gripped her arm and steered her to sit down on a wooden box.

"Oh, Michael," she wailed. "Oh, no, no, no!"

She covered her face with her hands and gave herself over to a few moments of unbridled grief.

"It ain't the first time I've seen such a thing," said the old crone. "I'm sorry, lass. It's a cruel old world."

"I should have stopped them." The old gentleman's voice was filled with regret. "I knew something like that could happen, so I went to the barkeeper and begged him to stop it. He cursed me most dreadfully and thrust me from the inn. Yet I should have returned... I did return, this morning, to see what had happened, if my fears had come true."

Katie summoned control over her keening voice and lowered her hands to her lap. "I must go after him. Which of these ships is going in the same direction as the *Lucky Jane*?"

The crone and the gentleman exchanged a glance. Revulsion registered in the gentleman's face, but his tone was gentle. "I'm afraid there's no chance of that, my dear. A sailing ship is no place for a tender young lady."

"Aye, lass. All you can do is to wait here for him to come back," said the crone.

"*Wait*! And how long will that be?"

"Weeks at the very least," said the gentleman softly, "if not months, or years."

Years. The word winded Katie, leaving her shaking. She clutched the edge of the box to keep from falling.

She had so recently returned to Michael's life. They were married now. They were meant to be inseparable. Surely nothing could divide them again! And yet, appallingly, it had.

The world spun around her.

"Watch out," said the crone. "She'll faint."

"Dear lady!" The gentleman grabbed her arm. "Come, you're not safe here. Do you have any family here?"

"Molly will come," said Katie faintly. "Molly will come. Please... please... someone, send for her. The farm's near a village outside Bridlington."

"That's not far by fast horse." The gentleman helped her to her feet. "Let me take you to a different inn, the one where I stayed last night. You'll be safe there. I'll send a messenger to your Molly, if you can remember her address."

Katie mumbled it as the gentleman slowly walked her over to a brighter inn nearer the docks. Terror and suspicion kept her alert until she stepped through the doors and a motherly figure rushed over, saying how pale she was.

When the strange man released her arm and the sweet innkeeper's wife grasped her hands, Katie could no longer stand it. The world slipped away and she tumbled into oblivion.

CHAPTER 20

CHAPTER NINETEEN

*P*apa's voice resounded from the floor below Katie's room, plucking her from the fitful doze that had wrapped around her. The innkeeper's wife had been sitting in the corner of her room, knitting, ever since she woke here thanks to some sharply applied smelling salts. The old woman straightened now, alert, at the loud sound of the voice downstairs.

"What's all that kerfuffle, then?" she wondered.

Katie shakily stood. "That's my papa."

Relief flooded the old woman's features. "Oh, mercy! Thank goodness for that."

Katie stumbled to the door. "Thank you," she managed. "You've all been so very kind."

She stumbled downstairs to find Papa at the bottom, red-faced and wide-eyed. He ran to her and flung his arms around her. Tears overwhelmed her as her father cradled her against his strong, broad chest.

"They took him, Papa," she wailed. "They took him!"

"Oh, my darling. Oh, my pet!" Papa cradled her close and kissed her hair. "My poor, poor little poppet."

He allowed her to weep into his chest. All of her trembled, but his presence anchored her. Papa was here at last. She knew he would protect her, no matter what came next, and yet at the same moment he could not save her from the most essential hurt deep in her spirit: the hurt of Michael's absence.

"You say some sailors shanghaied him?" Papa asked.

"They made him drunk and took him away. Oh, Papa, don't blame him. He didn't know. It wasn't what he meant."

"I don't blame him for a second, my poppet." Papa brushed tears from her cheeks. "Such things have happened to older and wiser men than Michael, and he's never had to be alone, not like you. His father... his family always stayed with him." His voice broke. "I should have come to get you. That cursed harvest! I could have left it in the field."

"You're here now, Papa." Katie clutched his coat. "Don't let me go. Please."

Papa's arms surrounded her. "Never again, my love. I promise."

"What shall we do? How will we get him back?"

"There's no way to contact the *Lucky Jane* for now, my love. We'll have to wait until they put in at port here in England again."

"No," Katie whispered. She feared she might faint again.

"I'm sorry, pet, but there's nothing else to do but to take you home. We must have faith now that Michael will come back."

The word bled from Katie like a haemorrhage from a wound. "*How?*"

"My dear, the same way you and your sister had faith that I would someday return to you."

Katie covered her face with her hands and sobbed. She felt not one ounce of faith in her aching bones.

The carriage rattled on and on. Katie's weary joints jarred with every step. Her head leaned against the window as she sought comfort in the velvet seats—a luxury she'd never known to dream of. She had underestimated just how prosperous the farm had become.

Yet the luxury mattered little to her. She imagined how she and Michael would have giggled and grown excited over the velvet seats and the curtains on the windows of the pretty brougham that clattered from Grimsby to Bridlington at a bold pace. They would have smiled at every animal grazing in the field, laughed at every passing cloud.

There was no smiling or laughter now. Katie had felt the cold, cruel hand of this world many times. But never before had her fate stung so desperately as it did now, with her precious husband wrenched so heartlessly from her grasp.

She slid in and out of something akin to sleep as the long day passed in clopping hooves and rolling wheels. They stopped at times, she knew, and Papa kept trying to offer her food and drink, but Katie wanted nothing—nothing in the world but for Michael.

She must have fallen asleep at last, because it was twilight when there was a gentle touch on her arm and Papa said, "We're home, my darling."

Katie knew she did not remember the farm. Yet as the carriage came to a halt and Papa opened the door for her, she felt a great wave of familiarity wash over her at the sight of the cozy house with its thatched roof and the barn to one side with lamplight glowing within. The yard was cobbled and swept clean. A great haystack stood beside the barn, golden in the light of the carriage's lanterns.

Katie could not truly remember laying eyes upon this place, but the moment she did, she knew Papa was right. She *was* home.

The farmhouse door swung open and a fat-footed puppy lumbered forth, the white tip on its tail as bright as a firefly as it gambolled across the yard. Close on its heels came Molly, her apron failing to hide the growing curve of her belly.

"Katie!" she gasped.

"Mol!" James appeared in the doorway. "You shouldn't be running, love!"

But run Molly did, almost tripping over the puppy, and flung her arms around Katie. The tears came again then as her sister's warm love allowed everything inside Katie's heart to boil over. She clung to Molly, weeping.

"Hush, hush, pet. He'll be back. You know he'll be back." Molly was stroking her hair.

Katie had struggled to believe it when Papa said so, yet something about Molly's voice slowed her tears.

"Auntie Katie!" a little voice shouted.

Katie released her sister and gasped with surprise. Alfred had grown impossibly in the year since she had last seen him. She held out her arms to the little boy and spun him around, then set him on her hip and stared, amazed, at the new length of his hair and the new sparkle of brightness in his eyes.

"Oh, look at you!" she said.

Seraphina hastened outside, cradling her infant

daughter in her arm. She said nothing, but embraced Katie close and fervently.

"Sera." Katie swallowed the lump in her throat. "Look at her. She's absolutely beautiful."

"Isn't she?" Seraphina smiled. "We've named her Ella."

"Ella." Katie traced a finger over the baby's pink, plump cheek. "It's perfect. It's just enough like Ellen. But where's Henry?"

"Here he comes." Papa pointed with a deep chuckle.

An old wagon horse came galloping stiffly across the dusky field, his massive hooves flying, his blinkered head swinging left and right in great consternation. Henry's figure was bent over on the horse's harnessed back. He rode with speed, determination, and a total lack of skill, and it was only a miracle that he didn't spill clean off the horse as the big beast came to a slithering halt in the barnyard.

"Katie!" Henry thundered.

He dismounted in a great leap and charged toward her. Before she could protest, he wrapped her in an embrace that smelled of dust and showered her with bits of corn husks.

"Henry, for goodness' sake, you'll smother her," Molly chided.

Henry's arms faltered.

"No," Katie whimpered. "Don't let me go."

Her brother hugged her all the more tightly.

"Never," he said, with fierce love.

PART VI

CHAPTER 21

CHAPTER TWENTY

Two Years Later

"Ella!" Katie called. "Ella, slow down!"

The little girl stampeded down the church aisle, arms in the air, her toddling steps carrying her at speed toward the door.

"*Ella!*" Katie ran after her, arms extended.

Ella's giggles filled the church, drawing indulgent smiles from the congregation. It was a puny little stone church nestled at the heart of the village, and Ella crossed it in mere moments, Katie sprinting after her.

She caught the child at the very edge of the steps leading directly onto the cobbled street. Ella squealed with excitement as Katie swept her off her feet and planted a kiss on her shiny golden hair.

"You naughty thing," Katie scolded.

"Good catch, Katie-pie." Henry slapped her on the back as he strode out, Seraphina's arm around his. "Ellie, are you misbehaving?"

"Papa!" Ella held out her arms.

Henry allowed her to climb into his embrace, her little arms around his neck. "Have you been a silly girl?"

"The silliest little girl." Seraphina tickled the child's tummy, triggering a belly laugh.

The little family proceeded down the steps, leaving Katie behind, Ella's laughter wrapping around them like an embrace.

"Alfred! Alfie! *Alfred Harrison, get back here this instant!*" Molly bellowed.

Alfred bounded down the steps past Katie, merrily ignoring his mother as he tore off his tie.

"Alfie! Alfie! I'll take a switch to that Alfred, so help me," she snarled, storming after him.

James chuckled as he followed, suntanned and smiling. Papa was next to him; it seemed his hair had grown thicker over the past two years, his wrinkles easing, as though joy had made the years turn backward for him.

"Alfie's a proper little farm lad," said Papa in tones of deep approval. "There's nothing of the city in him."

"Molly's determined to make him into a little gentleman," said James.

"Well, heaven help her, for no Turner boy was ever a gentleman."

Katie watched as James hurried over to help catch the rampant Alfred. Papa slipped little Alfie a boiled sweet when he thought his mother wasn't looking.

It was a beautiful scene, she thought, joyous and filled

with love, yet she struggled to force her limbs to carry her down the stairs and join them. The hollowness in her made her feel untethered to the world, as though a wrong gust of wind could blow her clean away. She had been emptied into a dry husk by Michael's absence.

The thought of his name was enough to make her eyes tear. *Oh, Michael.* Everyone had said he would come back after the winter. But summer had come and gone, then another spinning year, and autumn blazed now in yellows and reds on the trees lining the village's only street, and still there was no sign of him.

Perhaps the gentleman had been wrong. Perhaps Michael had left purposefully to see the world.

"Good morning, Katie!"

Katie turned, plastering on her smile. Two sweet little old ladies approached her, one bent and frail as she leaned on her stick, the other tall and stately with traces of handsomeness remaining in her sagging jowls.

Mrs. Hawkins and Mrs. Dawson were sisters, and Katie had never seen them apart, not now that both of their husbands had died.

"You're looking so well, dear." Mrs. Hawkins, the bent one, reached up with a shaky hand to pat her cheek.

"Thank you. That's kind to say."

"It's true," said Mrs. Dawson. "You're in the very heart of the flower of your youth."

"A beautiful time." Mrs. Hawkins beamed.

"A perfect time. A time to be fruitful," Mrs. Dawson added.

Katie wasn't in the mood to talk to them. She edged away, but they kept going.

"Why, it's such a terrible pity to waste a body like

yours," Mrs. Dawson went on, "such a tragedy that a young womb should lie barren!"

Katie blushed. "I beg your pardon?"

"We're just commiserating, dear," said Mrs. Hawkins, "about how terribly sad it must be to find yourself without a husband."

"I... I have a husband," Katie stammered. "He's just not here."

"Of course, dearie, of course." Mrs. Hawkins patted her arm.

"You poor thing. Even talking about it has you all upset," said Mrs. Dawson. "Why don't you come over and have tea with us at our cottage?'

"That's an excellent idea, Ophelia," said Mrs. Hawkins. "Why, isn't your grandson working in our garden today?"

"He certainly is. A fine, strapping young man, is our Richard." Mrs. Dawson smiled. "You might like to meet him, Katie. He's a hardworking young man and very handsome. I believe he's about your age, too."

Katie drew back. "I can't come today."

"Tomorrow, then," said Mrs. Dawson.

"Oh, yes! Richard will be there tomorrow, too," said Mrs. Hawkins.

Anger flared in Katie's chest. "I'm married," she snapped, far more harshly than she knew she should speak to her elders. "How dare you treat me like a young widow?"

"Poor Katie." Mrs. Hawkins shook her head, tutting.

"My dear girl," said Mrs. Dawson, more sharply, "your little husband is gone, but Richard is right here. Come and meet him."

"Everyone knows that those sailors never come back," said Mrs. Hawkins.

Her words drove through Katie like a dagger in her belly. She stumbled backward, almost fell from the top step of the church, and turned around to bolt toward home.

"Katie!" Molly gasped as she brushed past her sister.

Katie didn't stop to listen to whatever her happy family with their blossoming marriages and children wanted to say to her. She ran until she reached the willow tree overlooking the river at the back of the farm, where she used to play with Molly, Henry, Tessie, and Michael.

She was alone there now. And the weeping willow trailed it's sad fronds into the water below in solidarity with her as she poured out her grief.

The new barn was almost full.

Papa, James, and Henry had built it for the upcoming harvest, when their crops were so abundant that they could not fit all the hay they had grown for their animals into the first barn. Now, a towering haystack rose to the rafters in the second. Katie helped herself to an armful of the hay and carried it across the yard.

She felt old, slow, and tired with grief. It was Wednesday, but Mrs. Hawkins' words still haunted her incessantly, snapping at her heels with every step like a wayward dog.

Everyone knows those sailors never come back.

There were ten thousand reasons why not. Ten thousand terrifying possibilities out on the high seas and in the strange continents those ships visited. Storms and sea monsters and all kinds of exotic diseases, predators, and people awaited her dear Michael when they carried him out senseless to a fate he had not chosen.

Had they wrapped her husband's body in old sailcloth and lain him to rest in the sea?

Katie's heart stung so fiercely at the thought that she had to stop for a moment, trembling in pain, halfway across the farmyard. She shakily inhaled, trying to be calm. The sheepdog lay stretched out in the sun, enjoying its unseasonable warmth. Chickens pecked around him, unperturbed. In the paddock across from the barn, the ageing plough horse rested limbs grown tired from the previous day's raking.

Katie carried the hay over to the plough horse and tossed it over the fence. The big animal gave her a friendly nicker and touched her with his nose before he lowered his head to eat.

"Good old chap." Katie petted his neck.

Michael loved horses. He would have loved this one. She'd always hoped she would be able to show him the old fellow one day, but Mrs. Hawkins' words would not leave her.

What if he never *did* come back?

The thought was too heavy for her to carry, and she had to milk the cow if they were to skim the milk tomorrow morning for butter. Katie was amazed that her legs did not buckle as she trudged across the yard to the barn.

Hooves clattered in the lane.

"Katie!"

She looked up.

"Katie-pie, I have something for you!" Henry rode into the yard, lithe and elegant in the saddle after two years of practice. His prancing hunter, a gift from Papa, tossed its fiery head as he halted it near Katie.

"Oh?" Katie tried to look excited for Henry's sake.

"I met the postman along the way." Henry vaulted

down from the horse and withdrew a pale envelope from his jacket. "Here. A letter for you."

Katie's heart leaped. She snatched it up, breathless, and turned it over to see the return address.

Disappointment cut her. It was from Peter and Joan at the Welcome Hearth.

"Thank you, Henry," she said politely, placing the letter in her pinafore pocket. "That's kind of you to bring me."

"Aren't you going to read it?"

"Not right now, thank you. When I've finished my chores, I will. You're kind." Katie turned away.

Henry touched her arm. "Katie, tell me that you'll read it."

Katie looked up at him with every intent of lying, but she found no untruth would pass her lips as she gazed into his concerned eyes.

"Are you angry with Peter and Joan?" Henry asked softly.

"No. Not at all. I... I'm ashamed to hear from them." Katie's throat swelled. "I'm the one who lost their son."

"Oh, Katie, you know they don't see it that way. Look how kind they were to you when we visited the inn this summer."

"Of course they were kind. They're good people. But they never lost Michael. I did." Katie walked away.

"Katie, wait! What if they have news about him?"

Katie stumbled to a halt. "Please, Henry, I beg of you, don't say that."

"Why not? It could be true!"

"It won't be true." Katie swallowed against her tears. "I can't hope anymore, Henry. Hoping hurts too much."

Henry laid a hand on her shoulder. "Do you love him?"

Katie gasped. "What?"

"Do you love him, Katie?"

"Of course I love him! How could you ask such a thing?"

"If you never plan to stop loving him, then don't stop hoping, Katie-pie. Love and hope are the same thing." Henry smiled. "Seraphina taught me that."

Katie pulled the envelope from her pocket and stared at it in her shaking hands. Hope was unbearable to her, but love... She could not stop loving Michael. It was an impossibility.

Henry was right. Whether or not she ever saw Michael again, he had adored his parents. She could honour him by at least reading this letter.

A strange peace came over her as she slit open the envelope. She had received a few letters from Joan and Peter, especially in her first few months at the farm, and they were always long missives written in Joan's meticulously tidy hand.

This time, however, there was only one page. The words were scribbled in Peter's messy, shaky writing.

Katie, come at once. He's come back!
Michael is in London. He longs for you!

Katie let out a shriek, her hand flying to her mouth. She dropped the letter as though it had burned her and stumbled back a few steps. The shock was so terrific that she thought for a second she might fall.

"Katie!" Henry seized her shoulders. "What is it?"

"He's back, Henry!" Katie clung to him. "Michael's back. He's in London!"

Henry stared at her, his smile slowly growing until a

guffaw burst from him. "Then we must go to him now. At once! We'll take the train. First-class tickets. I'll go with you."

Katie flung her arms around her brother and hugged him. She had not known it possible to experience such joy so shortly after such sorrow.

CHAPTER 22

CHAPTER TWENTY-ONE

*K*atie was trembling, but she could not stop smiling. She hung onto Henry's hand to anchor her in the joyous madness of the world as the steam train huffed and puttered its way into the heart of London, following its shiny tracks with puffs of white steam trailing behind.

London had changed so little in two years. It was still a wasteland of grey and brown, with smoke filling the sky from the dozens of factories, turning the air murky yellow. The Thames still sprawled, sticking its tributaries like grubby fingers into the disorganized mass of the streets. In the distance, the taller, grander buildings jutted against the smoggy sky.

But those buildings were for those who wanted to gape at grandeur. This, Katie thought, was the real London, the grime and the filth, the darkness.

A sudden shudder crept over her despite the elation in her heart.

"It's strange to be back, isn't it?" said Henry.

"So strange. We had some happy times here, of course. But each time we're here, I can't help but think of all of the hard ones. The long hours in the cotton mill. The fire..."

"Tessie."

"And then the cholera."

"The Larks."

"The mudlarking. The workhouse."

"Fred... then Seraphina." Henry's smile flickered.

Katie clung to his hand. "I'm so glad we found each other and brought the family together."

"The family's not quite together," said Henry gently. "Not yet. Not until your husband is with you again."

"That could be today."

"It *will* be today."

The train shrieked and moaned to a halt, and Katie gazed across the platform at the beloved inn where their hopes and dreams had lived and died. Peter and Joan had repainted the sign; its flames were bright yellow, more welcoming than ever.

In all the darkness of London, the Welcome Hearth was a pool of brightness. Suddenly, Katie longed to be inside, to stand next to that beloved hearth and hear Michael's voice laughing upstairs as she had done so many times before.

She pressed through the crowd, almost leaving Henry behind. He caught up to her as she rushed from the platform and paused to glance at the traffic. Her brother matched her every step as she hastened to the front door.

She flung it wide open. "Where are you?" she cried. "Michael, my love! Where are you?"

The afternoon patrons looked up in surprise. Several

familiar faces beamed and waved at her, but Katie didn't look at them. She almost ran across the inn to the bar. Peter stepped out from behind it and caught her in a swift embrace.

Katie scrambled out of it. "Where is he, Peter?"

"I'm sorry, dear," he said, and her heart plummeted. "He's gone down to the docks to buy fish for supper. He wanted Joan to make you the fried fish you like best to welcome you here. Your train was a little early."

Joy and relief spilled as tears down her cheeks. "The docks—the fish market, the one we always used?"

"The very same, but it's a dangerous part of town, Katie. Wait here until he gets back." Joan emerged from the cellar. "He'll be here in a moment. It's good to see you, Henry."

"I've been waiting two years. I can't wait another second!" said Katie.

She vaguely heard Henry telling her parents-in-law that he would go with her before she sprinted from the door. Skirts hiked up high, she ran down the street, Henry shouting at her to wait for him. But it was true what she had said; she could not bear another moment's waiting. She not only wanted to be in Michael's arms. She *needed* it.

Familiar landmarks whipped past as Katie sprinted down to the docks. Two years' hearty eating and hard work had made her strong, and she was barely breathless when she rounded the corner and saw the great ships leaning before her. And yes, on the bow of one stood the accursed name, *Lucky Jane*.

Katie's steps slowed. The fish market was around the corner to the right, but the sight of the *Lucky Jane* arrested her. This was the boat that had carried her husband away from her for two endless years. She stared up at it, her heart jabbing her ribs. Part of her wanted to spit upon it.

Part of her wanted to burn it down.

The shadow emerged from a pile of barrels nearby, moving so quickly that Katie didn't notice his presence until he was right beside her, a faint prick at her neck telling her of the sharp glass shard he used as a weapon.

"Money," the mugger hissed in her ear, the word coming out with the stench of fermenting ale.

Katie cried out, but the mugger seized her by the hair and wrenched her head cruelly back. "Your *money*, wench, or I can think of something else I'd like to take from you."

"Take it! Take it!" Katie yelped. "In—in my front pocket. Take it."

She felt the queasy pressure of his fingers reaching into her apron pocket, heard the jingle as he took the few coins she had stashed there.

"Let me go," she whimpered.

She heard Henry shouting her name. She had run too fast; her brother had lost her in the crowd. He would not see what was happening now.

"On second thoughts..." The mugger's words huffed, hot and damp, on her neck. "Maybe I'll have something more from you, too."

There were people everywhere, and yet they did not glance at Katie beneath the shadows of the *Lucky Jane*'s prow. No one spared her a second glance or offered succour from her terror.

"I'll scream," she hissed. "Let me go or I'll scream."

The sharp edge lightly pierced her skin, and she felt the hot trickle of blood.

"If you scream, I'll kill you," the mugger hissed.

"Katie!"

It wasn't Henry.

It was Michael.

He stood before her, not the sickly and scurvy-stricken creature she had feared, but stronger and browner and more beautiful than ever before. The sun had painted bright streaks in his hair, and his muscled arms looked as though they'd been cast from beaten bronze. He wore a fine leather coat with breeches and boots, and the handle of a knife jutted from his hip.

He ripped out the knife. "Let her go."

The mugger clutched Katie tighter. "If you hurt me, I'll kill her!"

"Michael, help!" Katie yelped.

"Let her go! I won't tell you again!" Michael thundered.

"I'll kill her!" the mugger screamed.

Michael threw the knife. It hissed in the air, faster than Katie could see, and she heard a meaty sound as it met the man's leg a few inches from hers. He screamed, the glass faltering at her neck, and Katie twisted away.

Michael's strong arm surrounded her. He smelled of the sea, but also, wonderfully, of himself.

"Police!" he cried. "Police! Help! Thief!"

The mugger lay curled on the cobbles, groaning and clutching his wounded leg.

Bobbies came running. Katie barely saw them. She barely felt the sting of the small wound on her neck. She felt only Michael's arms around her.

"Katie!" Henry pushed through the fray, fists up, ready to attack anyone who threatened his sister. "Ka— Oh!"

He vanished into the periphery of Katie's world. She raised her hands to Michael's face as his arms encircled her. She explored it with her fingertips, finding his soft sun-bleached hair, the precious shelf of his brows, the aquiline line of his nose. She cared little who was watching or could see this public affection; instead, she traced her fingers over the curves of his cheekbones, finding a new scar low down on his jaw and the hint of stubble along his upper lip.

It was when she felt his breath on her fingertips that she truly believed he was here and real.

"Oh, Michael," she whispered.

Michael said nothing. He merely pulled her close and kissed her as fiercely as if no one was watching.

THE AFTERNOON PASSED in a delightful whirl of laughter and love. Katie stayed close enough to Michael to touch him, never leaving his sight, half fearing that he might evaporate into thin air once more if she allowed him to step away. For his part, Michael had no protests. He held her hand or touched her arm or brushed her knee with his for every moment of the walk home, the fortifying cup of tea at the fire, and then the celebratory dinner Joan cooked with the fish Katie liked best, just so.

It was all a glorious blur to her. She barely tasted the fish. She barely heard the conversation flowing around her. All she could focus on was Michael's presence beside her—his hand in hers, his voice mixing with the others, the miracle of him being here at all.

"How did you get away?" Joan asked softly.

"We were little more than slaves aboard that ship. We sailed hither and thither across those seven seas, sometimes capturing more unlucky men like us, usually when one of us succumbed to the hard work and meagre food." Michael's hand found Katie's. "Why, if it wasn't for the fever that broke out aboard, I fear no one would ever have known what had happened to us. The *Lucky Jane* was quarantined in London harbour." His voice was quiet. "When the port authorities came aboard, some of us told them we'd been taken against our will."

"They believed you?" Peter leaned forward.

"Enough of us had the same story. The authorities released anyone who could prove they were from London." Michael's thumb traced over Katie's knuckles. "Captain Matthers and his first mate were arrested on the spot—apparently we weren't their first victims. They're already in Newgate Prison awaiting trial."

Henry shook his head in disgust. "Good riddance."

"I came straight here," Michael continued, his eyes never leaving Katie's face. "I was afraid you'd moved on, that I'd lost you forever."

"Never," Katie whispered. "I never stopped believing you'd come back."

Joan's eyes filled with tears. "When we got word that you were coming to London, we could hardly contain ourselves. Michael's been counting the minutes."

"I was buying fish to make your favourite meal," Michael said, his voice thick with emotion. "I wanted everything to be perfect when you arrived."

Katie felt tears spilling down her cheeks. "You're here. That's all I need."

Later that evening, when they were finally alone in their room at the Welcome Hearth, Katie couldn't stop staring at him. He was perfect in every conceivable way, healthy and whole, all hers.

"Katie, I need to tell you something," he said softly.

"What is it?"

Michael's eyes welled with tears. "I'm sorry."

Katie touched his face. "Michael..."

"I'm so sorry. I should never have stayed downstairs in that bar. I thought the sailor was only friendly, but it didn't matter. I should have gone up with you in any case, not left you alone even for a second. Anything could have happened to you, my love, anything, and it was all my fault." Michael was openly weeping now. "Please, I beg you, forgive me. It was a stupid, stupid thing to do, but I never thought—"

"Michael, hush." Katie kissed his teary cheek. "How could you have known? It was only a mistake."

"It took me away from you for far too long. You must know that I missed you for every second, every moment. Everything I did was to get back to you, Katie-pie."

"I know." Katie smiled. "I never stopped knowing that. I never stopped believing in how much you love me, Michael."

He wrapped his arms around her and drew her close to his chest, where his heart beat hard against her. "I love you."

"I love you always."

"This will never happen again, my love. I will always be with you." He kissed her head. "We can go anywhere you like now. Anywhere in the whole world."

"The whole world!"

"I have a ship now." Michael laughed. "The world is ours to explore. Do you like the sound of that?"

Katie cuddled closer. "I like the sound of anything as long as I'm with you."

EPILOGUE

Ten Years Later

THE LAUGHTER of grandchildren filled John Turner's orchard.

He sat in a rocking chair, a patchwork blanket covering his aging knees. His eyesight was starting to fade a little, too, but his vision still easily made out the wide smiles of the children playing tag beneath the orchard's boughs.

There were so many of them. John knew them all; they were the most precious jewels in his life.

Alfred, the eldest, led the way. The boy was fourteen now, growing lithe and suntanned. Though his mother forced him to read and do his sums, all Alfred wanted to do was farm. He could already drive a plough horse and handle stock better than most of the grown men John knew. The boy was John's shadow, dogging him everywhere. When he was little, that closeness was occasionally inconvenient.

Now, Alfred was John's right hand.

Ella darted among them like a little dragonfly, her

bright blonde hair trailing behind her, pretty with ribbons. At twelve, she had the makings of a woman as breathtaking as her mother. It was sad, John thought, that Seraphina had only ever been able to have the one; but perhaps it was also Providence. Heaven knew that Seraphina had been ill enough when she had Ella. Perhaps not having children had been key in her continuing health.

There was little Johnny too, of course, eleven and full of life. Molly's twins, six-year-olds, followed their big brother like two little tails shrieking with joy every time they followed Johnny around a fast turn.

Alfred tripped dramatically, allowing several smaller children to catch up. They thought themselves the strongest, fastest children in all the land as they swarmed him, laughing and squealing. Three of Katie's were among them: Pete, Maggie, and Joanie.

Sweet little Hannah seldom wanted any part of rough-and-tumble games. The little girl padded over to her grandfather now, holding a dandelion in one hand, the other cupped around it to protect it from the breeze.

"Grandpapa, look what I found." She gazed up at him with hazel eyes so like her mother's.

"That's beautiful, darling." John ran a hand over her hair. "Did you know that they grant wishes?"

"They do?"

"Of course. You close your eyes, make a wish, and then blow on it. The little seeds will fly away and make your wishes come true."

Hannah stared up at him. "Won't it hurt the dandelion?"

"Not at all, pet. It'll only spread the seeds. You'll be helping the dandelion, not hurting."

Hannah closed her eyes tightly, wishing hard, and then

blew. Her laugh at the spinning seeds was melodic, miraculous, perfect. John closed his eyes and listened to it, feeling so humbled that he almost felt he could fall from his chair onto his knees and give weeping thanks for this splendid moment.

"Papa." A soft hand touched his arm. "Dinner's almost ready."

John looked up at Katie. She and Michael and the children were freshly back from their travels—Spain, this time, he believed—and there was a healthy, ruddy flush on her cheeks.

"In a minute, darling." He cupped his hand over hers. "Stay out here with me for a moment and listen to the children."

"Katie! Did you call him?" Molly emerged from the farmhouse behind them. "Are you all right, Papa?"

"All right!" John smiled, admiring the glints of grey in Molly's hair. He knew how hard she had had to fight for the privilege of growing older. "I'm the best I've ever been, darling."

"Grandpapa..." Hannah began.

"Oh, there you are." Henry appeared in the back doorway. "Are we ready to eat? I'm starving."

"Hush, Henry." Molly teasingly slapped him with a dishtowel. "You're ruining the moment."

Henry seized the dishtowel and playfully chased her with it.

"Stop it!" Katie giggled.

John smiled and closed his eyes again. *On the contrary, Molly*, he thought, *nothing could ruin a moment like this.*

"Grandpapa," said Hannah insistently, tugging his sleeve.

"What is it, pet?"

"Do you want to know what I wished for?"

John smiled. "Of course." *That way, I could make it come true for you.*

Hannah gripped his arm with both her hands and leaned her head on her little fingers. "I wished that we would always be together."

Katie picked the little girl up, spun her around, and kissed her forehead.

"We always will be," she said. "Trust me. Us Turners always keep our promises."

The End

THANK YOU FOR READING

I hope you enjoyed *The Forgotten Daughter Book 3 in the Turner Family Saga Series*

If you would like to be informed of new releases please **Join My Newsletter Here.**

As a thank you, you will also receive an **exclusive subscriber-only book!**
OVER THE PAGE YOU WILL A LIST OF MY OTHER BOOKS

LIST OF BOOKS

The Turner Family Saga Series
    The Daughter's Silent Promise Book 1
    The Lost Son of London Book 2
    The Forgotten Daughter Book 3

Victorian Romance Saga Series (Three Books)
    The Widow's Hope Book 1
    Little Jack: Book 2
    The Lost Mother's Christmas Miracle Book 3

Other Books
    The Forgotten Match Girl's Christmas Birthday
    The Christmas Pauper
    The Little One's Christmas Dream
    The Waif's Lost Family
    The Pickpocket Orphans
    The Workhouse Girls Despair
    The Wretched Needle Worker
    The Lost Daughter

Printed in Dunstable, United Kingdom